LOST CROWS AND FALLEN STARS

ABELIA SUMPTER

Note from the Author

Lost Crows & Fallen Stars is not suitable for those under 18 years of age. Please see abeliasumpter.com for a full list of content warnings.

Chapter 1

4060 D-AR

"Would you like some more tea?"

I jolt out of whatever trance I was in and tighten my fingers around the chair's armrests. Inside the bright, sterile room, there is nothing but the table in front of me, set with crystal teacups and a teapot made of black hexagons and triangles.

That, and a guy sitting at the table across from me, looking somewhat amused.

His legs are crossed as he rests his temple on his fist and his elbow on the armrest. "Have you paid attention to a single word I've said?"

"Yes . . . I mean . . . No. I'm so sorry, can you repeat it?"

"Girls with their heads in the stars don't tend to last too long around here." He laughs and adjusts in his seat. "You know how coveted this place is?"

"Yes, I understand."

"And that it's a good place to visit this time of year?"

"Um . . . yes. Of course, I completely agree."

The guy tilts his head and leans onto the table. "You're so . . . malleable."

"Excuse me?" I narrow my eyes, debating whether I should just get up and leave. "What is that supposed to mean?"

But then it occurs to me. The surrounding room is completely unfamiliar. In fact, I can't even recall what building I am in.

He picks up the teapot and pours himself a cup of pink-tinged tea. "Your name is Margot, isn't it?"

"Shouldn't you already know my name?"

The smile on his face disappears as he sets the pot down. "I believe I'm the one asking the questions here."

"Well then, what do you want to know?"

"Don't be foolish."

I slam my fist down on the table, making the tea set rattle. "Just ask me the damn questions so I can go, all right?"

"Careful now." His jaw softens. "I won't ask again. Would you like some tea?"

I relax back in my seat. Is that all? Drink his stupid tea? At this point, I'll say anything for him to let me leave. "Sure, I'll take some tea."

"Excellent." He stands and picks up the pot, slightly bending over the small table to reach my glass.

The tea starts out rosy, just like his. I smell the floral notes and can feel the warm steam swirling up my nostrils. But, as the tea reaches the halfway point of the cup, a metallic stench takes over. The soft-pink tea turns a thick red. It looks just like . . .

I smack his hand as fast as I can, making him lose his grip. The teapot flies feet away, shattering open on the ground. The blood is everywhere like some kind of crime scene, staining the white floor. Some of it flies so far that it sprays the hem of the man's pants.

"Now look at what you've done." He sighs. "Send in the maid."

"Wait . . . why is there blood?" I try to stand, but my wrists are strapped to the armrests with leather restraints, as are my ankles. I wasn't tied up before. *What is going on?*

The man slumps back into his seat and shakes his head. "Now that we're more than past formalities, we can begin the real questions."

"Who the hell are you?"

"Answer my questions, and *maybe* I'll entertain yours."

"Then ask me!" I practically scream the words.

Just then, a maid enters with her hands folded in front of her. She keeps her gaze on the ground in front of her as she approaches the mess of shards and blood and kneels in front of it.

Her stare is blank and unfeeling as she reaches for the shards and begins to scoop it up with her bare hands.

"What is she . . . stop her!" I yell at the guy, but he is completely focused on me. To him, the maid may as well be invisible. "Please, don't do that. You'll hurt yourself!"

She doesn't listen, and the jagged edges slice her skin open, adding more crimson to the mess.

He looks to the maid, tracing the edge of his cup. "She's simply doing her job. Now, tell me what I want to know. This doesn't have to be difficult."

Something in me shifts when I realize I cannot make out the man's features. Even his hair color is unidentifiable to me. It's like I'm seeing him without really seeing him. A face on the tip of my tongue.

Then I remember the question, the *real* question.

How could I ever forget?

The memory triggers something. As if sensing my thoughts, the room turns a deep red and sirens blare loud enough to make my ears ring. I struggle even more to escape, but I'm stuck to my seat.

He starts laughing maniacally, the sound bouncing off the walls.

Then my head pounds while a high-pitched noise overtakes my mind, and I know it's not from the sirens. It's painful, almost unbearable, making my head throb and my neck tip back as I cry out. "Please stop!"

But I don't mean my words. Truth is, they can torture me. Kill me. But I will never tell them the answer. I will not betray my planet.

When he releases me from the pain, the table is gone, as is the maid. The man stands in front of me with his hands gripping the armrests, nearly nose to nose with me. He tilts my chin up with two fingers. "The clock is ticking, Margot."

Behind him sits a trough filled with water and my lungs hurt just at the sight of it.

"Go to hell." My body begs me not to say those words. There isn't much more I can take. But I'm willing to die if it means protecting the people I love.

"Oh, I will." He undoes my restraints and forcefully drags me to the trough.

Before I can get a full breath, he shoves me under the water, holding my head under with all his strength. I grasp the edges of the trough, trying to force myself out, but his grip is unwavering.

My head goes fuzzy, and my muscles weaken. Just as the water is about to take me, he rips my head up. I heave for as much air as I can get.

He's kneeling behind me now, one hand gripping my hair and the other holding the front of my neck. His mouth nears my ear. "One more chance is all you'll get."

"Never," I say the word weakly. If he wasn't holding me up, I would have already toppled over.

Before I can catch my breath, he submerges me again. I hear him laughing, almost satisfied that I didn't tell him.

The water turns into an endless ocean. In the distance, sitting on the ocean floor is Death, tipping his hat to me, then reaching out a hand. I shake my head, resisting his presence. Then he grips it forcefully, bubbles of screams stealing my remaining air as I disappear into the dark cavern.

Beep

Beep

Beep

I toss around, sheets tangling around my legs, and a headache splitting through my skull. The nightmare has dissipated. A numbness prances through my limbs, leftover from the adrenaline of the dream.

Whatever room I'm in is pitch black. I can barely make out the source of the machine that's beeping.

Where am I?

I try not to panic as I fumble around for some kind of light but get tangled in wires. There is a plastic clamp around one of my fingers and, when I remove it, the machine beeps loud enough to make me flinch.

The door cracks open, letting in rays of light. "Margot?"

"Who's there?" I back up in the small bed until I hit the headboard.

The lights ignite overhead. A woman dressed in a white shirt and equally white pants enters. The room comes into focus. I'm in some kind of medical ward attached to machines.

What happened to me?

She approaches me and places the clamp back on my finger. "Breathe, your heart rate is too high." Then her hand is on my shoulder.

The hairs on my neck stand up as I smack her arm away. "Who are you?"

"You've been unconscious for weeks," she says with concern in her voice. "I'm your medic."

My breath hitches. Weeks? I try to remember what happened before I fell unconscious, but no answers come to the surface. In fact, nothing does except my first name.

She picks up a translucent tablet off the counter and taps around the screen. "Do you know where you are?"

"I—remind me."

Her lips form into a straight line. She pulls a communicator out of her pocket and speaks into it. "Please send for her lady's maid."

Lady's maid? Now she's making me angry. Is this some kind of joke? "Tell me where I am, or so help me—"

"You're on the Imnicus."

The Imnicus? I can't recall the word. It feels familiar, but I can't place any images or memories linked to it. I slide to the edge of the bed, staring at the floor.

And that's when I realize . . . I don't remember anything at all. All of my memories stick to the tip of my tongue. I press my hand to my chest, my breathing becoming unsteady. "I can't remember."

"Can't remember what?"

"Anything." My jaw shakes, and a tear runs down the side of my cheek. I attempt to yank the IV out of my arm, but it's taped down firmly. Wherever I am, I have to get away. I motion to stand.

"Don't try getting up." The medic quickly sets her tablet down and rushes over to me.

I ignore her, but the second I try to stand, my legs buckle, forcing me back onto the bed.

Where are my memories?

The door slides open and a girl enters. Her brown hair is braided in rows from her scalp to the ends. Her skin is dark and smooth. She wears some kind of uniform—a white dress with gray sleeves and a skirt that runs slightly shorter in the front. Whoever she is, she's well put together, from her manicured nails to her glittering eyeshadow.

"Oh, Margot. Thank the heavens you're awake!" She quickly steps across the room and tries to wrap her arms around me.

I push her away, shrinking back.

"Margot . . . " She holds back a crook in her throat. "Don't you recognize me?"

I bow my head and bite my inner lip, shaking my head slowly. The last thing I need is to care about hurting some girl's feelings.

The medic goes back to typing things into her tablet. "Think. Is there *anything* you remember?"

"My first name." I hold back any more tears. "Will someone tell me what happened already?"

"I'll give you and Lleu some privacy," the medic says.

I want to throw a pillow at the medic. Why won't she just come out and say it? Why hide it from me?

The medic runs out, leaving me alone with this young woman. Lleu.

I hug my knees to my chest. Lleu is the only line to my memories at the moment; that is, if she's even willing to tell me why I can't remember a single thing.

"If you won't tell me, just leave," I say to her.

Lleu shuffles over to me before sitting down on the edge of the thin mattress and folding her hands in her lap. "Terrorists from the planet Lavenai invaded through the west wing docks. They trapped everyone unlucky enough to be in that wing for hours. Everyone locked inside was either killed or injured, including you. Though they singled you out and interrogated you until you were close to death. If it weren't for the proditors, the entire palace may have been taken out. Unfortunately, they escaped."

Lavenai? Imnicus? Proditors? My head spins, and I press my fingers against my temples. *Focus on one thing at a time. Ease into it.*

"What is the Imnicus? Some hospital?" I ask.

Lleu covers her mouth like she expected me to at least remember those little details. "It's your home here in space. It's the palace and also the military hub for Ashtanabo. You're married to the Colum. Ring a bell?"

Married? The room spins. Colum is a word I recognize. It's as ingrained into my vocabulary as any basic word would be. The Colum is the leader. The king. The ruler.

A pulse of nausea hits my throat. I signal to Lleu to bring something for me to vomit into. She scrambles around the room, then chucks an empty basin at me. I dry heave into it, tasting nothing but bile.

Chapter 2

This entire week has been nothing but poking and prodding from a handful of medics—human or otherwise. No matter how many scans they do, I already know the verdict—inconclusive. Though they suspect a head injury caused my amnesia, there are no scrapes or bruises on my skull itself to support that.

On day eight of my stay in the medic bay, Lleu shows up with a box full of nail polish and plops down in the chair next to my bed. When she sees the untouched bowl of soup on my bedside table, she immediately leans over and pokes one of my ribs. "You need to eat something before you become skin and bone."

"I'm not hungry. Give it to the patient next door." I push the bowl of cold soup further away.

Lleu frowns and sets my lunch tray by the sink. "Has the medic said anything else?"

"Besides that there is nothing they can do?" I don't tell her about the entire interaction I had with the humanoid medic, where he finally admitted what I already knew. He tried to give me some hope, that maybe if I tapped into my muscle memory, fragments could possibly return.

"I'm so sorry, Margot. Really. It was unfair that you got caught up in Laven affairs. They targeted you, and the worst part is, you don't even know why. But you need to take care of yourself. Have you at least been sleeping?"

"On occasion." I don't burden Lleu with recounting my recurring nightmare. Sometimes, additional elements stack onto it, but in every single one, I die. The shadowy man haunts what little sleep I get. One medic gave me a sleep tincture and said it would help, but it did nothing but make the horrific dreams linger even longer.

"At the very least, let me paint your nails. I don't like to see you like this, all bed bound and sunken-eyed."

I sigh. "If it will stop you from scolding me about food."

She patters her hands together, smiles wide, and pulls a handful of glass nail polish bottles from her purse, spreading them across the bedside table. "Have your pick."

Without even looking at the bottles, I point to a random color.

Lleu nods. "It suits you." She takes hold of my hand and begins to paint. "Do you remember watching Dames of Ashtanabo?"

"No, but I saw an advertisement for it on television." It's just some dating show, but I can see why Lleu would like it.

She scoffs. "Ugh! What a shame. I suppose that just means we'll have to watch the entire series again."

I force a smile.

The white polish dries within seconds of Lleu applying it on each nail, leaving behind light gray swirls.

From another room, I hear a man yelling. Four medics in the hallway run past my doorway, one pushing a cart in front of them. Anytime I hear commotion from the other rooms, my heart drops. I can only assume he's another soon-to-be casualty from the Laven invasion.

Lleu tries her best to ignore it as she places gems on the edges of my nails. There's no doubt she's good at what she does. Every morning when she arrives, her hair is always in a new style—braided, flat-ironed, or curled. Even with the constraints of wearing a uniform, she finds ways to make it her own, sometimes with a scarf or with body jewelry placed around the waist. I've come to enjoy having her around, no matter how much she nags. It distracts me from the more pressing question.

Where is my so-called husband?

I don't know what he looks like, or even his name, but I don't care to know. What kind of husband doesn't visit his wife after an attack? Shouldn't he be concerned about me? A part of me worries I woke up into the nightmarish reality of a loveless marriage, maybe an arranged one. When I try to concentrate and remember his face, pain splits through my head.

I bring my hand to my forehead and wince.

"Are you all right?" Lleu leans forward with concerned eyes.

I stretch my neck and massage the base of my skull. "Yes, just a headache. It seems to happen anytime I try to remember the past."

"The medics told you not to strain."

"It's still just a lot to take in."

"Whatever the Lavens used to erase your memories, the medics will figure it out. I'm sure of it. And when your memories come back, those terrorists won't stand a chance."

Lavenai. The planet responsible for my memory loss, my fear. I may not remember what happened, but my body does. The way I flinch when medics try to touch me. Just last night, a medic tried adjusting my top sheet while I was asleep and I came close to strangling her.

"Yeah? Well, Lavenai can burn for all I care."

Lleu frowns. "You don't mean that." She finishes placing the last gem. "The Colum rules them as much as he does Ashtanabo. As do you, need I remind you?"

As the Columess, I'm supposed to love all my people, but I can't help but despise them. And why should I love them? I don't even know them. Hell, I don't even know myself right now.

"Did the medics say when you're going to be discharged?" Lleu asks.

"Well . . . " It was supposed to be yesterday or whenever I felt comfortable. I chose the latter. I don't want to find out what my life looks like outside of these four walls. Of course I knew discharge has always been in the future; I just didn't expect the medics to recommend it so soon. Outside of here, I don't know my role, how to act, or anyone's names outside of Lleu.

Lleu . . . who is my lady's maid and probably knows that I was supposed to leave before I did.

"Margot?"

I can't look her in the eye. "I am supposed to leave when I'm comfortable. That's what they technically said."

Lleu frowns. "Life will keep moving, whether you're there to join it or not."

"I know," I sigh.

"You won't be alone. I will be there to guide you every step of the way, and even in the times I can't, I will be there to listen to you vent after. That's what friends are for, isn't it?"

Something about the way she says it really does put me more at ease. Like I really do have the strength to make it outside of the medical bay. As Columess, or whatever. But mostly, I don't want to face my husband alone.

"If I don't like it, I'm coming straight back here," I say firmly.

Lleu laughs. "I'm sure they'll love that."

Chapter 3

As Lleu pushes me out of the medic bay in a wheelchair, a medic shouts goodbye. I force a smile, waving back, keeping my shaking legs at bay. There's a cold burst of air when the doors open. Lleu leads us into a long hallway made of glass from floor to ceiling.

We're surrounded by the void of space filled with glittering stars that form constellations. Far-off in the distance floats a planet swirling with different shades of purple, and even I have to admit it's beautiful. There's another planet far off in the opposite direction. It's dark green and encapsulated by a ring. Both planets stare at each other like two forbidden lovers. My mouth gapes at the sight.

Lleu leans down toward me, her dark brown braids brushing against my shoulder. "See what I mean? A change of scenery can do wonders for the mind."

"We've barely left the infirmary."

"And we still haven't seen anything yet."

Once we reach the next door, Lleu skips through the threshold as she pushes the wheelchair through it, causing me to hold on tight to endure her movements. Blue lights shine against white industrial walls. The hallways are wide enough that each white tile could fit my wheelchair four times over. There are engraved letters over one of the archways that read, *Imnicus: South*. The brass engravings shine like the sign is polished every day.

Soldiers dressed in dark green uniforms hastily walk past us as if we don't exist. On either side of the archway of the command center, two guards stand like statues dressed in light gray armor, their faces hidden behind helmets made of black mesh triangles while they keep their grip firm on long circular guns.

The command center is enormous with stations that tier up like stairs. A man, whom I can only assume is a commander, mumbles curses under his breath as he stands over a lower-ranking officer who is frantically typing commands into a keyboard.

A few soldiers recognize me, their eyes lighting up. Some of them nod or give me a small bow. More approach me, offering their support and condolences.

"Lady Arris, I'm so glad to see you're well."

"Columess, we're so sorry that this happened. We are doing every-thing we can to ensure the future safety of the Imnicus."

I thank them, but inside I hate their pity.

The more we travel, the more palace-like the Imnicus becomes, while still maintaining its ship-like roots. There's a library in the center of the Imnicus that contains seemingly more books than there are stars. Each of the four walls has spiral-shaped shelves that resemble the pinwheel shape of a galaxy, and in the center of the spirals are circular mirrors that make the library feel infinite.

I look away when I see my disheveled reflection. I can't remember the last time I've run a brush through my hair. My face is paler than yesterday, and all I want to do is change into something that doesn't reek of the medic bay sanitizers.

"Lady Arris," a voice says from behind us. "Lleu."

"Proditor Alarik." Lleu turns my wheelchair to face the voice.

I'm slightly taken off guard by his dark, armor-like attire. A metallic mask engraved with triangles covers the lower half of his face. He wears a hood with dark gray embellishments, and dark red hair peeks out from under it.

Seeing him makes me feel even more self-aware at my unkempt hair, and I want nothing more than to hide behind one of the bookshelves until he leaves.

"Margot, this is Proditor Alarik Walsh. He's one of five proditors that live on the Imnicus."

A proditor? I've heard Lleu mention them before, but whatever I was imagining, it wasn't this. He's a ray of darkness, yet I can tell by his eyes alone that there's a soft and gentle nature about him.

I ignore the urge to finger-comb my hair or sniff myself.

"I'm glad you're recovering. I wanted to visit when I heard you were awake, but the Colum said to let you rest." Alarik folds his hands in front of him and bows his head sympathetically.

"It's nice to meet you." I bite my tongue. *It's nice to meet you? You already know him.* But something about not being able to recall who he is, or what kind of dynamic we had, paints my face in a reddened shame.

"I was told you had some memory loss . . . well . . . complete memory loss. You really don't remember me?"

I shake my head. "No. I'm so sorry."

So the Colum is more than aware that I'm awake. For a moment there, I had given him the benefit of the doubt, that maybe he was so busy, nobody had time to tell him. But he even had the gull to deny others access to me. My threads of mercy are fraying at the seams.

"What is a proditor?" I ask, more so to quell my anger about the Colum.

Alarik stiffens slightly, like he's not used to being asked. "We serve the Colum and are gifted with abilities that go beyond the natural realm. Not only do we fight with the body, but also with the mind."

I wince and press my hand to my forehead. I'm taking too much information again, and yet my curiosity is getting the better of me. "The mind?"

"I think that's enough for now, Margot. I will explain more later when you're ready," Lleu says.

I nod and the headache dissipates.

"So, how have you been?" Lleu asks Alarik, almost nervously.

"Busy," he answers. "But I'm looking to take leave within the next few months, if time permits."

"That sounds lovely." A blush creeps across Lleu's dark skin. "Will you take a holiday anywhere in particular?"

Alarik shrugs. "I try not to get my hopes up until the day before my leave."

The conversation that follows is strained, surface level, and somewhat awkward, yet neither one of them wants to let go of it. Normally, Lleu doesn't have trouble holding a conversation with anyone, but with Alarik, she stumbles over her words.

It's enough to make me uncomfortable. "Lleu, I think we should be going now. My headache is worsening."

"Yes . . . right. It was nice talking to you, Alarik."

"You too, Lleu." I can see the smile in his eyes.

Lleu wheels me to the north wing, and it takes everything in me not to pry her about Alarik. Or to admit that I don't really have another headache.

This north wing is more elegant than the industrial south wing. Dark gray geometric shapes protrude slightly from the walls. Some points stick out enough that if one were to walk too close, they may nick their shoulder. It's a strange design choice for a levitating ship, or space station, or whatever the Imnicus truly is.

Lleu takes a sharp right, stopping before a set of large double doors. She taps her beaded bracelet over the security sensor.

"Welcome, Lleu Todd," an intercom says.

She wheels me into the dressing room. It's filled to the brim with luxurious furniture, gowns of every color that hang on the racks like a darkened rainbow, and shelves lined with shoes. A vanity sits against the wall, necklaces dangling from racks and rings stacked on the fingers of a dark gray mannequin hand.

Lleu brushes past all of it and guides us into the bathroom. "I think it's time you had a proper shower."

Every day in the medical bay, I sponged off sweat leftover from nightmares, as if that were enough.

She helps me out of the wheelchair and guides me into the bathroom. I'm wobbly on my feet from the weeks I lay in bed, even with the medics making me walk laps around the room once or twice a day to keep up my strength. The pain from my injuries made walking hard, so even now I'm still sore.

Inside the bathroom is a curved chamber that resembles the letter C, and the wide glass door is tinted with shades of blue.

Lleu shoves towels and toiletries into my arms. "Take your time, and when you're finished, meet me out here."

"Thank you."

She nods and leaves me all alone in the oversized bathroom. When I slip out of my plain gown in front of the octagon mirror, I gasp.

Everywhere imaginable, I'm covered in faded bruises, and the skin is darker along my neck and collarbone. Then, there's the monstrosity on my back—a long, half-healed wound that runs from my shoulder to the middle of my spine. It's what makes me stiffen most.

What the hell did Lavenai do to me?

I enter the chamber, letting the warm water soothe my shaky muscles, though also making me wince in pain. It brings to light how serious my injuries really were and makes me thankful I never stepped into the shower in the medic bay.

I lather shampoo through my hair, washing the remnants of the attack down the drain once and for all. The water running off my legs is a soft shade of crimson, the color deepening while I scrub my body, grimacing every time I pass over a sensitive spot.

Once I'm finished, Lleu has a gown picked out for me, lying over one of the lounge chairs. She directs me to sit so she can do my hair.

I slump down at the gold vanity. Did the girl I was before really need all of this? I'd have to wear two dresses a day for three years just to get through every gown.

Lleu taps my chair. "Sit up straight. I know it's hard, but you must return to your role eventually. You are the Columess, after all."

I fix my posture the best I can. Maybe I could blame it on the bruising.

She refreshes my natural golden curls by placing them inside rollers, then applies a shade of red across my lips.

Lleu assists me in stepping into a dark, navy-blue dress, then she places a sheer hoodless cloak over my head that connects across my chest. It's adorned in countless rhinestones and crystals, simulating the glitter of a starry night.

"What time of day is it?" I ask. I've been all over the Imnicus, and I have yet to see a single clock.

"Well, now that would depend. In the capital city of Ashtanabo, Heidl, it's almost dinnertime. It's the time the Colum follows, as do I. For others, it's nearing breakfast."

So she's getting me ready for dinner? And she's not just throwing me in another simple day outfit, but a gown. My body trembles.

Is it really time for me to meet the Colum?

I don't know if I'm more terrified of what he'll think of me or if I'm excited that I can finally give him a piece of my mind.

When Lleu pulls a glass box out of the vanity, I swallow. Inside is a crown, one that fits across the forehead, made entirely of diamonds. I bend down for her to secure it around my head, then look in the mirror.

There's a disconnect between the girl in the reflection and myself. Just an hour ago, I was covered in dried blood and stench. Now, I am adorned with the wealth and status of royalty and feel entirely undeserving of it.

Chapter 4

Knots constrict inside my stomach the entire way to the north wing's dining room. The Colum's dining room. My legs feel wobbly again, but this time I know it's not because of my strength. Still, part of me wishes I hadn't refused the wheelchair. I chew on my nails, and Lleu slaps my hand down.

"What was that for?" I fold my arms together, and Lleu slaps them back again, until they hang by my sides.

"You're the Columess. It isn't proper to show signs of nervousness. Or any signs of discomfort or annoyance. Even if you're cold, you should keep your hands to your side . . . " Lleu has her hands laced together near her ribs. A lot of the maids walk like that, with their backs overly straight and necks stiff. "Also, biting your nails is gross."

"I'm not nervous," I lie. "It's just dinner."

Lleu raises an eyebrow at me. "It's only natural. You're meeting your husband for the first time . . . again."

The cape attached to the back of my dress drags against the swirling embossments of the tile. "I haven't thought about it that much." I can tell Lleu sees through my lie, but she keeps her lips pinched shut.

Marriage is intimate. Emotional. Maybe even sacred to some. But I don't know this man, even if I once did. I've thought of every scenario about how meeting him would go, and in almost every one of them, I feel angry. Isolated. I mean, he didn't visit me once.

Colums are cold, hunched-over middle-aged men with a graying-brown beard, a round belly, and eyes framed by wrinkles from the toll of a long rule. He rules two planets. He has to be at least in his forties.

I crinkle my nose, thinking about him trying to kiss me. Or worse, take me to bed.

As we approach the dining room doors, they slide open automatically. There is a large table that looks like it could fit nearly twenty people, but it's set only for two at the opposite ends. I sigh in relief that the Colum hasn't arrived yet.

Servants, both human and robotic, are working on the finishing touches, straightening holographic candelabras with blue fire emitting from virtual wicks.

A small cleaning robot, an A.S.O.P. unit I deduce based on its lettered markings, zips by my feet, almost making me trip. One of its wheels hits the tile's groove just right, and it falls on its side. I bend down and hold its circular, dark-blue exterior, and set it back on its wheels.

A human girl shoes the A.S.O.P. and it speeds away. "I'm so sorry about him, Columess."

I shake my head. "No need to apologize."

She thanks me and pulls back her curly red hair as she gets back to work.

Lleu pulls out a chair at the head of the table furthest from the door. "Sit, he'll be here shortly."

I adjust my dress as I plop down into the tall black chair that matches the equally black plate and silverware. A blue fiber-optic table runner stretches across the length of the long table. "What should I say? When he first arrives, I mean?"

Lleu's bracelet beeps and she ignores my question as she quickly stands against the wall with the rest of the servants.

It takes me off guard. It isn't until now I really processed Lleu's role. In the medic bay, she felt higher ranking. Alone with me, she was simply a friend. But here, she is the servant class, far beneath the Colum, and she has to act like she's under me too.

All this time, I've been depending on her help, and without it, I feel naked. Vulnerable.

Then I hear it. The resound of footsteps and two male voices bickering with each other just outside the door.

My heart pounds as the mechanisms inside the door whirl before sliding open.

"We have an entire battalion bolstering the outer defenses. Pushing for further patrols and security checks on the inner checkpoints would spread us too thin."

Two men enter. The one speaking is a short and age-worn commander with many pins upon his lapel. The other, a tall man clothed in dark armor-like attire, walks ahead of him, eyes furrowed in concentration.

Is that really him? The Colum?

He notices me a moment later at the head of the table, his raised fist stopping the commander's next words as his eyes meet mine. My legs buckle together, his expression impossible to read—a strange mixture of shock and apathy.

The commander glances my way and he pales. "Forgive me, Lady Arris. I did not see you there." He bows low, lower than I would expect from a man of his station.

"Commander Aisil," the Colum snaps, not taking his eyes off mine. "Upon the matter we discussed, I want no excuses. You are dismissed."

The Commander, Aisil, stiffens, words upon his lips. But his eyes dart once more to mine before they clamp shut. He offers one last bow before shuffling out the door, the hiss of metal following behind him.

All the while, the Colum has not torn his eyes from mine. When I imagined him. I thought he would be old and worn out. But he can't be more than five years older than me. Twenty-seven, maybe twenty-eight. Like me, he wears a long cloak connected to the shoulders, screaming of royalty and status. His longish hair is a charcoal-black. He moves his gaze away, and my breath returns.

"Lleu, why was I not informed?" he asks shortly.

Lleu's eyes widen and she steps out from the line. "Colum, I thought you were aware. Proditor Crux said—"

His glare was almost enough to kill. "We'll speak of it later."

"I'm so sorry, Colum." She bows her head, clasping her hands back together as she steps back to rejoin the other servants.

He didn't know I was coming? And he blames Lleu? He still has yet to say a single word to me. Something in me shifts from nerves to anger. "Is there something strange about your own wife dining with you? I wasn't aware I needed an invitation."

His lips form into a straight line. If his gaze is any indication, he's pissed at me too. He pulls out his chair and signals a servant to fill his chalice with wine. "Considering *my wife* has been in a coma for weeks, I would have preferred some notice."

I bite down on my tongue and almost laugh. "I've been awake for weeks, too. Recovering. Alone." Is the Colum even aware I have memory loss? I'd like to find out.

"And it seems you're just as mouthy and stubborn as you were before. While you were still asleep, I did visit you. Many times. But I rule two planets, and I couldn't just sit around waiting for you to recover while Laven terrorists are on the loose."

"Well then, with all that time, did you manage to apprehend them?" I fold my arms and legs, taking a comfortable position in my chair. An entirely unladylike one, based on Lleu's expression. But in reality, it's taking all my willpower to stop the trembling in my limbs.

He narrows his eyes and I glare right back at him as humanoids set out appetizers in front of us. Even with how good the food smells just beneath my nose, I can't break my stare, even when I try. Then, to even my own surprise, a sly, uncharacteristic smile washes over my lips and I rest my jaw on my fists.

For a second, he looks paler, as if he's just seen a ghost. He clears his throat and reaches for his drink with his ring-clad fist. Some rings are silver, others gold, and the one around his ring finger—a band of black diamond.

The curious side of me wants to play along. How far can I go before he realizes I do not remember him? I only manage to get a few bites in before the servants bring out the next course—a dish of purple noodles.

I straighten my shoulders more and spin noodles onto my fork. "They carved a knife down my back. Beat me. Starved me of air." All of that I deduced from wounds, and he doesn't seem to suspect a thing as he takes a few large gulps of wine.

Lleu looks like she's holding her breath.

He tilts his head. "Oh? Tell me more about your brave show of valiance."

"I survived Lavenai. You should be relieved."

He doesn't react, concentrating on his own plate of food, swiping butter across his dinner roll with a knife. "Yes, the cruel and heartless Laven from the planet of, oh, what color was it again, Margot?"

Color drains from my face. I can't remember. I'm sure Lleu told me earlier which planet was green and which was purple. I force a laugh. "What a ridiculous question."

"Are our planets ridiculous?"

"That's not what I meant."

"Then tell me." He sets his roll down but doesn't look up at me. His expression is stoic and unbothered.

I bite down on my bottom lip. "Like I said, it's laughable for you to ask something like that."

"Then how about something easier?"

I roll my eyes. "Yes?"

"What's my name?"

Redness crawls up my neck as a servant sets the main course in front of me. What was I thinking? What was I even trying to do? Humiliate him when he clearly has the upper hand?

"There's no need to be embarrassed." The Colum signals a servant to refill his chalice. "I gave you a fair shot. Let you have your fun with whatever game you think you're playing with me. But you lost. And like before, you're just as conniving."

I fly to my feet, the chair screeching back. It takes all of my energy to hold back the tears that form in my eyes. Gods, to do something so weak and pathetic like cry in front of him would be the last straw. I feel grief for the woman I was before who jumped headfirst into a loveless marriage. Was I really the type to marry for fame and riches?

"I am going to bed." I swipe my plate off the table and signal Lleu away from the others and head to the door, waiting in agony for the motion sensor to detect me.

The Colum scoffs. "Would you like a map? It would be a shame if you got lost."

I have half a mind to pour the dinner plate over his head. When the doors finally open, he clears his throat, turning to face me fully, his dark eyes settling on mine with cold resolve. "My name is Milo."

Chapter 5

Lleu leads me through the long hallways of the north wing while I stuff my mouth full of food. No matter how flavorful the dish is, it doesn't stop me from replaying every second of my interaction with the Colum.

Milo Arris.

"The Colum will have my head after that." Lleu places the back of her hand against her forehead. "Why didn't Crux inform him? He swore he would. Gods, he must have done it on purpose just to spite me."

I've not met Crux, but whoever he is, I'm glad he forgot. If he had remembered, I may have never learned how horrible Milo truly is. Or maybe I would have. "Lleu, why didn't you tell me he was a complete assshole?"

Lleu glances up and down the hallway, both her hands clutching the end of one of her braids. At least she was the nervous one now. "He's the Colum, Margot. For me to speak that way of him is close to treason."

As my appetite withers away, an A.S.O.P. unit passes by, and I set my plate on top of its flat, square head without slowing my pace.

My trek to the bedroom becomes aimless. Lleu has to keep pulling on my arm to direct me down the correct hallways. All I can think about is Milo. How cruel he was to me.

Once we're finally to my quarters, Lleu unlocks the bedroom door. The sight of it is enough to make my jaw soften and make me forget all about Milo.

The room is more of a suite than anything. The walls are dark and the furniture luxurious, yet neutral. None of it compares to the extra large bed that seems completely useless for one person. Near the window, there's a lounge area like a platform, fitted with chairs and couches.

Lleu sorts through a wardrobe near the bed and pulls out a nightgown. "Tomorrow, we're working on your manners."

I turn so Lleu can unzip my dress. "You're mistaken if you think I will show Milo a single ounce of respect after the way he treated me."

"I've found with him it's best to keep my words short and simple."

"*You* are not the one who has to be married to him."

Lleu remains quiet, a stark tension forming between us. But I quickly remind myself that she is not my enemy here. When I think about being in her position, it seems even more exhausting—the way she's expected to balance her station, my memory loss, and our friendship.

I take a deep breath to clear my head. "Why did I marry him, anyway? Politics? Money? Power?"

She hits a snag on the zipper and wrestles with it. "You married him because you were in love."

In love? The thought is laughable. "Now isn't the time for jokes."

"It's true." She throws my gown to the side and helps me step into the silky nightgown. "You used to work in the south wing, you know. Even before I was your lady's maid, you and I were close friends."

"The south wing? So I was—"

"A soldier. Yes."

I don't know how to feel or how to react. I've had my own theories about who I was before Milo, but soldier was not one of them. Did I fly ships? Patrol the Imnicus? Escort the Colum on trips to Ashtanabo?

"And you never found it weird to be serving your best friend?" I ask.

"Not at all. Besides, if you hadn't personally requested me, I would have been stuck scrubbing toilets." She sticks her elbow in my side. "I know this brings up a lot of questions, but I think you have enough to process for one night."

Lleu winds my hair into a low bun and folds back the corner of the bedsheets. It's my first night not sleeping in a hospital bed, and just the sight of the mattress makes my eyes grow heavy.

After Lleu leaves, I go up into the lounge area and stand in front of the ceiling-high window out at the twinkling stars. In the distance, I can see Lavenai. I squint one eye shut and pretend the planet is in between my thumb and pointer finger. Then I squish it.

My attackers are still on the loose. Anytime I sleep, I could wake up to another invasion where I'm tortured and marked again. Maybe if they were gone, I wouldn't have these nightmares anymore. Without Lavenai, maybe I would know peace.

I curl up into one of the lounge chairs. I want to remember who I am. What I like and dislike. So far, every answer has left me with even more questions. I make the mistake of trying to remember the past and induce a mind splitting headache. Instead, I focus on the present.

Somehow, I climbed the ladder from an Imnicus employee to a Columess in a loveless marriage. But according to Lleu, I once loved Milo deeply. It makes me wonder how the servants and soldiers reacted to my engagement to him. Do I have enemies I don't even know about?

The bedroom door whooshes open and I'm too exhausted to turn my head. "Lleu, did you forget something?"

"Sorry to disappoint."

My stomach drops at the sound of Milo's voice. I quickly stand. "I may not remember a lot, but I know it's rude to enter a woman's room without knocking. What do you want?"

Milo undoes the clips holding his cloak, and it falls to the floor. Then he reaches for the top clasp of his top.

What is he . . . My mouth gapes. "What do you think you're doing?"

He lets out a long, drawn-out sigh. "Surely you don't expect me to give up my bedroom just to appease you?" His words don't stop him from undressing, the top coming undone, exposing his chest. "Or should I say, *our* room?"

My gaze dips to his abdomen a moment too long. I spin around and face the window. "This is insanity."

"Don't tell me you thought we had separate bedrooms?"

How could I have been so naïve? We're married, so of course we share a bedroom. The enormous size of the bed makes sense now—to maintain the illusion of a stable couple with the staff, when really our hearts are miles apart. Milo may be willing to put up with it, but I refuse to sleep in the same bed as him.

I take a decorative pillow off one of the lounge chairs and rush to the bathroom.

Milo undoes his belt buckle. "Where are you stomping off to?"

"I'm sleeping in the bathroom."

"Suit yourself."

I shut the door behind me and lean against the sink. The bathroom is fit for a Colum—eggshell walls with wainscoting, a jade claw-foot tub, and a golden-framed mirror.

Undressing and being naked in front of me may mean nothing to him, but to me, it means everything. He may know me as his wife, but he may as well be nothing more than a stranger to me. And I don't sleep in the same bed as strangers.

I nestle myself into the jade tub, laying my head on the pillow, the jewel in the center scratching my face. It's hard to ignore the chill in the bathroom, so after the first hour of tossing and turning,

I fashion one of the towels into a blanket, though it barely covers more than my torso.

Sometime deep in the night, my thoughts finally turn into dreams and my dreams into nightmares.

Chapter 6

The hallways of the Imnicus north wing are completely empty this time of night and the lights are dimmed. Not even the low thrum of the engine system is audible. I run my hand across the geometric walls, taking in the sensation of the protruding points.

It's strange though. The floor is raised in parts it shouldn't be, like small sets of stairs. The walls are cracked open to where I can see outer space.

I freeze as the halls become endless and more complex with paths disappearing and reappearing each time I turn.

Suddenly, the geometric labyrinth turns into a maze of mirrors, sharp and broken, protruding like icicles. When I turn too quickly, one of the points thinly slices my upper arm, making me curse.

My arm stings, the pain entirely familiar. I look at the mirrors again, and this time I'm able to hear their whispers.

They're trying to guide me to my memories, even if I encounter wounds along the way. They remind me that my memories aren't lost but shattered.

I take my pick and step into one of the mirrors, and the glistening floors turn to dirt and then moss. There is a large hill with swampy gray grass covered in mist. Even with limited visibility, I trek forward, stepping slowly.

In the distance, I hear caws getting closer and closer by the second.

A large bird zooms past my ear, brushing against my hair and cawing frantically at me. I shriek and jump back. Another whooshes past, then another, as if they're surrounding me like a tornado. I grab my hair and sink to my knees.

Finally, the cawing and talons stop, but the density of the fog increases and I can't see a thing. Still, I run, the nightmare beginning like it's breathing down the back of my neck.

I run into the thick, blinding mist, not caring if I could run off a cliff or into a tree. It isn't until I'm near the top of the hill, and completely out of breath, that I stop.

I'm not alone on this hill.

A male figure, as indistinguishable as a phantom, crouches on top of a tall stone fixture. Behind him, red-and-black berries hang from the branches of a white, leafless tree.

He raises his forearm and a large bird lands on it.

"Margot, Margot, Margot. We really need to stop meeting like this. It's no fun at all."

When I try to take a step back, my legs are heavy like lead. I can't move nor escape him. Static encases my limbs and I twist, falling onto my chest.

I try to pull myself forward on my forearms back in the direction I came, yelling at the dead weight of my legs. "Come on, work!"

"Haven't you learned anything yet? There's no point in running." Heavy boots hit the ground behind me, but instead of the dull sound of grass, I hear the echo of his heels landing on metal.

All it takes is one prolonged blink for my surroundings to change completely.

Where there were once foggy forests and mountains, there's now metal walls with torturous instruments hanging from racks. Rain falls from the ceiling as my arms go numb too, and I can't do anything more than blink and speak. The metal floor is cold against the side of my face. I need to move, fight. *Anything.*

"I won't give you what you want," I say without thinking. It's like a different part of me has taken over that I neither know nor recognize.

An arm wraps around my waist, pulling me up into his chest. "Is that so?"

I can move a little more now, but no matter how much I thrash and scream, his hold stays tight.

He runs a finger down my temple and my body immediately goes slack. *No, gods, no.*

The figure repositions my dead weight, carrying me bridal style across the dark room toward the cold metal table. "It seems you're due for another lesson. Maybe that will get you to talk."

My breath trembles. *Please.*

The water from the ceiling beats down harder, soaking my hair and masking my tears.

My body doesn't listen, no matter how much I want to fight back.

He lies me on the table, smoothing back my hair, and watching my lower lip tremble.

Click. Click. Cuffs around my wrists.

Click. Click. Another set around my ankles.

When I try to scream, nothing except a whimpering squeak exits my throat.

"Shhh," he hushes. "I know you're scared, but you can stop this. Just tell me what I need to know, and I can make it go away. All the pain. All the nightmares. Just answer my one simple question."

All I manage is one simple word. "No."

The guy smiles. "So be it."

His hands slam onto my temples, an indescribable pain piercing through my skull while high-pitched screeches saw through my head, like metal scraping down my mind.

I shoot up, gasping for air, my fingers gripping the sides of the jade tub. My back aches from the night of sleeping on its hard surface, and my head is pounding the way it does when I'm trying to remember the past.

Thank the gods. It was just another dream.

There's not a single night that I've gone without having a nightmare. Even the sweetest dreams eventually turn sour.

Too dizzy to step out of the tub, I rest my head against its curved edges. Beads of sweat coat the back of my neck, and my nightgown is completely damp.

Something about waking up like this, perspiring from head to toe, makes me burn with anger. It makes me wish I had the ability and resources to take care of Lavenai myself.

Not knowing *why* they tortured me is what really makes me shudder. They broke into a highly guarded ship, had access to the Colum's wife, and chose not to assassinate me. For some reason, they thought it better to erase my memories instead. What did they really want? And will they eventually come back for more?

I look down at my body and startle. All I had last night to warm me was a towel, but now I'm covered in a thick comforter. But I recognize this linen . . .

It's Milo's comforter.

Did I scream in my sleep? Did he hear? My skin crawls at the thought of him gazing over me while I was caught in my nightmares. The comforter's so heavy that it takes all my strength to haul it off of me.

I cautiously step out of the bathroom and breathe a sigh of relief when I see the bed empty. The Colum is the last person I want to see right now.

For a few minutes, I stand in the center of the room, unsure what I'm supposed to do or even what time of day it is. My stomach growls.

Should I wait for Lleu to arrive? Or maybe call her with the communicator on the wall? No, for all I know it could be early morning and I'd be disturbing her rest.

I open the in-room wardrobe, searching for anything to wear. Though not stocked with dresses like my dressing room, it has nightgowns along with casual clothing. Finally, I find a pair of black pants and a white top that seems acceptable enough.

After refreshing my curls in the bathroom with some water, I hit the button and the door slides open.

With five wings and ten-thousand employees, every section of the Imnicus bleeds into the next. When I was dressed as Columess, or had Lleu by my side, everyone we passed nodded or bowed. But dressed casually like this, nobody bats an eye, not even a lieutenant who walks by, as if they're so engrossed in their jobs that anyone who's not bedazzled in fine clothes is not worthy enough to catch their attention.

After an hour of walking in circles, with no luck finding any kind of kitchen, I make it to the south wing. This part of the wing is quieter than the rest, almost like it's abandoned. The blue lights that line the halls are darker and there's not a soul around.

The lights start flickering with a low buzz, sending a shiver up my spine. I would think that a ship with such heightened technology would be up to date on changing its bulbs. It makes me pick up the pace when rounding a corner.

Into a hall that's darker than the last.

The lights flicker so rapidly, I can hardly see. Each movement makes it seem like my arms and legs are moving at half the speed.

I stop in my tracks as something appears at the end of the hallway. All too dark and all too familiar, except this time I know I'm not dreaming.

The hooded figure walks toward me with urgency in his steps, like a waking nightmare.

To me, with the flickering bulbs and the inability to make out his face in the low light, he's nothing but the man from my nightmares. The one who haunts me night after night, finding more ways to torment me. A Laven.

I back up but lose my step, tumbling to the ground. I look over my shoulder, his steps still filled with purpose.

Why is he here? What does he want from me?

"Stay back!"

He bends over and reaches out for me.

I spin onto my back, lacing my legs around his, tripping him to the floor.

He grunts but recovers quickly, crawling over me and grabbing my wrists that can't seem to land a punch. "Margot."

"I said stop!" I close my eyes, unable to bear what he may look like.

He pins me down, using his kneecap to stop my thighs from kicking him between his legs. "Hey, hey, you're safe. It's just me, Knox. Don't you remember?"

I go still and stop yelling. *Knox?* The flickering dwindles, and soon I'm left face to face with who I thought was the monster under my bed.

His eyes are soft and his mask is made of embossed paisley designs. A proditor, just like Alarik. With their obstructive uniforms, combined with the flickering lights, it's easy to see why I mistook him for something horrible.

"You scared the shit out of me." My breaths still sound like I'm hyperventilating.

He sits back on his knees. I push myself up while he removes his mask and hood, which I thought was forbidden.

And it only takes a half-second look at Knox's true face to vanquish my anxieties completely. His curly golden hair frames his sharp face and dark blue eyes. He seems to be around Milo's age, in his late twenties.

He's as beautiful as the sun, yet I just treated him like a spawn of Hades.

I go red in the face. "I can't begin to tell you how sorry I am."

"Don't mention it, Columess. I know, after everything, you must still be on edge."

"It's just . . . you looked like something out of a nightmare."

Knox laughs, rubbing the back of his neck. "Well, I didn't think I was *that* ugly."

I rethink my remark. "No! I'm sorry, I didn't mean it like that."

Knox stands and helps me to my feet. "Now, now, there's no reason to apologize. In fact, I should be the one apologizing. Some of the bulbs in the south wing are old. When their frequency hits me just right, the electricity goes ballistic."

"Proditor magic?"

"Hey, see? You remember stuff already."

"Not to cheat, but I already met Alarik."

Knox starts walking. "Ah, well, still. I believe your memories will return in time."

"That's what they all say." I follow after him.

"What were you doing out and about anyway dressed like . . . " Knox points to my clothing. "That."

"Trying to find a kitchen. I'm starving. What time is it anyway?"

"There's no time here, so in a way, you can never miss breakfast. It's also never *too late* for breakfast." Knox replaces his disguise.

Knox escorts me to the north wing and into a smaller dining room where a servant girl immediately stands the second we enter, as if her only job is to serve Milo and the proditors at their whim. "Sloane, would you be a dear and ask the chef to whip us up something nice?"

Sloane nods. "Yes, Proditor Knox." She disappears out the side door.

"You really didn't have to do this," I say. "I could have settled on a snack to hold me over."

Knox pulls out a chair for me. "Please, what's the point of being a Columess if you can't have pastries whenever you'd like?"

I laugh, taking a seat. "You have a point."

Knox sits across from me, kicking his feet on the table and leaning back into his chair. "So, how are you adjusting? Or readjusting, I should say."

"Good," I say. *What am I saying?* It's been hell since I've left the medic bay. "Well, to be honest, it's been a challenge." Since I have no good words to say about Milo, I keep it to Lavenai. "I keep trying to remember what happened, but I keep hitting roadblocks, and the effort gives me horrible headaches. Sorry, that's probably more than you wanted to know."

"Not at all. It's only natural to wonder, and I've been worried about you."

It's strange that someone whose name I just learned is concerned about me. But compared to Alarik, I feel strangely close to Knox. Maybe we were close friends? Or was he assigned to me more than the other proditors?

Sloane and a few other maids bring out breakfast soups, pastries, fruits, and meats, along with refreshments. I take a sip and immediately taste the alcohol. "Isn't it too early to drink?"

"Remember what I said? There's no time. For us it's breakfast, and for others it's dinner. Why not pretend it's both?"

"Well, I can't argue with that." I smile. "What time is it on Lavenai?"

"Does your mind always go to your attackers?"

"How can it not?" I take another sip. "I don't even know why they did this to me."

Knox waits until the servants leave and the door is secured before he yanks his mask off and tosses a berry in the air, catching it in his mouth. "It's because they blame us."

"For what?"

"Many years ago, an Ashtanaban immigrant on Lavenai made a mistake in one of their power plants, causing a detrimental explosion. It wiped out thousands."

"So they want revenge? That's why they attacked the Imnicus?"

"Revenge, definitely. But it's starting to get to the point where they want Ashtanabo itself as rectification. The remnants of the explosion spread all throughout their planet, causing pollution and poisoning many of their plants and wildlife. Their planet is basically unlivable without our assistance."

"And was Milo always their Colum?"

"No. Lavenai's former Colum lost his mind, blamed us for the explosion, and considered it an act of war. They attacked us, we retaliated and we won, taking control of the leadership of Lavenai. To this day, Ashtanabo continues to try to restore Lavenai, but all they do is resist us."

I shove down the sympathy that forms for Lavenai. Though, it was horrible that happened, all as a result of one person. "I don't understand why they chose not to kill me."

"Neither do we."

"What if I told them confidential information?"

Knox takes a bite of a pastry. "That's what Milo is worried about. On top of the fact that we haven't found the breach yet."

At any moment, it could happen again. If I could just remember the moment before I lost my memories, maybe Milo would know who to hunt down.

Before I know it, I've already finished an entire glass of the fruity drink. Knox is staring at me, as if waiting for me to say something in response to his last comment.

"Oh, I'm so sorry. I have found conversions to be difficult to maintain without my memories."

"Then ask me a question." He leans on his forearms and pours me another glass from the bottle the servants left. "I find it helps. Besides, I can assume you have many."

He's not wrong. "Why am I allowed to see your face and the servants aren't?"

"See, was that so hard? The only people allowed to see my face are the Colum, Columess, other proditors, and a few exceptions here and there."

"I don't see the mask's purpose. Doesn't it make it hard to fight?"

"It's proditor code, but mostly meant for our safety and well-being. You see, we're feared on both planets. There are not many types of magic out there, which gives us the upper hand on humans. If I wear the mask, I can still have days off, maybe go to a nightclub on land or take a nice holiday. I can pass through cities without people recognizing my face and seeing me as an angel of death."

Knox becomes a vessel of information that I can't help but take advantage of, and he seems happy to oblige. I ask him more questions about the workings of the Imnicus, more efficient ways to get around, the hierarchy of servants and soldiers, and a little about the other proditors.

Next we move on to more personal topics and since I have nothing to share, he tells me things that annoy him about the Imnicus—tedious traditions and protocols. Sure, he does most of the talking, but there's more than enough air for me to contribute to the conversation.

Soon, I'm on my fourth glass and him on his fifth. We're laughing hysterically, and I'm having more fun than I ever have on the Imnicus.

"So, wait, what are they called again?" I can't stop laughing at the description of the animal he gave me. They're native to Lavenai but misshapen from pollution. Their heads are so much bigger than their bodies, that when they crawl the wrong way, they fall on their faces.

Knox grabs his stomach, trying to hold back. "Waddle bears."

Both of us start laughing so hard that tears are leaking from our eyes. I know what we're talking about is not funny in the slightest, but I can't help it. My body needed laughter more than I even realized.

"Knox, what the hell are you doing?"

Knox and I stop laughing in the presence of the stern voice at the doorway, which I didn't even hear open. Even with the many drinks I've had, it doesn't stop my shoulders from tensing. If I could have gone the rest of the day without seeing him, it would have been nirvana.

"Ah, Milo, join us!" Knox waves him in, his words slightly slurred.

"How many times do I have to remind you of your position? You're a proditor, not some servant who can afford to get drunk in the middle of the day."

"It's all just innocent fun. Lighten up."

Milo's gaze passes over the table, the glasses of wine, and then settles on me. "You should have waited for Lleu to escort you.

You're not well enough to be navigating the Imnicus on your own."

The anger alone sobers me up enough to scoff, though I can't admit to him that I got lost and then tried to attack one of his proditors. "I'm an adult woman. I don't need a nanny."

"You're not even properly dressed."

"Nobody even recognized me," I mutter.

"Knox, leave us."

"Come on, things were just getting interesting," Knox complains, but replaces his disguise anyway. "It was nice catching up again, Margot. Until next time."

Milo and I stand there in silence, the low hum of the ship audible.

"I thought you were too busy with your duties to worry about where I was," I say.

Milo rakes a hand through his thick black hair. "You're a girl with no memories navigating the largest space-naval vessel known to mankind. When Lleu asked me where you were, I had no choice but to track you down and make sure you were all right."

"How valiant of you. Do you want a medal?" I stand and walk to the head of the table in front of him, leaning back against it. "I'm not a prisoner, Colum."

"No, you're a Columess." Milo takes a step forward, placing his hands on the table outside of my hips, sticking his face near mine.

I didn't expect him to get so close. My heart pounds as I quickly lean back.

"And I expect you to act like one." Milo grabs a blue fruit from the tray behind me and straightens, taking a large bite out.

"And what you mean by that is dressing up in fancy attire, never going anywhere without a lady's maid, and having virtually no fun until the day I die?"

"You know that's not what I mean. You have every right to explore the Imnicus and to make friends. But you cannot strut around in civilian clothing or get drunk with proditors. People talk, and everything you do reflects on me. Including making a fool of yourself."

"A fool? How dare—"

"Colum," Lleu interrupts from the doorway. "I'm here to escort Margot to her dressing room."

Milo's shoulders drop, yet his dark eyes still pierce into me. He turns around to Lleu. "Don't let her out of your sight."

He whips around her, his boots clicking against the tile.

Chapter 7

Back in my dressing room, I slump down onto one of the couches while Lleu frantically searches for a dress.

"Margot, I'm so sorry. I should have told you the plan for the day. I didn't expect you to go off on your own."

I throw my hands up. "Why does it even matter to Milo? I'm the Columess. I should be able to do what I want."

"The people on the Imnicus can be horrible gossips, especially many of the servants. Milo may be cold and crass on the outside, but I know deep down he doesn't want people to speak poorly of you."

"What you mean to say is that he doesn't want people to speak poorly of *him*."

Lleu sighs, keeping her next words to herself.

She dresses me in a light-blue gown with a long, sheer cape attached to the back. The sleeves fall off the shoulder. Next, she directs me to sit at the vanity, where she loosely braids my hair down my back.

"I have something for you," Lleu says, as she ties off the end of my hair.

"If it's more news about the attack, I don't think I can take it."

"No, not news. An item." Lleu opens the vanity drawer and pulls out a small glass box with golden edges. "Milo wants you to start wearing this again." Once she shows me what's inside, my blood boils over.

Opal sits in the center of the rose gold band, surrounded by two diamonds set in silver. The silver veers into small spikes at the edges, resembling a star.

A wedding ring. My breath gets stuck on the inhale.

"I thought maybe it's time you wear this. You've not been the Columess long, so not many people on the Imnicus recognize you unless they worked with you directly. This may also help to integrate yourself into society as our Columess. Not to mention your security clearance is in the diamonds, so once Milo settles down, you'll be able to get around most of the Imnicus without my help." Lleu takes my hand and slides the ring on.

"This is ridiculous." But when I see her hand, I immediately forget about Milo and the ring. *Is that . . . a burn?*

"What happened to you?" I take her hand, inspecting it under the light. A blue burn covers her dark skin from her hand up to her wrist.

She yanks her hand back. "Oh, that? It's just a silly little thing that happened, is all. I was making moon tea last night and pressed it against the side of the kettle. Clumsy me!" Lleu forces a laugh.

"But why is it blue? You should see a medic!" I can't believe she hasn't. It looks horrible. I may not remember a lot, but I know even the worst of burns aren't usually blue.

"Margot, I'm more than fine. It happens all the time. Now face the mirror, I need to touch up your makeup."

I don't speak to Milo for the next few days. Not when we sit across the table at meals, or when I race into the bathroom as he strips out of his clothes for the night.

The worst part about sleeping in the bathroom, besides my back aching from the hard tub, is how stuck I feel when the sleepless nights hit, which is most of them now. If it isn't from fear of my nightmares, then it's from thoughts of Lavenai.

Nobody seems to be any closer to finding out how they got in, what they wanted in the first place, or even what information they tortured me over. I wish I could start my own investigation. How can anyone expect me to sit idly by while my attackers roam free? And if I find them, they could be the key to restoring my memories.

Milo seems to be more concerned with making sure I'm kept under lock and key until I become *more acclimated*, whatever that means. If I'm not in my room, he orders Lleu to watch over me, and even on a ship as large as the Imnicus, there isn't much to do besides read and stare at the stars. It's been mind-numbing torture.

In my dressing room, while Lleu cleans, I scroll through a tablet, brushing up on current events and past ones in Ashtanabo. Though, most of what is easily searchable is celebrity related.

Lleu hums a tune, sorting through dresses that are in need of steaming.

Bored out of my mind, I set the tablet on the nearby table. "Do you want any help?"

"No, Margot. It isn't proper. The Colum was very firm with me that he wants you to act more like your title, and a Columess does not clean her own dressing room." Lleu places a silver-black dress on the rack.

"Think about it—if you let me help you, you'll be done quicker, and both of us will get to relax for the rest of the day."

"Nice try."

"Don't servants go insane with all the monotony? Living the same day over and over?"

Lleu laughs. "It's a completely different world in the east wing. Drama and theatrics. Servants gawking over soldiers. Parties. And of course, there is the nightclub."

"A nightclub?" I've gone on many walks, but I haven't seen a nightclub or anything remotely resembling one.

"Yes. It's called the Jupiter. The former Colum named it after his favorite planet from a neighboring galaxy."

I like the way Lleu describes the east wing. It may be beneath my station, but something about it feels right. Familiar, even. The idea of visiting the nightclub fills me with a sense of normalcy. "We should go."

"Wait, what?" Lleu raises her eyebrows.

"Tonight. I mean, why not? As long as you're by my side, I'm still technically following Milo's wishes."

"His wish was to stop you from making a fool of yourself in front of his subjects. His words, not mine."

"When I'm not dressed like a Columess, nobody even recognizes me. They won't even know I'm there."

Lleu rubs her temples. "I don't know. The Colum would have my head if he found out."

"And that's why he never will. I'll even have you straighten my curls to blend in more."

She still looks uneasy.

I stomp my foot and overly straighten my posture. "Lleu, as your Columess, I command you to bring me to the Jupiter."

Lleu laughs and then I do. Both of us not being able to take my commands seriously really shows how my title is nothing more than a decoration for Milo.

"Fine, Lady Arris. But you need to be subtle and discreet. Eat dinner with him like normal, and then I will take you."

Chapter 8

At dinner, I pierce my fork into the crispy, purple leaves of my salad. It isn't until some of the dressing goes down the wrong pipe that I realize I'm eating too fast, sending myself into a fit of coughs.

"Are you trying to choke yourself? Slow down," Milo says.

I take a sip of water. "I can eat at whatever pace I choose, Colum."

"Not if you're going to hurt yourself."

Lleu is off to the side with the other servants, but even she mouths to me to tone it down.

I pray to the gods that this meal will be over soon. Lleu and I will finally have a night where we can ignore responsibilities, and, most importantly, avoid Milo. But it feels like every course is taking longer than usual.

I finish the last bite of my salad and signal a humanoid to take my plate. "You know, I had a large lunch, and I'm completely stuffed. I think I will take my leave now." I push back my chair.

"Sit," he commands without looking up from the table.

"I'm not hungry."

"You will wait here until all the courses are complete, even if you choose not to eat them. My chefs and servants work hard on every meal for us. It's the least you can do."

A deep shame washes over me. In all my complaining and being bogged down by my own issues, I've hardly acknowledged or thanked the staff.

The rest of dinner feels like an eternity. To respect the servants, I finish every bite of my food, even after I'm long stuffed. But Milo is still only halfway done. It's like he's taking his sweet time just to taunt me, savoring every last crumb, as if he knows how much it's pissing me off.

The second his dessert fork hits his empty plate, I stand and turn to the staff. "Thank you for everything. It was delicious."

The servants and Lleu bow and curtsy. An A.S.O.P. unit beeps something unintelligible. In all this, I hope I did not offend them. Though it still hasn't tapered my excitement for the Jupiter.

When I walk past Milo, he shoots me a suspicious glare.

Inside the dressing room, I yank my heels off, grumbling about how slowly Milo ate.

Lleu hands me the dress she's letting me borrow. "You need to be more careful. You were writhing around like an asylum patient."

"You saw him. He knows we're up to something." I stand to face the mirror.

Lleu unzips the back of my dinner dress. "Listen, the Jupiter is fun, but it's not worth pissing Milo off over. It's open all the time, so there's no need to rush."

"But if I'm not back before Milo retires for the night, he'll come looking for me." *I think.* "I've been cooped up almost this entire week. Can you blame me for getting a little excited?"

Lleu laughs. "All I know is that you're paying for every drink tonight."

She prepares items at my vanity while I slip myself into the tight dress. It has a maturity that none of my own dresses have.

It's much more provocative than anything in my wardrobe, featuring metal mesh material ending mid-thigh. It comes with a band made of hanging chains that fit snug around my thigh where the leg slit is, as well as another band for my upper arm. From what I've seen around the Imnicus, Ashtanabans seem to love body jewelry.

Lleu uses hot moon rocks to straighten my hair, then ties it into a high ponytail. She uses her artistry to paint my eyelids a shimmering gray, contouring the eyeliner to give the illusion of a different eye shape.

At first glance, I'm unrecognizable as the Columess. In fact, I barely recognize myself.

I do what I can to help Lleu get ready, but she doesn't seem to need any assistance. Lleu has a natural beauty to her—dark skin and hair, plump lips, sparkling eyes. She's far too pretty to be stuck in the role of a servant. It makes me wonder why she chose this life.

"Tonight, don't treat me like a Columess. I want to have fun and forget," I say.

"Okay, *Margot*." Lleu grabs a pair of heels and throws them at my feet instead of helping me into them like she normally does. "Put these on and let's get out of here."

Lleu leads us to an area tucked away between the east and south wings, which explains why I never stumbled upon it during my walks. Electronic music thumps and gets louder with every step closer. Our footsteps fall to the steady beat of the music. It thrums in my chest, increasing my already excited pulse.

We squeeze our way through the Imnicus employees congregating in the hallway, but without their uniforms, I cannot tell who is military and who is servant. In a way, I like it. It makes us all feel like equals. Most of them are dressed in shiny, glittering, casual outfits. One guy burrows out the crowded entrance with a girl on his arm, headed toward the east wing dorms.

Lleu takes my hand. "Come on." She raises her voice a few times at other partygoers to get us through, and finally, we make it into the club.

The Jupiter is lit by gold, cylindrical lights. One of the club's walls is all window and overlooks the galaxy, the stars and satellites giving the illusion of glitter. People linger against the bar, paneled with alternating rectangular mirrors and gold pipes. Two girls laugh together, their hands full with gold-tinted wineglasses.

Nobody bats an eye at me. Just like I suspected, I am completely unrecognizable when dressed like this.

Lleu finds us seats at the bar and waves at the bartender.

"So Margot," Lleu says. "Is it everything you thought it would be?"

I watch the men and women on the dance floor moving to electronic music. Something about it feels familiar, especially when the strobe lights turn a deep red. "I'm enjoying myself so far."

"Just you wait until we get our drinks." Lleu finally gets the bartender's attention and orders.

The bartender makes us two drinks in tall-necked glasses and slides them over the mirrored bar. The liquid swirls with pink and silver glitter. Sugar crystals stick to the rim of the glass, and a small skewer pierces through Ashtanaban fruit.

Lleu sips her drink, glitter staining her upper lip. I stir my drink with the skewer. It's so extravagant, it doesn't even look edible.

"Drink it already!" Lleu pushes the glass closer to my mouth.

I roll my eyes and take a gulp. Then another. It's after the fifth swallow that I finally feel warmth rushing to my head, and realize I should probably slow down. Whatever is in it is stronger than wine.

As Lleu finishes her drink, I spot a guy smiling at her across the bar, desire in his eyes.

"Who is that?" I yell.

Lleu glances over her shoulder and shrugs. "I've seen him around."

"You're not interested?"

"There's someone else I have my eye on." Lleu stares down at the bar, a small smile on her lips.

Who could it be? She's been so busy with her duties, I can't imagine who she'd even have time to crush on. It would have to be someone whose duties intersect with hers, like a—

"You like Proditor Alarik?" I shout over the music.

Lleu panics, looking over her shoulders and covering my mouth. "Don't say it so loud!"

I laugh into her hand, then pry it away. "Lleu crushing on a proditor. How scandalous."

"If you tell anyone, I'll pinch you. I don't care if you're the Columess." She buries her face in her hands.

I place a hand on her shoulder. "Let's just hope he's all you wish for beneath that mask of his."

Lleu rolls her eyes and takes another sip of her drink, but her motions are too quick, making her spill a few drops on her dress. "Dammit. I'll be right back."

I laugh. "Take your time."

After she leaves, I watch the people on the dance floor, jealous of how carefree all of them look. It only takes a minute for a man to approach me and ask to dance, but I dismiss him. Dancing with a guy, on top of defying Milo, will only make things worse for me.

I hop off the stool and roam through the club on my own, pushing past groups of people to a quieter area of the club with circular booths and tables. It has a smaller bar and only a few people strewn throughout. It takes one scan of the partitioned-off room to see why.

A proditor is here.

He sits in a corner booth, a woman on both sides of him. I back up, cursing to myself. But it's possible he may not recognize me dressed like this. Maybe he's as dense as the other staff. I don't recognize the cascading metallic waves decorating his mask, so I know he's not one I've met before.

The proditor doesn't even look in my direction, stroking the face of a blue-haired woman and holding the thigh of a pink-haired one.

I take a seat at the bar with my back facing the proditor. If I go back to the main area, someone may ask me to dance. At least here, I'll have some quiet time until Lleu returns.

"What can I get you?" the bartender asks while he shines a glass with a cloth.

"Which proditor is that?" I ask quietly.

He squints through the dim lighting. "Either Crux or Onyx, I don't know. They all look the same in this damn lightning. Ahh, great, and now he's waving me over. Please excuse me."

I look at one of the mirrored panels behind the bar to watch the interaction. The bartender approaches the proditor and leans close to hear him over the music.

The bartender nods a few times before circling back around the bar in front of me. He pours green liquid into a glass and slides the drink in front of me. "From Proditor Onyx, Columess. And I do apologize for not recognizing you sooner." He bows his head.

Dammit. This proditor, Onyx, recognized me. I look up at the mirrored wall to spy on him again, but his eyes are already on me.

Onyx winks.

Shit.

He grabs his drink and pushes himself out of the booth, squeezing past one of the ladies. My muscles tighten as the sound of heavy boots comes up behind me.

"Does Milo know you're here?" He leans against the bar, adjusting his hood enough for me to see his eyes, olive skin, and longish white-blonde hair.

I gulp. "I'm taking the night off from being the Columess."

He sits on the barstool to my left. "I didn't realize that was an option."

If he tells Milo, I'm done for. "How did you recognize me?"

"You expect old friends to forget each other so easily?"

I frown, but he holds up a hand. "Forgive me, poor choice of words. But your ring is also a dead giveaway."

I grip my ring finger to cover it. I didn't even think to take it off. "Right."

"Onyx Tanaka." He offers his hand, and I shake it. "Nice to meet you. *Again.*"

"I hope I can trust you to keep quiet about me being here?"

"Ahh . . . now my discretion doesn't come cheap. Thankfully, I am known to offer discounts for friends from time to time."

I raise an eyebrow. "What did you have in mind? I doubt it's money you want."

"I want you to drink. And I want you to dance."

It's not what I expected him to say. My brows narrow in suspicion. "Why? So you can humiliate me?"

"Never. Tonight, I want what you want."

"And what is it I want?"

"To relax, I presume," Onyx says.

My eyes steel over. Milo punishes people for simply relaxing, which I learned the hard way with Knox.

Onyx picks up on my apprehension. "Don't worry. I know Milo can be a stick in the mud, even on a good day. And he hasn't had one of those since . . . you know."

"Are you even allowed to say something like that?"

"I've known Milo since I was born. I've seen every tantrum and shameful moment of his. So yes, I know how he can be." His eyes crinkle as he smiles. He waves off the women in the booth, who scowl at him in return. "So, is my assessment right? You're here to live a little. Find yourself, as some may say."

"That's about right." I rub the back of my neck. "And it seems you're giving me no choice."

"You'd be right."

"But your second request . . ." I glance at the main area. "I'm not sure dancing is part of my agenda tonight."

"Well first, finish that." Onyx signals to my drink. "After one or two more, you'll know how to dance better than anyone on the Imnicus."

I stare at the swirling green of the drink before me. There's nothing but trouble at the bottom of it, yet I bring it to my lips. I drain the whole thing before I can stop myself.

"That's more like it." Onyx orders a round of shots.

The liquor has barely settled in my stomach before he's dragging me out of the lounge and back into the main room. His presence sets people on edge, but they keep dancing. He makes space for us right in the center of the dance floor.

Onyx grabs my hands and tries making me move. "Trust me, it will be fun."

I mimic the movements of those around me but feel entirely out of place. Minutes later, my body feels warmer and my head airy. I take a step back, laughing hysterically.

"There she is." Onyx smiles. "Now, move like your life depends on it."

It takes me a song to get into it, but finally I'm moving my hips and raising my arms, making Onyx clap and whistle. When I spin, I lock eyes with Lleu across the club, her jaw completely dropped. Even if she thinks I'm making a mistake, I don't care.

Soon, there's another drink in my hand. Lleu finally gives up on her scowling and joins us on the dance floor. Onyx cheers and gives her a spin.

I give her a big hug. "You know . . . I never told you how bad I felt about not remembering you. How could I forget my best friend? You're wonderful." My words slur.

"Gods, you're drunk." She shoots a glare at Onyx. "How much did you give her? I knew I shouldn't have left her alone."

"I gave her as much as she needed." Onyx nudges her shoulder. "Now both of you need to lighten up and enjoy the music."

The three of us find our rhythm, dancing in a circle together. All the while, I can't stop smiling. Lleu shuts down the advances of every guy who tries to cut in to dance with me.

Onyx's movements are more reserved. He seems much more interested in watching me, though he doesn't dare touch me in the way some on the dance floor are.

That doesn't stop him from coaxing me into dancing even more provocatively. He points at my hips, directing me to move more without a single word. I shake my hips around, running my hands up my waist and chest. Even the Imnicus workers finally relax and gather around in the circle, cheering me on.

The alcohol peaks, and I jump around and shout, feeling alive. I'm not a prisoner; I'm not a Columess; I'm not a pawn for Milo to control.

Onyx slides a small circular table into the middle of the dance floor and helps me onto it. I'm making a complete fool of myself, but I don't care. In fact, I'm willing to lie and scheme if it means coming back here every night.

The crowd is in awe. Some people laugh at my provocative dance moves on the table, while others stare in shock. But halfway through the next song, the expressions of everyone fade.

Lleu tugs on my dress, panic in her eyes.

What? I mouth. Did my dress rip? Did they realize I am the Columess?

The music stops and everyone goes quiet. Not a single murmur.

"Margot!"

Oh no. I spin around, nearly losing my balance.

Milo.

With his ring-clad hands clenched, he stomps through the club, his cape trailing behind him. Everyone parts a path for him quickly so he doesn't so much as graze them, as if his wrath is contagious.

"What the hell do you think you're doing?" Milo says through gritted teeth.

"So good to see you. You should dance with us." I attempt to hide the slur in my words.

"No, we're leaving."

"Perhaps later." I smile. In front of his subjects, he's not going to try anything. He said it himself—people talk.

"Get off the table *now*."

"No, thank you."

The humanoid DJ stands stiffly behind his setup.

"Play the music again!" I shout to the humanoid.

Milo takes a step back, as if I'm the first to question his authority. What is he going to do about it, anyway? Hit me? I'd invite it. It would give me an excuse to punch him right in his smug—

Milo wraps his arms around my legs, tripping me onto his broad shoulder. I hang over his back, and his tight grip keeps me locked in place. It's only when I'm inverted that I realize how drunk I really am.

"Put me down!" I pound on his back.

Milo scans the room. "All of you, back to your dorms. Now!"

They scatter like ants past us, his direction almost causing a stampede. Onyx and Lleu stay put, avoiding eye contact with Milo. I can hear Onyx cursing beneath his mask.

The blood is rushing to my head, and I finally stop fighting Milo. My body slumps and he adjusts me to support my near-dead weight.

"Onyx, what were you thinking?" Milo seethes through his teeth.

Onyx stands in formation, arms folded behind his back. "Colum, I thought you were aware."

"Don't lie to me, Proditor."

Onyx stays silent.

In a daze, I play with Milo's cape, rolling the cotton between my fingers. He shakes me, causing a wave of nausea to pass over me and my arms to hang again.

"And Lleu . . . " He sighs heavily. "Knox will deal with you two later."

Onyx could go to hell for all I care, but my heart aches for Lleu. What was I thinking, bringing her into my mess?

As Milo leaves the club with me over his shoulder, I can feel eyes on us in the surrounding hallways, but thankfully the stares don't last long. His presence makes everyone rush away or pretend like they are in the middle of some task.

Every step makes me sicker and sicker. His shoulder cuts into my hip bones, but anytime I try to fight him, I end up more nauseated than before.

"I can walk," I slur when we're halfway there.

He ignores me and moves me to his other shoulder like I weigh nothing, refusing to put me down as if I'm going to escape him.

When we're finally back in our bedroom, I groan as he offloads me onto the bed. My back lands hard against the mattress. He pours me a glass of water as I sit up and rest against the headboard.

"Drink." Milo shoves the glass into my hands.

"You sound like Onyx." I bring the glass to my lips, taking small sips, careful not to overdo it.

He undresses himself while I rehydrate. Normally, I'd look away, or yell at him, but in my drunken haze, I can't seem to look away from his chest. The sight makes my stomach tighten.

I pretend to look at something else when he turns in my direction.

"I hope you know I can never let you go back there," Milo says firmly.

I scoff. "Wouldn't expect anything less."

Milo sighs. "I'm only doing what's best for you. *For us.* In letting them see you like that, it undermines my authority."

My title holds no power. I have more authority over Lleu's dress than I do over anyone on this ship. I saw how they trembled in front of the Colum. "Nobody even recognized me until you barged in."

"Onyx did. And do you think they'd say a word even if they had? When it's so obvious you're trying to sneak into their club undercover? Not to mention, in Lleu's attire."

His eyes dip to my dress, making me overly aware of my cleavage and exposed thighs. I fold my arms over my chest.

I stand, still hugging myself. "Put yourself in my shoes and try to understand for one second what it's like to be in my situation. To not remember anyone or anything, then to be kept in a cage!"

"To be in our positions comes with great sacrifice. It's the life you chose when you accepted my proposal."

I laugh sarcastically, and as I open my mouth to say something, I retreat, a wave of nausea gripping me. I cover my mouth.

Milo reacts before I can, wrapping me in his bare arms and hauling me to the bathroom. He makes me kneel over the toilet bowl just in time for me to purge. I hear him pull up a small stool and sit behind me, his coarse hands pulling stray hairs away from my dampened face.

"Anytime I drink with Onyx, I end up exactly the way you are now." His words are sharp. He grabs a towel and dabs up the sweat on the back of my neck. "You'd do well to remember that the next time he starts shoving drinks down your throat."

I heave again, finally accepting I drank too much. Did I drink often before the attack? *I can't imagine why.* When the purging gives me a break, I start shivering.

Milo leaves and comes back with a blanket and wraps it around my shoulders. "Maybe you're right. You've been too cooped up on this ship. Perhaps we'll visit Ashtanabo soon, but until then, I need you to take care of yourself. All right?"

I slowly nod into the toilet bowl.

The rest of the night is hazy. But I remember Milo waiting for me to empty my stomach. And I remember him wrapping me tighter in the blanket, hauling me in his arms, and tucking me into his bed.

tighter in the blanket, hauling me in his arms, and tucking me into his bed.

Chapter 9

When I awaken, my arm is sore and a near-empty indigo IV bag hangs from a metal pole above me. My head pounds and swirls like I've tumbled down a flight of stairs.

As I look to my left, my mouth goes dry.

Milo is fast asleep next to me, his arm resting above his head, black locks slightly covering his eyes.

I cover my mouth. Over my clubbing dress is a long black shirt. One of Milo's. *He dressed me?* Well, somewhat. He had enough sense to not get me naked.

But still, I can't believe we slept in the same bed.

I shake my head. This was a one-time thing. Something to quell his conscience. I mean, what kind of husband would make his sick wife sleep in the bathroom? Even he knows better.

As I try to tiptoe out of the bed, Milo stirs. I silently curse.

"Where are you off to?" His morning voice is raspy as he runs a hand down his face. "You need to rest."

I hold on to the IV pole. "I am going to call Lleu and get ready for the day."

Milo sits on the edge of the bed for a moment before circling around in front of me. "With that in your arm?"

I look down at the transparent film dressing and the catheter in my vein. "I can remove it."

Milo steps forward, making me take a step back until my knees hit the bed, and I'm forced to sit.

"I'll remove it for you." He bends down, his warm hands gently taking hold of my forearm, sending a buzzing sensation up my arm and down my chest.

Stop it, I say to myself, biting down on the inside of my lip.

Milo clamps the tubing and detaches it from the catheter. "The medic says you were dehydrated before you even arrived at the club."

I think back to the week before. It's true I haven't been drinking enough water lately. "I'll be more careful."

He takes some gauze the medic left on the bedside table and begins removing the dressing. "I'll be making sure of it."

I wince as he rips the dressing off. "Dammit, that hurt."

"Then take care of yourself and you won't need another infusion." Milo removes the catheter and compresses the site with gauze, then he tightly secures it with some tape. He stands and heads to his wardrobe to pull out a new set of garments for the day. "After you passed out, I spoke with Lleu. She isn't feeling the best either, so one of the proditors will escort you around the Imnicus today."

"I don't need an escort."

"You're still readjusting. I insist."

I look away as Milo dresses from his lounge pants into his royal attire.

"Wait in here until someone comes to get you. And Margot, I mean it."

I huff. "Yes, Colum."

Milo heads to the door.

"Wait." I stand quickly, nearing him.

Milo stiffens before turning to face me. "Yes?"

I fold my arms, refusing to look him straight in the eye. "I just—thank you. For last night."

Milo nods and after he leaves, I fall onto the bed, staring at the ceiling. The motion leaves me able to further smell the woody notes of his cologne on the sheets, making me feel things I don't want to. "What is wrong with me?"

Minutes later, an automated voice informs me that there is someone at the door. I answer, and the door slides open, revealing Knox leaning against the doorframe with his legs crossed.

"Ready for our day out, Columess?" His eyes rake over my clothing, or rather, Milo's.

Day out? I scoff internally.

"Throw on something presentable, and I'll take you to your dressing room."

"Are you going to doll me up for the day?" I joke.

"Of course, if you don't mind looking like something out of nightmares."

I slip on a pair of lounge pants and a tank and meet Knox outside the room.

He leads me down the hallways of the north wing. We pass maids scrubbing floors with the help of robots and servants pushing carts of metal boxes into kitchens. Some of them whisper to each other when they see me, making me cross my arms over my chest.

When we get to the dressing room, I use the security clearance on my ring to access it when Knox's doesn't work.

He sits back onto one of the couches, kicking his legs up.

"You know, I don't need an escort or a babysitter. You're a proditor. I'm sure there are better things you could be doing."

"What? Don't want to spend time with me?" Knox chuckles.

"It's not that." I sort through the racks of dresses. "I just don't understand how long Milo expects me to live like this."

"It's only until he deems you well enough to roam around on your own. And for you to relearn Ashtanaban manners. It seems you reverted back into one of a soldier."

"Maybe being a soldier is my natural state."

"Hence why you need to relearn. It wasn't easy the first time either."

"You're saying before all of this, I behaved exactly as Milo wanted?" I pick a gray dress off the rack.

"After lots of lessons, somewhat." A stray blond curl falls from under his hood onto his face. Even at twenty-nine, Knox is too young to be right hand to a Colum. Though it could also be argued that Milo himself is too young to be the Colum at the age of twenty-seven. I'm not even sure how one becomes an Imnicus proditor and the Colum's closest friend. At least, I assume they're friends.

I step behind the dressing partition. "The only thing I'm concerned about now is learning more about the attack, not manners or traditions. Those can wait."

Knox laughs. "Spoken like a true soldier. Leave that work to your old comrades. You're the Columess for a reason."

"Is it so bad that I want to remember my life before all of this?"

"Have you tried tapping into that muscle memory of yours?"

I forgot all about that. The medic said it was one of the few memory types I retained. It's why I was able to attack Knox in the hallway so easily when I first met him. "What about your powers? Could they help me?"

"You don't remember what my magic does?"

"Obviously not." I finish changing and emerge in a solid gray dress. It's simpler than the other dresses Lleu has picked out for me. Less glitter and embedded metals. I sit down at the vanity and sort through the lipsticks and eyeshadows. "So, tell me, what does your magic do?"

Knox sits up, removing his proditor disguise. In the reflection, I can see his dimples. "Do you want me to show you?"

"I—sure." Truthfully, most of what I know about proditor magic is that it can somehow interfere with light bulbs and electricity. But I've been too preoccupied to care what they can really do.

I watch as Knox stands and paces behind me. When his leather-clad hands wrap around my shoulders, I stiffen. He leans down, his head next to mine as he looks at me through the mirror. "Are you sure?"

I swallow. "Yes."

Knox reaches around me, taking off both his gloves and setting them on the vanity. He moves his fingers near my head. "Let's begin." He presses them against my temples.

Within a split second, my eyes roll into the back of my head, then I'm engulfed in darkness.

My breath hitches as everything comes into focus. The beach and the crashing waves. The pink sunset on the horizon. White sand between my toes.

I turn around, and Knox is nowhere to be found.

"Knox?" I run down the sand, stepping on seashells that break like glass under my toes.

Is this place real? Did I fall asleep?

Every second that passes, my heart rate increases. Even with all the beauty surrounding me, I feel scared and out of control as the tide breaks against my ankles.

"Knox!"

I startle as his hands grab my upper arms, making me yelp. Quickly, I turn around, clutching my chest as I come face to face with Knox on the beach. I take a sigh of relief and slap his chest. "Don't sneak up on me like that! You almost gave me a heart attack."

Knox laughs, his face still free of the proditor disguise. "Enjoying the scenery? I figured you may have missed the sun."

"It's lovely, but where are we?" I move a seashell around with my toe. "Is all of this real?"

"No. We're in a projection I placed inside your mind. In fact, we're still in your dressing room."

The wind sweeps through my gray dress. "Can you read my mind?" If Knox can place illusions into me, maybe he could search my mind and restore my memories. Perhaps he could surpass any doctor on Ashtanabo.

"No," he says. "There are rumors of disciplined proditors who have such abilities. I am not one of them."

I hold back any looks of disappointment. "I'm struggling to understand what the Colum uses your powers for."

"Ashtanabo uses my powers for the good of the planet."

"A very diplomatic answer."

"To a very diplomatic question. But in all honesty, the answer is complicated."

"You owe me an answer, at the very least."

Knox sighs and stares at the horizon toward the glowing sun, forever on its course to setting but never arriving. "Proditors find their use in methods soldiers don't often resort to. Or can't. We're enforcers, we're agents, we're spies. But what we're known for most is our interrogation."

I glance around at the beach and the sand. "How can something like this harm someone?"

Knox pauses and turns to me. "Would you like to see?"

I nod slowly. Maybe I should be more reluctant.

He steps back, unfolding his fists by his sides. The scenery starts to change, the sky turning gray and the tide picking up. Ink beads on his fingertips while he raises his arms.

The grains of sand darken, resembling crystal-like dirt. Darkness pools above his cheekbones. His hands shake, almost like he's holding back something much more vile.

A murkiness forms along his under eyes. Black liquid drips down his fingers onto the ground. The beach rumbles, skulls emerging from the sand. Blood leaks from the eyes of some of the skulls. Bones shoot up from the surface, making me shout and cover my mouth.

My heart thumps. It may be fake, but my body trembles as though it's real. "Stop it. I don't want to see anymore."

By the shake in his chest, it's apparent that Knox is restraining himself, but I could see how easy it would be to torment someone using his powers. With the ability to project any image, the possibilities for interrogation are endless.

He drops his arms, and an image of a large crow appears behind him, giving the illusion of Knox with wings. The wings curve forward, as if they are about to swallow us whole.

I slam my eyelids together, frightened the crow will overtake me. But as instantaneously as we entered the hallucination, we're back in the safety of the dressing room. In the vanity mirror's reflection, I see my chest heave with deep breaths.

So does Knox's as he takes a step back. "I'm sorry that I frightened you. But now you know what my magic can do and why everyone on both planets fears us."

An unsettling sensation nips at my stomach. I turn in my chair to look up at him. "Don't be sorry. You were only doing what I asked." Still, there is a tremble to my limbs.

"You must be starving," Knox extends a hand to me. "Shall we?"

I nod. I wonder why magicless humans like Milo serve as the Colum instead of a proditor like Knox. His magic is horrifying and something I would never want to be on the receiving side of.

Chapter 10

One morning, Lleu dresses me in a dark-green gown that's fancier than my normal day dresses. She even spends more time than usual dolling up my hair and perfecting my makeup. Lleu gets in these moods every so often, usually when she's learned a new technique, so I don't think much of it at first.

That is until the dressing room door opens and Milo is leaning against the wall with folded arms like he's been impatiently waiting for me. "You took your sweet time."

I put my hands on my hips. "Excuse me?"

"Come on, we're already running behind." Without even waiting to see if I'm going to follow him, Milo strides down the hallway.

I huff and concede, following him blindly. As I catch up to him, I narrowly keep up as we turn corners in the direction of the south wing.

"Where are you taking me?" I ask.

"To the arbitors."

I recognize that word. They're the governmental leaders of Ashtanabo, responsible for relaying Milo's decrees and ruling planet-side. According to Lleu, Milo and I weren't married long enough for him to introduce me to them. We had no wedding, but an elopement after a whirlwind romance. With the way we're at each other's throats, it seems like we rushed into things too fast.

"Why do they want to see me?"

"Well, for one, they won't stop sending correspondence that they want to meet the rumored Columess. I can also assume they want to offer their condolences regarding the attack."

"Wait . . . does that mean you're taking me to Ashtanabo?"

"I told you I would, though you may not remember. Last we spoke of it, you were expelling a nights-worth of alcohol."

I almost can't believe what I'm hearing. In fact, it makes me feel like I can breathe again. I'll feel the sun on my skin. Fresh air in my lungs. Maybe defying Milo at the Jupiter was worth it after all.

The docking bay is larger than I could ever imagine and filled with more ships than I can count. The ceiling is nearly as high as a large building, and Milo has to pull on my arm a time or two to keep me from bumping into pilots and robots.

We approach a white ship where technicians appear to be performing last-minute safety checks. Milo goes up the ramp before me. I huff and follow behind him.

The interior of the ship is lined with white leather seats, a bar, and sleeping quarters for a long journey.

I take a seat near the window and he sits beside me. An A.S.O.P. unit immediately brings us sparkling beverages. This all seems like too much for a trip that won't take more than a few hours there and back, including the meeting. Then again, Milo is the Colum.

I lie my head against the window.

"Sit up straight." Milo commands as he fastens his seatbelt.

I mouth a stern impression of the Colum's words when he's not looking, making a nearby guard suppress a smile.

I grip the armrest when we take off; the sensation of flying is so foreign it almost makes me sick. When we enter Ashtanabo's atmosphere, I clutch my chest at the quick changes in altitude.

The ship descends further, and I press my hand against the cold window as I watch the scenery. Buildings emerge inside the bustling city. Every structure is stone white and covered in luscious greenery, vines crawling up the oval homes. There are pools of crystal-clear water between the spacious properties.

Central to everything in the city, there is a singular skyscraper larger than any building in view. Small lakes branch off into streams that snake around its fixture.

Our ship touches down on the flat landing platform of its bulbous roof with a soft rumble.

I fiddle with the seat belt, but the latch won't come loose as if it's damaged. I yank and pull at it.

Milo unbuckles himself and watches me struggle. "Are you almost done? They're waiting."

"Just give me a second." I grit, fumbling even more under his gaze.

Milo rolls his eyes and leans over me, releasing the buckle with a single motion. "Come on." He takes hold of my hand and pulls me toward the exit.

"You could be more patient with me, you know." I jerk my hand out of his, stopping his purposeful stride.

"As stubborn as always," Milo mutters.

"What was that?" I stomp forward, hands on my hips.

"You've never taken your title seriously. Not before you lost your memories, and not now. Do you have any idea how much of a headache that is? When I have the lives of billions of people in my hands?" His expression isn't angry anymore, but hurt.

Guilt pangs in my chest.

Was it really me who caused the rift in our marriage? It makes sense, though. I was a soldier who married a Colum. With how I feel now, there is no way I could have been happy decreasing my Imnicus responsibilities back then in favor of tea parties and gown fittings.

"I—" I'm at a loss for words.

"We don't have time to discuss it. The arbitors are outside waiting." He offers me his arm.

I hold on to his bicep as the ramp comes down, but thoughts continue to race in my head. Was I really that stubborn and horrible?

We descend the ramp, and the sun warms my face. I try to forget my conversation with Milo as I savor the warmth. The air passes through my nose and lungs, and it feels completely different from the stuffy air of the Imnicus.

Waiting for us are three men and two women wearing extravagant royal attire. Guards stand around them at attention with the same uniforms as those on the Imnicus. Servants, donning loose tan or white outfits with robe-like sleeves, line our walkway.

The center man approaches us and gives a light bow. "So good to see you again, Colum, and what a pleasure to meet you, Lady Arris. It's a shame it's taken us this long to meet." He jovially takes my hands in his and squeezes them in delight. His smile accentuates his crow's feet. "I am Arbitor Gareth Monicas, and with me are Arbitors Cedrick Lorne and Joaquin Bruis, as well as their wives, Lady Anya Lorne and Lady Ida Bruis."

"I apologize for my delay in introducing myself." I smile.

Monicas turns to Milo. "Colum, we were beginning to think you'd die a bachelor."

Milo politely ignores his remark but barely hides the flash of annoyance in his eyes. "Let's convene inside, shall we?" His hand touches the small of my back and guides me forward.

"Ah, certainly. This way then," Arbitor Monicas says.

Our group travels down the winding stairs into an indoor garden. The sunlight passing through the floor-to-ceiling windows gives the illusion of strolling outdoors. Whatever glass the window is made out of allows sunlight to shine brightly inside, still keeping the building a comfortable temperature.

Vines hang from every fixture, and flora mixes in with every shade of green. Gardeners are everywhere, some high on ladders and others bending over to trim overgrown plants.

Like the north and west wings of the Imnicus, the white walls and ceilings of the garden follow a geometric pattern with bulging shapes piercing out in every direction.

"So, Margot, how have you been faring?" Monicas asks.

I turn my attention toward him. "It's been an adjustment, but in time, I hope to be completely reacclimated."

"That's the spirit, if I do say so myself. There's no point in sulking about when there's nothing to be done. All we can do in these situations is hold our heads high and move forward, wouldn't you say?"

I guess I never thought of it that way. His words only add to my looming guilt of failing as a Columess.

When we reach the meeting room, there are throne-like chairs in a circle with a holographic projector in the middle. The small tables between the seats are filled with teacups and pastries.

I sit in the chair next to Milo. Monicas thanks a servant who fills his glass with wine.

During the meeting, there isn't as much talk about the attack as I expected. The arbitors focus more on the rising crime rate on Lavenai and how more soldiers have been deployed to calm the increasingly restless cities.

I can't stop thinking about how each of the arbitors' wives are also referred to as "lady." It shows just how little influence the three of us hold, nothing but accessories in the conversation.

Lady Lorne takes a bite of an apple and leans her body weight onto the armrest while still emitting elegance. Her dramatic look of boredom entertains me more than it should. She plays with her braided brunette hair that flows halfway down her back, tied together with a gold pendant. Lady Bruis is much more reserved, with her black hair tied tightly on top of her head, one hand in her lap, and the other taking a sip of moon tea. Both women are at least fifteen years my senior.

"We have too many proditors pulling double shifts as it is," Arbitor Bruis adds to whatever was said last, making me realize how long I've been tuned out of the conversation.

Lady Lorne chimes in, letting the apple roll off of her hand and onto the table. "Men, as intoxicating as this conversation is, I think it's time for us ladies to get to know each other a little better." She pushes herself out of the chair and grabs my hand.

I look over at Milo, unsure of what to do. I want to stay and listen to their conversation about Lavenai.

Please don't make me go, I plead through my eyes. If they do end up discussing the attack, I want to be here. I *need* to be here.

He gestures for me to follow her. *Damn him.*

Lady Bruis curtsies to the Colum as she follows us out of the room.

Lady Lorne leads us into the gardens outdoors with their many bridges, streams, and plants. The scenery, combined with the warm breeze, almost makes me forget how upset I am. Almost.

"The Colum has kept you quite the secret for some time," Lady Lorne says as we step onto the walkway.

"Yes, well, I've been adjusting to my new title, Lady Lorne. Not to mention, there was the attack, the coma, and the loss of my memories."

"Don't call me Lady Lorne. It makes me feel like an old lady. Please, call me Anya." She runs her fingertips over the tall flowers as we stroll. "So you really remember nothing from before?"

I shake my head.

"It seems you have a lot to learn about yourself." Lady Bruis butts in. "Do you know your wedding anniversary?"

My breath hitches. It's not something I ever cared enough to ask. "No, unfortunately."

The women giggle, making me grit my teeth.

"Don't tell me you and the Colum haven't had a heart-to-heart discussion since the attack?" Anya asks.

"Milo isn't the mushy type," I counter.

"Just like his father." Anya nudges my shoulder. The women laugh in unison once again.

Gods, I hate them.

We approach a bench overlooking a small pond and take a seat. Colorful hybrid birds decorate the lake; clusters of lily pads surround them.

"Ida, could you imagine losing your virginity to the same man twice?" Anya asks Lady Bruis.

I practically absorb into the bench as the women laugh together. The last thing I want to talk about with them is my sex life. Could I use my status to shut down this conversation? No, it'll only cause more problems for Milo if they get offended.

And who says I lost my virginity to Milo? I could have had other men before him. Though sex with Milo is the last thing I want to be thinking about. Just the thought of it makes me tense.

"Now, let me ask the real questions." Lady Bruis scoots closer and takes my hands in hers. "Can we expect little ones to be running around in the future?"

All the color drains out of my face. At the rate Milo has wined and dined me, I'm closer to being ejected out of an air-lock than having his children. "We haven't talked about it." *And we never will.* I swat at a bug that lingers by my ear.

"If you don't, Monicas will be next in line for the throne if something happens to the Colum. Not that we dislike him, but the Colum's father always preferred his own kin. Such a shame he died so shortly into his rule," Anya says. "Speaking of his father, he always loved attending parties, balls, and lavish events. The Colum isn't the same way, however."

I still have a lot to learn about Milo's past, but I'd rather hear it from a turtle than from the gossiping mouths of these women.

"He simply stays tucked away up in space, sometimes unreach-able for days at a time." Lady Bruis adds, "It's maddening."

Anya throws her hands up. "He didn't even attend my fortieth birthday party. Can you believe it?"

"I still think of his absence on occasion."

"It's in my opinion that a leader should attend such events, and do so willingly. I mean, what are we supposed to think when he's holed up there for sometimes weeks on end, leaving our husbands to run Ashtanabo?"

Something rises in me. A strange protectiveness. Milo is a lot of things, but he's far from some lazy Colum who sits around doing nothing on the Imnicus all day.

Anya continues, "Of course, you can't ignore the social aspect. How can our husbands make solid connections with other leaders if the Colum doesn't attend or even *plan* anything? How else can he expect to really understand his subordinates?"

Lady Bruis opens her mouth to speak. Her expression shows her next words are going to be equally insulting. I need to defend Milo without coming across too rude. *Quick, think of something . . .*

"*Actually*, the Colum and I are planning on hosting our first ball soon." Of course, I am lying through my teeth. There is no ball, but as long as I don't give too many details, it will stay up in the air and hopefully never happen. If it's enough to stop the rumors of Milo being dismissive to Ashtanaban affairs, I'll say anything.

The women look so ecstatic their heads almost fly off.

"Tell me all the details," Lady Bruis exclaims. "What are your color palettes?"

"Is this to celebrate your introduction as Columess?" Anya jumps in.

"Yes," I lie. "But we don't have all the details together yet, or a date . . ."

The women ramble on about guest lists, music, and decorations. It was a bold lie of me, but nothing will come of it. I know the Imnicus has a ballroom, but considering the attack, I doubt Milo would actually let us host one anytime soon.

"Between the representatives from each sector, the delegates, and the celebrities I mentioned, you will be at about two hundred people," Anya says.

"That seems like the perfect amount," I say.

"Perfect amount of what?"

I hold my breath and turn my head. Milo stands there with the arbitors.

Oh no, I should have chosen another lie. Wait, maybe I can get out of this. Perhaps . . .

"The guests, of course." Lady Bruis stands and links arms with her husband. "For the ball you're hosting to officially introduce your wife as Columess."

Milo's lips part, his stare lethal. "Oh . . . really?"

Arbitor Monicas taps his hands together in a gleeful clap. "I thought you swore to never have one during your reign. Why, this is the best news I've heard all day!"

My face must be completely pale now. "Yes, *dear*. Don't you remember?" I'm completely putting him on the spot and I'm sure he'll have my head on a platter later this evening.

"Yes . . . a ball to celebrate my beautiful wife." Milo forces a smile and nears me. He pulls me from the bench and into his arms for a tight embrace.

"How sweet!" Arbitor Lorne proclaims. "Why, I never thought I'd see Milo Arris being so affectionate."

Milo lowers his voice to a whisper. "You'll pay for this."

I swallow down the lump in my throat.

As we wrap up the visit and say goodbye to the delegates, I can think of nothing but Milo's hand on my lower back, tensed against my spine. His speech is coarse. And maybe, just this once, I'm afraid of what he may do.

When we enter the ship, a bead of sweat runs down my neck. The doors shut and Milo comes up behind me, backing me up into my seat until I have no choice but to fall onto it.

He grabs the armrests and lowers his face at level with mine. "You have some explaining to do."

I keep my head pressed firmly against the headrest, not wanting to be even a centimeter closer to him. I'm hyperaware of his body heat, which seems to be growing warmer with his anger.

"It was just a ruse to get them to stop talking about other things. If you hadn't interrupted, they wouldn't have asked about it again."

"Do you understand how tight the Imnicus security is? How many people want both of us dead simply for leading? Hosting a ball is dangerous. What could have possibly been so pressing that you had to put everyone on the ship at risk?" His breaths grow angrier.

"Stupid things. Invasive things."

"Like?"

I swallow. There is no way I'll tell them about the gossip or the horrible things the women said about him. The last thing I want is to cause political tensions. A part of me is also too stubborn to admit that I was trying to help him. Instead, I tell him everything else we spoke about. "They were hounding me about my loss of memories. Our anniversary date. *Sex.* Bearing your children. Just to name a few."

Milo is silent for a minute. His eyes contemplate then shift to an emotion I've never seen from him before—fascination. "You're so uncomfortable with the thought of me touching you that you lied about hosting a grand ball?"

"Absolutely not—" I suck in a breath as he moves a hand to cradle my face. *What the*—I don't know what to say or do, or even how I feel about his holding me like this. I stay completely frozen.

His voice grows lazy and whisper-like. "This is what you're so afraid of?" He passes his thumb just below my bottom lip, his eyes staying locked on mine with amusement.

I straighten my shoulders. "I'm not scared of you or of being touched *by any man*."

Milo pauses and laughs without smiling. "Is that so?" He moves his other hand to my waist, circling his thumb there. "I am still your husband, after all. A man who is just like every other man. A man with *needs*."

My breaths are deep and I internally curse at myself for the warm feeling building in my lower belly. I should be shoving him off but I'm completely frozen.

A guard clears his throat. "Sir, we're about to depart. The captain requests that everyone buckle up."

Milo doesn't move at the guard's words and continues to hold me. "We'll host that ball, just like you want. I'll even go through the trouble of dealing with the security preparations. But don't think for a second that I'm even remotely happy about it." He pushes off of me and buckles himself into his seat.

Within minutes of takeoff, he's completely dozed off.

I stay completely still, reeling from the way he touched me.

And the way my body responded.

Chapter 11

When we arrive back at the Imnicus, I stomp off the ship, and Milo doesn't try to stop me for once. Right now, I need to be alone, not escorted by Lleu or a proditor but simply alone.

I find an unfamiliar hallway, and when I'm far away from prying eyes, I lean against a wall and touch the spot below my lip. The memory of his finger makes me flush.

Stop it, he doesn't deserve it, I think to myself. He was teasing me. If anything, there was a touch of humiliation.

Still, I can't stop thinking about it. I bite down on my tongue and force myself to walk again to clear my head.

I pass under the *Imnicus: East* sign and the dorm rooms come into view. Off-duty soldiers whisper to each other as I walk by, and I feel more self conscious than I care to admit.

Part of me views the soldiers as people I once knew. They were my comrades and fellow workers. But how do they see me now? Some former soldier who was power and money hungry enough to seduce the Colum? Or perhaps Milo was right about my night at the club. That they lost respect and cannot view me as a leader.

Nobody is in uniform and they incessantly apologize when I pass them, to which I tell them not to worry. There's a door left half-open where two Imnicus employees are going at it, completely unfazed by who might be watching. I somehow find myself unable to look away. But it isn't their nakedness or even what they are doing that keeps my attention sealed. It's the way he looks at her. Like she's the sole reason he's close to breaking.

When I think about how there may have been a time where Milo looked at me that way, a warmth encircles my inner thigh. Even if I don't want to think about it, we're married, which means we've definitely—

My throat and mouth go completely dry. I shake my head, forcing myself to look away from the couple and flee deeper into the Imnicus before anyone else sees me.

Right now, all I need is a sip of water, so when I find a darkened kitchen, I quickly disappear inside.

It's such a large kitchen, I'm surprised it isn't running twenty-four seven. But it seems older and maybe now used only to store things for other cafeterias. Most of the cabinets have all the essentials, like flour and sugar, and the fridge is stocked with raw meat. Finally, I find a cabinet full of glasses.

As I reach for one, a sob leaks in through the doors of the cafeteria. It makes me flinch, and the glass falls out of my grip, shattering onto the tiled floor.

I curse at the shards, but as the crying continues, I can't help something rising in me. The part of me that was once Columess, or perhaps just the part of me that cares.

But comforting a servant could be overstepping. I turn to leave the kitchen, but then I stop short, curling my fist.

If what Milo said was true, it's about time I step up as the Columess I am supposed to be. And maybe the servants are a good place to start. As I near the other door into the cafeteria, it automatically slides open.

A servant girl is on her knees, sobbing and cradling her hand. She bites down on her lip to stifle her cries. I recognize her as one of Milo's personal serving staff members. Sloane Fairfax. Her curly red hair is piled on her head in a loose bun. She wears her usual servant uniform—a mid-length silver dress. One sleeve of her dress has fallen off her shoulder, like the fabric was overstretched.

When she sees me, she startles and stands, swiping a tear away. "Lady Arris, I'm so sorry. I'll get back to work immediately." She seems intimidated by me, as if I have actual authority over her.

"No, there is no need for that." I close more distance. "You're not in trouble."

When Sloane nods, there's a little relief in the movement. "Is there anything I can get for you, Columess?"

"I'd like to ask you the same thing."

She hides her hands behind her back. "N-no. Just lost control of my emotions for a second. It will pass."

"Were you hurt?" I motion to her arm.

That makes her eyes widen. "It was nothing! Really. I am fine."

"May I see your hand?"

Her eyes widen. "I need to finish my preparations—"

"Let me see it now," I say with a firmness that even surprises me.

With reluctance, she raises her arm. I take her hand in my own and inspect it. A distinct blue scald mark, just like the one Lleu had. My expression hardens, and she pulls her hand back, arms folding over her chest.

Could it really be from the same source? Not to mention, Sloane is being just as secretive as Lleu was.

"What happened?" I signal for her to sit next to me at one of the bulky, octagonal tables.

Her hands tremble as she takes a seat, and it's enough to tell me that these blue burns aren't simple occupational injuries.

"It was simply—"

"And there's no need to hide it from me. You won't be in trouble. I promise."

Her voice shakes. "I'm not sure. I was ironing uniforms in the laundry room, then the lights went out. The doors slid shut and locked. And then—" She points to her wound.

"A person did this to you."

Sloane nods. "It was a man, but I couldn't make out his face. He grabbed me and pushed me to the ground. I tried to scream, but he covered my mouth."

"Did he . . ."

"No!" The word is quick, but I can tell she's telling the truth.

That, at the very least, makes me relieved, but what kind of sadistic person prances around burning servants? The thought makes me numb. "Do you remember anything about this man?"

She shakes her head. "The room was pitch black, and he struck me once more before dashing away. He was strong. Stronger than any of the male servants I know."

I stand. "Allow me to escort you to the medical bay, Sloane."

Sloane stands quickly. "Please, Lady Arris, I beg you. Don't make me go there."

"Why?"

"Being a servant on the Imnicus is a coveted position, and if the medics find that I'm too injured to work, it will mess with my tenure. I will heal, in time."

I don't push her further, even though I know I should. I'm hesitant to leave. She could have a stalker. What if he's watching us right now?

But Sloane could be right? What if mentioning the burns would complicate life for her and Lleu? If they are too scared to report what happened to them, then I need to tread carefully. Being the Columess who runs off to tell her husband everything won't serve me well in the long run. The best way I can help her is by using my position to investigate these burns more.

"At the very least, please use the sink in the kitchen to cool your burn." I adjust my dress as I head out to leave.

"Lady Arris?" she stammers.

Turning, I see her trepidation. "Yes?"

"Be careful. Dark things happen aboard this ship."

I rush back to the bedroom thinking of nothing except Sloane's burn.

Is there a stalker aboard the ship? Some man who is targeting the servants?

Or what if it's something worse? A Laven could have stuck aboard the Imnicus, picking off servants until the terrorists can organize another attack. The thought feels more like my own paranoia, but I can't let it go.

The only way I could know if the burns are related is if I had my memories back. Maybe my captors burned me before they erased my memories, but they healed before I woke from my coma.

Now, more than ever, I want a second opinion on my memory loss. Sure, the medics on the Imnicus are great, but there could be someone on Ashtanabo who could be of even more help. Milo should be in the bedroom right now to freshen up. Though, after the ball incident, it's probably not the best time. But with him, there's never a good time.

When I enter the room, he's spread out on the bed, shirtless, pinching the bridge of his nose. "You again?"

I fold my arms. "I need to talk to you."

He moves to lie on his side, resting the side of his face on his fist. "If this is about the ball, then your apology is still not accepted."

I narrow my eyes. "It's not about that in the slightest. I want a second opinion on treatments for my memory loss."

"Why? The best medics in the galaxy work on the Imnicus."

"There could be someone with more unique treatments that could really help. Besides, my memories could be of use to you and the arbitors. If I got them back, it could help us identify the Laven who attacked us."

"Just do what the doctors here have said. Tap into your muscle memory. Perhaps you'll find something of use."

"My body doesn't feel like a soldier. My muscles wouldn't remember a thing even if I tried." Though, there was the time I knocked Knox to the ground. But that could easily be blamed on adrenaline.

Milo climbs off the bed and closes the distance between us. "Want to bet?"

I take a step back. "What are you doing?"

"Margot, I'm going to swing at you. Block it."

He's going to hit me? "Wait . . . Milo!"

Before I can do anything, he raises his hand back and throws his fist in my direction. A portion of my brain I had forgotten was there lights up. My forearm blocks the blow.

I stumble back. *What just happened?*

My arms shake. It felt so natural. So instinctive.

A headache forms in my temples. I sit on the edge of the bed, unable to connect myself with the person who just took over my body.

"I told you. You're stronger than you think." Milo regains his stance. "You were one of the highest-ranking spies on the Imnicus. To say the least, you *enthralled* me." He spits his last words out like they're coated in poison.

I was a spy? That can't be right. I'm easily spooked. My emotions are always on edge. Though that could be a result of the attack, something I'm not even close to recovering from. "You're lying."

"When you were first posted here, you climbed the ranks faster than anyone expected. Soon enough, you were placed in meetings with commanders, and then with proditors, and then finally me. I admired you and how you were years ahead of anyone who shared your rank. No matter what exam or mission we threw at you, you always found a way to overcome it." He looks lost in the story, speaking of the woman he once loved.

My heart skips a beat.

"We did our best to keep your true profession a secret, even to those who lived on the ship. It's never good to give too much notoriety to someone who's supposed to be anonymous. Most thought you were just another soldier."

Milo meanders over to his nightstand and unlocks the bottom drawer with one of his rings. He removes a tablet, then saunters back over to me, offering me the device. "I wasn't sure if you were ready for this yet, but you have retained more than even I realize. Try unlocking this."

On the touchscreen is a keypad requiring a passcode. "But I don't know it."

"You logged into this device hundreds of times a week. You may think you don't know it, but your body may surprise you."

"Sure, okay," I say with heaves of sarcasm.

He pushes the device into my hand, and a sense of familiarity rises, but a firewall blocks it. I try to lock onto the memories attempting to surface, but like usual, they fall out of reach. This item really was mine, something I used every day. Holding it feels like running into someone you recognize but being unsure where you know them from.

"Relax, don't force it. Don't use your brain. Let your hand take over."

I close my eyes for a second and let all my thoughts dissipate. *Relax, don't force it.* I repeat Milo's words to myself in my head.

I hover my fingers over the screen and air poke a few times before my fingers adopt a mind of their own. They touch the glass screen, and in a swift movement, type the numbers: 5826.

The tablet unlocks, showing a black home screen filled with gray nameless applications.

Milo stands stunned for a minute, his breathing ragged, like he didn't actually expect his pep talk to work. Like maybe a part of him didn't actually believe in me.

He snaps back to his normal self and takes the tablet back from me and places it back in the locked nightstand. "You see, your mind is in better shape than you think."

I'm still in disbelief, not just over how intact my muscle memory is, but from everything that happened today. The things I learned about myself. In order to truly step into the role of the Columess, I have to do more than simply want it. I need to learn what it takes.

"Milo, can I watch you in action soon? I think . . . " I want to bite my tongue, but I swallow my pride. "I think I want to learn more about what you do every day, and more so, what I should be doing."

"If you insist." Milo folds his arms. "Soon, most of my duties will involve securing the Imnicus to make sure everything is safe for the ball, thanks to you. So maybe it's only fair that you tag along."

I rub the back of my neck. "Sorry about that, again."

"Save your apologies for another time. For now, focus on being the Columess."

Chapter 12

I follow the Colum around like a lost puppy, studying his rounds and sitting in meetings with various commanders about tightening Imnicus security for the ball.

Milo's strides are so long and purposeful as we journey to different locations on the Imnicus that I have to pick up the pace every few hallways to keep up, sometimes in a light jog.

"Goodness, can you slow down?" I ask, clearly out of breath.

He doesn't stop. "Every second of my day is valuable, and the Imnicus is large. I don't waste my time on slow strolls between tasks."

I huff and jog up next to him. With his tall height, I have to take two steps for each of his. "Where are we off to now?"

"To the command center again. It's part of my rounds."

"Why? So you can make them piss themselves every time you enter?"

Milo side-eyes me. "It's your ball that has me in there more often than not. Besides, the simple reminder of possible discipline is far more effective than discipline itself. Maintaining standards on this ship is one of the most important things that keeps it functioning. The second I start to slack, so do they."

It sounds exhausting on both the staff and Milo.

Like expected, when Milo enters the command center, his presence makes everyone stiffen and their conversations cease. Officers type quicker at their keyboards, and the commanders' postures become pin straight. I've not seen Milo discipline anyone yet, but whatever he does has to be terrifying.

Milo paces behind the tiered stations, inspecting the computer screens and the officers as they press hundreds of buttons. He stops between two officers and leans in between them, inspecting their work with greater scrutiny. I'm not even sure what he's looking for.

"Change the camera angle there," Milo commands, his voice still soft.

One of them types quickly and then moves a few inches away for Milo to get a good look.

I half expect Milo to lash out. To tell them they are doing something wrong. But he simply takes a step back.

"Do you two need anything?" he asks, not a hint of strife in his voice.

"No, sir!" they chant in unison.

I follow behind Milo, careful not to trip over my dress, as he descends the stairs of the stations.

"What were you looking for?" I ask Milo.

Before he can respond, an officer rushes up to him with a tablet tucked under his arm. "Colum, so sorry to disturb you, but this matter is urgent. There is a water pipe leaking in the east wing and the technicians can't seem to get it under control."

"Where?" Milo asks.

"It's in area B, sir."

Milo turns to me. "Come, I'll need help carrying supplies."

Supplies? I narrowly keep up with his long strides down a small south wing hallway to a utility closet.

Milo opens the closet and sorts through the shelves, then hands me an empty crate.

"You're repairing it yourself?" I laugh.

He narrows his eyes. "I know this ship better than anyone."

"There has to be someone in this palace besides you who can do it."

He pushes away prepacked wires and various cans of liquids to find tools, piling more items in the crate, and I do my best to pretend like it's not too heavy. When my crate is full, he fills another crate and places it on his shoulder.

We enter the utility room to pure chaos. The room itself is flooded up to my shins. Water is spilling out into the hallway. Technicians scurry around, one trying to tighten the pipe. Two men frantically point at an archive blueprint.

One man steps forward with a few extra pins on his uniform than the others. "We're so sorry to have disturbed you, Colum."

"The pipes on the Imnicus haven't changed since its inception. If you cannot contain a simple leak, what *can* you do?"

The man bows his head. "We will all go through additional training, sir. Please forgive our incompetence."

Milo looks furious. "All of you leave immediately."

The technicians rush out, leaving Milo and me alone in the flooded room. Milo fixing the pipe himself somehow seems more improper than my time at the Jupiter.

He removes his cape, which is already half-drenched from the flooding, and then his shoes. My dress, on the other hand, is a lost cause. I know Lleu will be beside herself when she sees the hemming soaking wet.

"What do you think is wrong with it?" I ask.

He grabs a flashlight from his crate and inspects the pipe. A few times, he presses his finger into different parts of the pipe until the water flow decreases. "A microscopic crack. That bastard made it worse by trying to tighten the mechanisms." The pipes appear to be made from a clear silicone-like substance, making them more mobile than metal.

He sets down his crate and ties the top half of his hair back. Milo digs through my bin, mumbling under his breath about which technique to use, before pulling out a long metal tool. He steps a few feet away, using the tool on a valve. The leak increases significantly, pouring out twice the amount of water than before.

I yelp and leap back, water spraying the rest of my skirts. "Did you just make it worse?"

Milo scowls as he steps quickly back to my side. "I know what I'm doing. If the flow is too weak, the patch won't stick." Milo reaches into the crate until he finds a long, tan tube and a thin metal needle. "It sounds paradoxical. It's why most competent plumbers fail onboard this ship."

"Then where did you learn to do this?"

Milo affixes the needle to the tube of paste. "My father. He knew I'd take the throne one day and wanted to prepare me. He built this place after all."

Milo probes the pipe one more time before carefully sliding the needle beneath the surface a few feet from the leak. A thick paste spreads into water and is caught quickly in the flow. I watch as the leak slowly weakens, the paste sticking to the inside of the pipe by the force of the flowing water. A few moments later, the leak had stopped entirely.

"It'll dry clear in a few hours." Milo reaches out and tentatively probes the leak area.

"Why did he want to live all the way up here in space anyway? It seems inconvenient."

Milo removes the syringe, and the hole is quickly filled by the paste left behind. "Security. It's much easier to prevent infiltration from up here. He worried about how Lavenai may retaliate after the occupation."

"So much for that plan," I joke.

Milo's lips stay in a straight line, enough to know that I pissed him off. "I'm handling it, Margot." He strides past me, splashing water against my dress. "Leave the tools. The technicians will put everything away when they clean up."

I set my crate on one of the small work tables and follow after him. Before we cross the threshold out of the flooded room, two voices from the hallway echo in our direction. As their conversation becomes more audible, I tense when I realize they are speaking of both of us. Milo places a hand on my shoulder to stop me. He stands there, listening carefully.

"That was Lady Arris with him, yeah?"

"Who else would it be?"

"How would I know? Hardly anyone has seen her. Only rumors, you know?"

"You didn't see her at the Jupiter? It was wicked hot."

"My gods, you're lucky," the first technician says, "though I heard the Colum was furious."

I hug myself, squeezing my upper arms. All along, Milo was right. I think that's what hurts the most. The servants really do respect me less because of it, and worse, it's rubbed off on Milo too.

"But damn, Lady Arris knew how to move her hips. Makes me wonder what else her body can do. I might hold that memory in me until I die," one of them adds.

I can feel Milo's eyes scanning my face, which must be a few shades paler. His fist tightens, and he storms into the hallway toward the two male servants.

"Wait!" I yell after him. If he acts in anger, it will only make things worse.

They don't even sense Milo stomping up behind them until his fingers are wrapped firmly around the back of their necks. He slams both of them into the wall. I shriek as I hear one of their noses crack, followed by a scream.

The crimson-haired one strains his head back, meeting the deadly gaze of the Colum.

I rush up behind Milo. "Please don't hurt them. They didn't know we were listening." A part of me finds a small amount of satisfaction in seeing them put in their places, but this seems extreme, even for Milo.

Milo moves his mouth between their heads, still holding them steady. "You'll hold that memory until you die, huh?"

Is this the Milo that everyone is scared of? The man who brings silence to every room he enters? I lean against the opposite wall, somewhat unnerved.

Milo releases them, taking a step back. They stay huddled against the wall, pure terror on their faces.

The white-haired one gets on his knees, blood dripping from his crooked, broken nose. "Please, Colum, we are sorry. I'll do anything to make it right. Anything. It was wrong of us to speak of you and the Columess that way."

The crimson-haired one stays against the wall, at a loss for words. He looks as though he's ready to pass out.

Milo doesn't look like he buys it. "After all the Imnicus has provided you, this is how you both act?"

Nothing they say will quell Milo's anger. I can see it in his eyes, his still-curled up fists, and his murderous glare. I have to stop him from doing something worse. I place a hand on Milo's shoulder, but he shakes it off.

Milo steps forward and grabs the guy's white hair. "My father would have considered speaking poorly about superiors to be treason. I could be merciful and send you to the Laven mushroom fields for this."

That's the merciful option? The way he's speaking makes it seem like he's close to having them executed. The thought makes my hair stand on end. I can't let him do something like this over me. "Colum, if you hear nothing else from my lips, listen to this. Let them go. Let them keep their positions. Do this for me. Please." I won't have their fates on my hands, even if he's willing.

The crimson-haired one finally speaks. "Her name will never leave our lips again. Not unless we're speaking of how merciful and gracious she is."

"I could have Proditor Knox make sure of that," Milo says.

The white-haired servant's eyes widen, and his breathing turns into a heave. "I . . . I'm so sorry, Lady Arris. I regret every word."

I remember Knox's demonstration of proditor magic and how gruesome the punishments could be. It makes my skin crawl.

The memories of their words still make my heart sink. I want to latch onto that anger. A horrible part of me even wants to see them suffer. But what kind of Columess would that make me?

"Both of you will mop the flooded room until it's drier than the Napane Desert. You won't eat until it's done, got it? Proditor Crux will check on you hourly," Milo commands.

"T-thank you," the crimson-haired servant says. They bow to Milo and sprint into the utility room like scared children.

"You didn't have to break his nose," I bite.

"It's not the worst thing I've ever done." He rubs his wrists.

That I believe. His temper, even if it was to defend me, was brutal. It makes me wonder more about his father before him and how Milo ended up taking the throne. Before I can find more words to reprimand him, a proditor strides in our direction. I recognize the triangular knot-like design on his mask.

"I thought I heard your voice," Alarik says, curious eyes settling on Milo's soaked clothing and my ruined dress. "Though it sure is tough to make out what I just walked in on."

"Proditor Alarik," Milo says, "summon Crux to monitor the buffoons across the hall. Tell him no meals until they're finished. In the meantime, take Margot back to our quarters. I must speak with Commander Aisil."

"Yes, of course, Colum." Alarik places his gloved hand on my upper back. "This way, Lady Arris."

I want to stay and confront Milo about what I just witnessed, but he's down the hall and out of sight before I can muster up any words.

Alarik clears his throat as we walk. "I heard through the grapevine that there will be a ball here on the Imnicus."

I almost forgot myself. With everything going on lately, I hoped it would have disappeared completely because the thought of entertaining politicians and socialites makes me want to hurl. But Milo was right. I am paying dearly for my lie.

"Yes. Lleu told you, I'm guessing?" I look over at him, remembering how she practically squealed when I told her about it.

Alarik nods. "I guess Milo put her in charge of all the planning and decorations."

At least some good came of it. But between her duties with me and her other tasks on the Imnicus, it doesn't leave her with much time for the ball. "She's going to be exhausted."

"She's the kind of girl who can muster energy from anywhere, as long as she's doing what she loves." There's a smile in his voice.

"You two seem close," I say.

He adjusts his mask. "Outside of the Imnicus, I don't know much about her, if I'm being honest."

I grin. "Well, maybe you should get to know her a little better. I'm sure she'd appreciate the questions. Though you better be prepared for an hour-long conversation."

That makes Alarik laugh. "You're right about that."

When I get back to my room, I change out of the soaked dress and hang it up in the shower.

I saw a side of Milo today that I didn't expect, though it didn't surprise me completely. People fear him for a reason, but I doubt he is usually *this* hands-on with the servants. Still, the memory of him defending my honor brings a strange warmth to my chest.

Chapter 13

Before I know it, it's the day of the ball. Lleu smooths out the bottom of my ballroom gown, fit with a floor-length cape attached along the hem of the gown's exposed back, completely showing my scar. Even with the many creams and healing baths from the medics, it's still visible. All they could do was fade it slightly. Lleu offered to cover it up for me, but I refused. I want to bear this mark to remind everyone of what Lavenai did to me.

I look at my reflection in the mirror. The black fabric is scattered with gold embroidery that resembles a shimmering night sky. A diamond armlet is secured around my upper arm, draped with loose chains. At the vanity, Lleu braids my hair around the crown of my head.

"And to add the finishing touches—" She secures my diamond crown around my forehead.

Though it ties everything together, I wish I could forgo it. There's something about it that makes me feel needlessly superior around the staff.

There's a knock at the door. Lleu hops over and presses the button to answer it.

A man with brunette curls stands there wearing a navy and gold mask that covers the majority of his face, though I can see his soft lips and sharp jaw.

"Proditor Crux Branwen will escort you tonight," Lleu says.

I turn to Lleu, completely ignoring the proditor. "What do you mean? Won't you be there?"

Lleu frowns. "Only servants actively working can be in attendance."

"But . . . you planned the entire thing!"

"Sure, I picked things out, made table arrangements, sent out invitations. The whole getup. But Milo hired a coordinator on Ashtanabo to take over the day-of arrangements."

"That's . . . that's ridiculous! You spend god knows how many hours planning, and you don't even get to enjoy it?" I curl my fists. Lleu is the only person I feel truly comfortable with on the Imnicus, and I wanted nothing more than for her to be with me throughout the night. Milo knows this. It's almost like he's not letting her go just to spite me.

"If I can interrupt, we should be getting to the ball now," Crux says. There is an air of shortness to his words that takes me off guard.

I breathe out slowly and nod. There's nothing I can say or do at this point to change Milo's mind. That much is certain.

Crux offers me his arm and I reluctantly take it.

"I'll tell you everything after. I promise," I say to Lleu.

"I look forward to it." Lleu smiles. "And don't forget to try the eel-wrapped celery. It sounds gross, but just trust me."

I give her a sympathetic look before letting Crux lead me out of the room and through the halls with my hand wrapped around his stiff upper arm. He doesn't say a word, only adding to the strange tension. He's the first proditor I've felt somewhat unwelcome around.

I need to say something, anything, to squash this painfully awkward silence. "Have you been working on the Imnicus long?"

"As long as the others."

"Which is to say?"

"A very long time." He doesn't look any older than the other proditors I've met. At most, he's worked on the Imnicus ten years if he started when he was an adult. The way he words it makes it sound even longer than that.

"Is it intentional that Milo sent a proditor to escort me?" I ask. "Or were you the only worker with an open schedule?" My words come off ruder than anticipated when they leave my mouth, as if my tongue is trying to match his energy for me.

"He'd prefer a proditor over a lady's maid as your escort when there's so many new faces on board." The frown he holds almost seems permanent. It's as if he's never smiled or even laughed once in his life.

I press my lips together. "Still, does Milo truly believe Lavenai could attack again tonight?"

"Before the attack, nobody had ever infiltrated the Imnicus." Crux stares down at me for a second. "But it's always a possibility."

"I used to be a soldier. A spy. Why does Milo assume that I am incapable of protecting myself? That I'm so weak?"

Crux stops us both. "Because you are."

"What is that supposed to mean?" I ask sharply. Columess or not, he has no right to speak to me this way.

Crux grabs both my wrists, almost aggressively, making me startle. He pulls them out between us, displaying my forearms for me to see, showing me the scars I bear. The ones I'd prefer to ignore.

"This is what he's trying to protect you from. You may not see it beneath luxury gowns and spa treatments, but he wants to ensure something like this never happens again." Crux runs his thumb over one of the scars firmly. I wince, surprised that they're still somewhat tender. "He doesn't want the person who did this to you, and whatever sick reason they had, to do it ever again."

"I get it." I pull my arms away. I want to slap him for being so forward with a stranger, but then I remind myself that I once knew Crux, even if I currently have no recollection of him at the moment. I can only assume he's being so cruel because maybe he blames himself for what happened to me during the attack. He's speaking as a friend, though a blunt one.

As we near the ballroom in the west wing, my mouth goes dry at the sounds of music and party guests, all of them here because of me. There are more guards than normal lining the walkways, meaning Milo sent for more from Ashtanabo for tonight only.

Crux escorts me up the stairs to a balcony just outside the ballroom. As we near the top, my heart skips a beat when Milo comes into view.

Commander Aisil stands across from him, the two speaking about something political in nature, but I can't hear it over the cotton forming in my ears.

Though Milo normally wears black, this time he's dressed in a suit that is the darkest shade of red. Black fur lines the cape attached to his broad shoulders. His dark hair is pushed back slightly. To my surprise, he's wearing a crown made of white ivory and shaven bones. I've never seen him wear it before.

I dig my thumbnail into my palm from the reaction. His attire is stunning; that's the only reason my heart leapt like it did. Still, I find it harder to swallow.

When he sees me, his face doesn't harden like it normally does. His lips part as he takes in my dress. "What took you so long?" He turns his head slightly, as if catching himself.

I narrow my eyes. "I'm not late."

Crux unlaces his arm from mine and excuses himself, as does Commander Aisil.

Milo opens his mouth, but a humanoid servant approaches us.

"Take your places in front of the door. I'll give Arbitor Monicas the cue," the humanoid says. It has silver and blue metal in place of skin.

Milo places his hand on my bare back, sending shivers up my spine, as he guides me to the balcony doors. "Behave yourself tonight." He takes my hand, lacing his warm fingers through mine.

"I will try my very best, Colum." I give him a nasally laugh.

His grip grows tighter.

Through the walls, Monicas's voice booms. My nerves kick into full gear. I can't make out his words as he makes a long and drawn out speech to proceed our introduction.

"Ladies and gentlemen, please welcome our Colum, Milo Arris, and his stunning wife, Lady Margot Arris!"

There're claps and cheers as the doors slide open, as well as a warm draft. My ears ring as my legs try to freeze up on me, but I force one stiff leg forward and then the other. Soon, I'm standing at the edge of another balcony, hundreds of eyes on me as I wave to the crowd.

Milo, on the other hand, is a natural, even though he could benefit from flashing even a single smile. His presence is royal and capable. Calm and collected. It surprises me that he insisted Monicas do all the speeches for the night.

Monicas shakes Milo's hand and then continues his speech. "Now that our esteemed hosts have arrived, why don't we start the festivities, shall we?"

As soon as the focus of the room breaks off of me, it feels like I can breathe again. Enough so that I can finally take in the room, or more so, the fruit of Lleu's labor.

The three-dimensional geometric walls of the ballroom project a moving, shimmering gold using holographic technology. Normally they're a muted gray. Moon-shaped chandeliers hang from the ceiling, though one central light structure in the center is made from three floating rings that are interconnected and move continuously.

The banquet tables surround the dance floor and are covered in black, glittering fiber optic table clothes that resemble a night sky. The wineglasses are decorated with stars, and there are more than enough white candles in silver holders. Table settings feature dark blue plates that rest on top of gold charger plates.

Many of the women wear structured gowns. Even though most in attendance are allowed to wear capes given their status, all of them forgo it in respect for the Colum and me.

In line with the soldiers on the top balcony are proditors keeping an aerial eye on the ball, far more than the five that live aboard the Imnicus.

Monicas takes my hand and kisses the back. "Lady Arris, you look ravishing." He looks at Milo. "And, Colum, it's been ages since I've seen you wear your crown."

"My father appreciated the lavishes of royalty more than I." Milo stares over the crowd, though not looking at anyone or anything in particular.

"That you're right. It wouldn't surprise me if the man slept in his." Monicas laughs. "Now, don't let me keep you. Dance, chat, eat. Enjoy your evening. And Lady Arris, I hope you can save a dance for me?"

I nod. "Of course."

He taps his fingers together giddily. "Splendid!"

When I turn to speak to Milo, he's already down the balcony stairs and approaching Ashtanaban diplomats. So much for keeping up appearances.

As I descend the balcony on the opposite set of stairs, people greet me with wide smiles and open arms. Women compliment my dress. And in no time at all, Lady Lorne and Bruis jump out of nowhere, their arms linked.

"Margot, you throw quite the party!" Lady Lorne beams.

"I certainly can't take the credit. My lady's maid—"

"The Colum looks absolutely dashing," Lady Bruis interrupts. "Was that your doing?"

Also Lleu's, not that these women care in the slightest. "The Colum can dress himself." I peer over my shoulder. Milo is deep in conversation with Arbitor Bruis and some other politicians.

For some reason, I find myself unable to look away. He's so different in settings like this, when he's nothing but a leader. His face feels more defined; he cracks small smiles more, even if they're all for show. I scan his broad shoulders and the way his attire hugs his firm stature. The way his crown keeps his long strands of hair out of his face.

"My, my, your Colum is handsome indeed," Lady Lorne adds.

Time stands still. The voices of guests dance around me, low and distorted. If I had any champagne in my system, I may have agreed with Lady Lorne out loud.

I want to get away from the ball. Away from these women. I can't feel like this, not toward Milo. I can't stand him, so why . . .

"Sorry to interrupt, ladies," a voice says. When I turn my head back, Knox stands there dressed in a navy blue suit and a silver mask, similar to the one Crux wore that covers the top half of his face as opposed to the bottom. Knox's golden curls are more defined than usual.

Lady Lorne eyes Knox from head to toe, taking in every part of him with parted lips. "Don't be sorry, Proditor Knox. It's been some time since you've graced us with your presence." She stumbles over her words slightly.

"Lady Arris, would you like to dance?" Knox extends his hand.

In the corner of my eye, I swear I see Lady Bruis swoon.

"Yes, I would like that." *Thank goodness.*

I take Knox's hand and let him lead me to the dance floor where others are already swaying and spinning. Knox pulls me into his chest and takes the lead, whisking me around the dance floor. I'm surprised I'm able to keep up.

"So, can I assume the Imnicus proditors are off duty tonight?" I say.

"Ah, so you've noticed the extra proditors, I see. Though how could you not? Milo thought we could use the security."

He spins me out, then reels me back into his chest. When he catches me again, one of his hands rests on my lower back over my scar. His eyes flicker as his finger traces lightly over the outline.

I thought showing my scar would be a way to show my strength, but after my conversation with Crux, it feels like a weakness. Knox probably pities me. Or maybe he feels guilty that the proditors weren't able to get to me before this mark was carved into my back.

"I'm surprised he could spare so many," I say.

"Well, hundreds of proditors live on both planets."

"I thought they were native to Ashtanabo."

"They're on Lavenai for work, not pleasure." Knox glides us across the ballroom floor.

"So many and yet so few postings aboard the Imnicus. How did you manage it?" I ask.

"Well, Milo's father practically raised me."

"So you're like brothers?"

Knox scoffs. "More like a cousin who has an awful lot of authority over me."

"Wait, you're an Arris?"

"Technically."

It makes sense now. Why Knox always seems to be so fearless even around Milo's worst temper. But if that's the case, it means Knox has royal blood, right? So why would Arbitor Monicas be in line for the throne if I don't have a son? Why not Knox?

"So we're essentially in-laws then, but it seems strange to say that."

"Then don't. I think 'friends' sounds better anyway," Knox says.

I smile. "Then yes. We're friends."

We're facing the other half of the ballroom now. The half where Milo stands between two politicians, but now he's not looking at either of the men at all.

Milo stares at Knox with his hand on my lower back, and Milo's stare turns into an icy glare. When I catch his eyeline, he snaps out of it and goes back to his conversation with the men.

Knox spins me, and I lose sight of Milo and the politicians. Soon, the song ends, and when I search for Milo again, he's nowhere to be seen.

That is, until a dark, long shadow towers over Knox and me.

Milo stands there, his posture straighter than an arrow. "If you don't mind, Knox, I'll be taking her now."

Knox brings my hand to Milo, as if presenting a gift to him. He bows his head. "By all means."

Milo rolls his eyes and steps toward me, elbowing Knox in the side as he does. Enough to make Knox grunt.

Yes, definitely cousins.

I take Milo's hand with reluctance, but feeling his palm against mine makes shivers run up my arm. The next song starts, and Milo pulls me into him. I'm overly aware of his hand on my waist as he whisks me around the dance floor.

I swallow as I do my best to keep up with him, avoiding eye contact at all costs. My heart pounds at every point of contact with his body.

The sight of the Colum and Columess dancing makes crowds gather around the dance floor. I'm no longer looking at Milo but at their beaming looks of adoration. It almost makes me lose my step.

"Look at me. Pretend they aren't even here."

I force myself to look up at him, and my breath hitches as he stares down at me. Somehow, this is even harder. His body heat, the scent of his cologne . . . It's almost too much. I need to think of something, anything, to talk about. "You're better at dancing than I expected."

"My father always said that a Colum should know how to do anything and everything, so I was given lessons. I even danced at a few of the balls he hosted." Milo dips me, and the crowd claps.

When he brings me back up, I ask, "And your mother?"

His lips press together tightly and his face hardens.

"I'm sorry," I say, "I shouldn't have asked."

"No, it's fine." Milo takes a deep sigh, but he doesn't say anything else, leaving me with more unanswered questions.

"Are you enjoying yourself?" I ask.

Milo tilts his head. "If I say yes, will you promise never to lie about hosting a ball again?"

I smile. "If you're being truthful, then yes."

"Fine. I guess I don't hate it completely."

His stare envelopes me, and for a minute, I'm lost within his gaze. It feels like we're the only people that exist in the ballroom, and that if we stayed like this, he could keep me trapped here for eternity with his eyes alone. The way he holds me as we glide across the floor sends icy-hot shivers across my body.

It isn't until the song ends and Milo steps away to bow to me that I snap out of it. *What am I doing?* Why am I feeling like this now of all times?

Milo steps forward and offers me his arm. "I believe it's time to take our seats for dinner."

I nod slowly and let him guide me to our throne-like chairs on a high balcony, the draft against my back extra sensitive.

When I sit at the table, I know there's no way I'm going to be able to eat a single bite. I don't know how Milo speaks and eats in the presence of so many eyes without even breaking a sweat.

I force down a few small bites of food and try not to look at the guests, but when I do, people are already staring like I'm some painting in a museum.

Milo taps the table near my place setting. "Try the wine."

I startle at Milo's voice. "What?"

Milo takes a sip from his glass. "I find it helps."

I try to steady my breath. "Is that how you get through things like this?"

"I manage fine without the wine, but it certainly takes an edge off."

As I reach for my cup, Monicas stands and clinks a golden knife against his wineglass as jolly as ever. "If I can have your attention for just a few moments, I'd like to say a word."

In the corner of my eye, I see Milo's jaw twitch.

Monicas continues, "Tonight we are gathered in this beautiful palace in the gorgeous ballroom to celebrate our new Columess. You know, when Colum Arris first told me that he was married, I practically fell out of my seat. It was unexpected, but I am delighted that he chose a girl as smart and lovely as Margot."

I smile at that.

"Some of you may have heard that our Lady Arris was once a soldier on this ship herself. Her placement led to love and our first Columess under the reign of Balistar Arris. And if I do say so myself, she is a beauty to behold." He places a hand on his chest.

Some guests nod. Others murmur. It's only now that I realize that my title holds mixed emotions with the guests. I knew it was the case for the servants, but I didn't think much about other politicians or even Ashtanaban citizens themselves. After all, Milo hid me for a while after we married, not just from the arbitors, but from both planets, and I see why. A lowly Imnicus employee fraternizing with the Colum is controversial in itself, let alone marrying her.

"Everyone, if you will, please raise your drinks." Monicas raises his and everyone else follows along, turning the ballroom into a sea of glass.

"To Milo and Margot Arris, a couple matched by the gods themselves. May their union be joyous and fruitful. To Arris Reign."

"To Arris Reign!" the crowd shouts.

I barely process Milo clinking his glass into mine. I keep repeating that word in my head . . .

Fruitful, fruitful, fruitful.

Light music plays again while guests return to their inaudible conversations. It gives me a second to catch my breath. There's no way to get out of being the Columess or my expected duties, which likely involve having children with Milo. If I don't, the Arris reign ceases.

My ears feel stuffy and my hands sweat. Everything becomes louder—the conversations and laughter, the small clinks of their utensils, the plucked strings of the electric harp.

I push my chair back and stand quickly.

Milo slowly sets his fork down. "Are you all right?"

I flinch when he touches my arm. "Yes, I just need some air."

"Should I come with you?"

"No!"

Milo's eyes widen.

"I'm sorry . . . but please, just give me a few moments alone. I will be back soon."

He turns back to his meal, his fork piercing into his food harder than necessary. "Fine, but don't stay out too long."

I hold on to the skirts of my dress and disappear out a door into the halls of the west wing. Once I'm around a few corners, I lean against a decorative table. *What is wrong with me?*

Lady Bruis and Lady Lorne said that if Milo did not have an heir, Monicas would be next in line. He would be an influential leader if anything would happen to us. As cold as Milo can be, I know he would force nothing on me. At least I can take solace in that.

But I wonder, wouldn't he be better off with someone else? Someone who wants to continue his line? Someone who actually loves him?

But my heart thumps remembering those eyes that followed me all evening. The small sparks of jealousy I felt anytime I saw beautiful women looking at him with more than simple adoration. And somehow, out of any woman he could have on two entire planets with actual titles, he chose me. Does he regret it now?

In the hallway, I test doors, trying to find an unlocked, empty room that I can sit in for a while, just to clear my head undisturbed. Every door in the hallway is locked, a way to deter guests from *alternative* activities. Or Milo's concern of hosting a ball—snooping.

Then I remember, I can just use my ring's security clearance on most of the doors anyway. In the distance, there is one door that is different from the others. In the crack of the door is a blue ribbon peeking out.

I bend down to pick it up and try to pull it out, but it feels like it's stuck on something. A light pull does nothing. I tug harder, with both hands this time, but it doesn't budge. Even pressing my foot against the metal door for leverage doesn't help.

I stand and tap my ring to the security sensor.

And then I see the reason I could not remove it.

It's attached to someone's hair.

The body of a girl falls back, landing on my feet. Her skin is pale, lifeless, with widened eyes filled with terror that's frozen in time.

Then I do the only thing I can think of—scream.

Chapter 14

I fall backward, scooting away, my limbs shaking as I look at the pale, cold body of a girl with tight black curls. Her maid uniform is ripped, like she tried to run and someone yanked her back forcefully enough to tear a seam. Not a drop of blood stains her clothes or the surrounding floor.

What happened? When did this happen? Gods, we were all drinking and dancing without a care in the world while she lay here like this, lifeless.

I can't seem to cry, but my throat constricts. Within seconds, Milo and Commander Aisil are around the corner, panting.

They look to me, and then to the body. Horror flashes in their eyes.

Commander Aisil pulls out his communicator. "Send the morgue team to room 602 of the West Wing."

It isn't until Milo kneels in front of me that I realize my bottom lip is trembling.

"Margot, start from the beginning. What happened?" Milo takes my hands into his.

I can't stop looking at the girl. It's not even her death that has me growing more and more dizzy by the minute. It's her fear. The way her face is contorted like she saw the worst thing to ever exist right before she passed. "I saw a ribbon, I pulled, and it didn't come out . . . then I opened the door—" I can't bring myself to say another word.

Milo simply nods and turns to Aisil. "We're in lockdown. Nobody leaves this station until you've cleared them personally."

Aisil spins around and presses his hand against a panel on the wall. His handprint glows blue, and an intercom appears. "Lock down the Imnicus immediately."

A second passes and the lights dim. Any hallway doors left open immediately shut, and I hear the distant yells of alarms from the ballroom floor. Milo and Aisil move off to the side to talk, leaving me alone with the corpse. I don't remember her name, but I've seen her around the Imnicus, cleaning a time or two. Now she's gone. Who could have done something like this?

Soon, the hallways are swarming with military personnel, assessing the hallway, the room beyond, and the body. None of them seem startled. Even Milo stands expressionless, as if he has seen death too many times.

"Someone strangled her to death. No rigor mortis," A mortician says to his colleagues. "I suspect she's been dead for less than an hour. Whoever killed the girl was likely at the party, given the proximity and the timing."

I try to piece the puzzle together and imagine the faces of party guests. Could one of them be a Laven? I scratch that thought from my mind. It wouldn't make sense for a terrorist to go this route, not with so many proditors on board tonight.

There are too many people to narrow down; it could be anyone. A personal enemy of hers, a ship employee, or someone who simply gets a kick out of making others suffer. Thousands of people live on the Imnicus, and I added hundreds more suspects by throwing a ball.

Soldiers roll the girl on a gurney and cover her body with a blanket. Before they conceal her head, Commander Aisil steps forward and kisses his little finger and then presses it to the girl's forehead.

I stand and hug myself, the air chillier than before.

Milo unsnaps his cape from his shoulders, swinging it over mine like a blanket. "I'll have a soldier secure you in our quarters. Don't leave until I say."

I want to stay behind to assist them, but I know I'll just get in the way. Whatever skill set I had before that would've been helpful remains locked behind an impossible barrier, lost to me forever. What remains is a timid Columess, dumbstruck by a body found in the hallway. Is this the woman whom Milo found intoxicating? I can't help but doubt it.

"You'll find the killer?" I ask.

Milo looks away. "We will do our best. That, I promise you."

It took all night and morning for Commander Aisil to clear the guests to leave. Still, many loitered, mesmerized at their rare chance to stay in the Imnicus guest rooms. It drove Lleu and the other servants mad.

In my dressing room, Lleu blow-dries my freshly washed hair, circulating the scent of jasmine throughout the room. I can't stop thinking about the girl with the black curls and her horrific expression. She must have only been a year or two younger than me, her entire life ahead of her, and now she is gone; for some reason, I can't help but blame myself.

"You're as pale as a ghost," Lleu says.

I turn in my chair to face her. "What if my ball brought some psychopath on board? If I had never planned this—"

"Stop that right now," Lleu places her hands on her hips. "Aisil said it himself. All the guests have been cleared of any suspicion. Not only that, but they are signing agreements to never speak of this again."

"Seems excessive," I say.

"You haven't caught up on the gossipy news networks then. Just try to forget about it. Leave it to the investigators."

So I try to do just that. For hours, I read in my bedroom, I write in a journal, and I even watch some television, but I can't stop thinking about it. A killer could be aboard, and I feel responsible. I need to see the victim, if not to gather evidence then to pay my respects.

When I step outside the room, Alarik is there, resting his upper back on the wall with folded arms. "Where are you off to?"

I curse under my breath. Of course Alarik is here, and by the book under his arm, it seems he's been standing here for some time. "I assume Milo has you guarding me?"

"Well, there was just a murder. Can you blame him?"

Of all the times Milo has assigned me an escort, this is the one time I agree with him. But I can't sit still today, not until I see the maid one last time. "Well, as much as I want to respect Milo's wishes, I have a morgue to visit. You don't need to come with me."

"I know you'd manage well on your own." I expect him to follow it up with, *but Milo,* but he doesn't. "Would you like me to go with you anyhow? Something tells me you need some company."

"That would . . . " *Dammit, why does he have to be so nice?* "I would like that."

I follow Alarik, lugging my blood-red gown behind me, all the way through the command center, which is buzzing with busy officers tapping buttons and speaking over intercoms. We pass through the research center in the south wing where there are odd machines and hybrid plants in glass incubators.

"Here we are." Alarik motions to the double doors.

"Thank you." Somewhere behind these doors is the body of a lifeless girl who didn't deserve to die. Hopefully they found a way to get that fearful expression off her face, but if they didn't—

"Well, are you going in?" Alarik tilts his head.

"I . . . uh yah, I just need a minute." Even though I know this is something I need to do, my legs remain frozen.

He places a hand on my back to guide me in. "I'll be with you the entire time. There's nothing to worry about."

Something about his words brings me genuine comfort. I believe him. Trust him. Truly.

A mortician approaches us with metal goggles on and quickly removes his gloves and bows his head. "Columess, I didn't expect to see you here. It's an honor."

"Sorry to disturb you. I know you're busy, but I was hoping to see *her* one last time." I feel ashamed that I don't even know her name, but at this point I don't want to. It would only make things harder.

"Of course. I have no reason to refuse you, as long as the Colum is all right with it." The mortician looks to Alarik, who nods.

Alarik just lied for me. Defied the Colum in a way I'm not sure even Knox would.

We follow the mortician into a cold room filled with metal tables, though only one has a body on it, which is covered with a white sheet. My skin crawls at the sight.

"Sorry about the mess." The mortician motions to the tables covered in instruments. "There isn't a lot of death on the Imnicus, you see."

"I can imagine not." My gaze is still pinned on the body.

"I will leave you two alone to pay your respects. Please, let me know if you need anything." The mortician disappears outside.

Alarik and I stand over the covered body, one I'm sure hasn't even been probably prepared yet for transport back to Ashtanabo. Gods, she probably has a family that Aisil will have to break the news to if he hasn't already. The thought breaks my heart.

I used to be a soldier, which means I've probably dealt with death before. But something about this feels more personal. Or maybe I hated death as much then as I do now.

"Are you sure you want to do this?" Alarik asks. "There may be things you can't unsee. There will be no going back."

I take a deep breath. "Yes, I want to see her."

Alarik nods slowly, taking the sheet off the girl and pulling it back to expose her naked body. It takes everything in me to resist the urge to look away. He didn't have to pull the entire thing off her, but it's like he knew I wanted to investigate.

And that's when I see it. Burns on the tops of her thighs. On her arms. Down her neck and chest. Not just any burns, but ones that are distinctly blue, just like the ones Lleu and Sloane had.

Alarik says nothing as he watches the expression on my face change to sadness to dark realization.

Whoever killed this servant was not someone who traveled from Ashtanabo. They've lived on the Imnicus for some time.

I don't know what to do or who to talk to, so I stay silent for days. Something is stopping me from going straight to Milo. If Sloane and Lleu have refused to report their burns, it means there is more going on than meets the eye. Something being hidden that is frightful enough for everyone to stay silent. I have to play this carefully. Not only that, but I need to stay safe from whomever this attacker is.

Inside the lounge area of my bedroom, Lleu sets a cup of moon tea in front of me before moving on to tidy up the area. Every day, I think the same thing—should I confront Lleu about her burns? Should I not?

"Lleu, what region on Ashtanabo are you from?" I ask.

She fluffs a pillow. "Msanii. It's beautiful with forests and clay buildings. We even have candlelight ceremonies for girls coming into adulthood. It's quite extravagant." Lleu walks over to one of the small tables and dusts a vase.

"That sounds lovely." I take a sip of my tea and watch her hand, no longer covered in blue burns.

Lleu sees where my gaze is pinned, and her posture immediately becomes rigid.

I turn my head away and clear my throat. "How are the other servants doing after . . . well, you know?"

"Oh, many of them have become a lot more antsy. A lot of the girls do their chores in pairs now." She picks up a vase to dust it.

"Understandable." I swallow, feeling the hard lump in my throat. "Your hand looks a lot better."

Her hand trembles as she sets the vase back down against the surface.

"Yes," is all she says. Lleu picks her cuticles raw, almost becoming a different person. One riddled with fear.

I stand and walk over to her, taking her hands into mine. "Lleu . . ."

Lleu pulls her hands back. "I don't have much time to talk. There are other duties to attend to." She's even more apprehensive than Sloane was, which means only one thing.

Lleu knows her attacker, and if that's the case, I'm willing to bet she knows who killed that servant.

She heads to the door with her back turned toward me. I can't help but feel somewhat hurt.

"The victim at the ball . . . she had the same burns," I call out.

Lleu stops, her fists tightening.

"If you just tell me the name of whoever burned you, it could lead us to the killer. You would be safe, and he won't be able to hurt anyone again."

Lleu looks over her shoulder, and a stray tear falls down her mocha skin. "I'm sorry, Margot, I am. But I cannot help you." She hurries out of the room, the electronic doors whooshing shut behind her.

I lean against one of the chairs. Not only is Lleu still in danger, but so is everyone on the Imnicus. For Lleu not to offer a single hint means that this person isn't some disposable servant or soldier. The attacker has status.

Though Sloane didn't see the man's face, she at least offered a few clues—the attacker is male and he is strong.

So far, he has three victims and one of them is dead. If I don't act quickly and tactfully, who knows how many more will follow. I can't run to Milo until I have more evidence or clues for him to go off of. I'll at least respect Sloane and Lleu in that.

In the meantime, I need to learn how to protect myself. I know that I am skilled in combat, it's just hiding somewhere within my mind. With training, maybe I can find that part of me, then I can protect Lleu.

I remember Slone's chilling words, *Dark things happen aboard this ship.*

Chapter 15

"**N**o, I can't train you," Milo says.

"Why not?" I furrow my eyebrows.

"I'm too busy." He walks away from me in the command center without so much as a goodbye.

"Milo, wait!" I follow up behind him and grab his forearm, pulling him back to face me. "I want training. After the murder, wouldn't it bring you some peace of mind to know I can protect myself?"

"We have proditors for a reason. There is no need to train."

"Proditors who aren't always around." I motion to my scars.

"I have duties from the moment I awaken to the moment I fall asleep."

"Duties you could easily hand off to an officer."

Milo pinches his nose and finally lets out a defeated sigh. "You were a spy, right? So why don't you . . . I don't know . . . try to sneak up on me at some point. Surprise me, though I doubt you can do it."

I scoff. "Is that a challenge, then?"

Milo folds his arms. "I guess so."

"How about this? If I'm successful, you'll train me personally?"

Milo rubs the back of his neck, contemplating before finally speaking. "Fine. But like I said, you won't be able to do it."

I smile. "Deal. Starting tomorrow, you better watch your back." I turn to stride away, smug with at least some semblance of victory. But I don't get far before realizing I have no idea how to get to my next destination.

I spin back to Milo. "How do I get to the library?"

Milo doesn't berate me. Instead, his brows just knit with confusion. "Library?"

"I have some studying to do. You can't expect me to be the Columess and know nothing about my own planet, can you?"

Milo waves over Commander Aisil. "I'll have him take you there."

"You can't walk me there yourself?"

"You told me I should start delegating."

I narrow my eyes.

Commander Aisil rushes over and salutes Milo. "Yes, Colum?"

"Escort the Columess to the library."

"Certainly, Colum." Aisil turns to me. "Right this way, Lady Arris."

Before I can gripe at Milo for handing me off again, he turns and walks up the steps of the command center to continue his rounds. I grunt and follow after Commander Aisil down the halls.

"I'm sorry to take you away from your duties," I say. A few V.I.X units pass by as we round a corner.

"It's really no bother. Besides, if Milo commands me to do something, it is my duty." Premature wrinkles line his eyes and forehead. It doesn't surprise me that I once thought he was in his early sixties. Up close, I can see that he's a decade younger against his subtle-Susukan features.

"But you're commander-in-chief. A *maid* can give me directions. This feels a bit extreme, wouldn't you say?"

"I never turn down an opportunity for a lovely walk." He passes a smile, and I see the truth behind his eyes. He'll never say it directly, but a chance to be away from Milo and his other duties is probably a blessing. "Besides, when we were at war with Lavenai, my title meant more. My position effectively takes care of itself most days."

"War?" Of course, it's not news to me. But I had never heard it referred to like that.

Aisil nods. "Back then, I was one of Balistar Arris's most trusted military advisors, though managing the Imnicus is a bit less hectic. I have to admit, it suits me better."

He sells himself short, I know. There's a strange depth beneath his words I can't quite place. I know Milo and the other proditors think he's a fool, but I almost get the sense that he wishes that to be the case. His facade is only an illusion of what lies beneath.

Once at the library, I thank Commander Aisil for his time. My short conversation with him was enough to spark even more desire to learn about Ashtanabo, and if time permits, Lavenai.

Of course, what I didn't tell Milo is that I'm also interested in researching burns.

There are no books specifically about burns in the computer's directory. Even when I search for virtual articles, nothing comes up in the electronic records. I have no choice but to read book titles on the shelf manually until I find something that may be of use. The medical section may have what I'm looking for.

I run my hands against the hardback spines as I line the circular shelves. An A.S.O.P. unit follows behind me, carrying my books on its flat head. The military staff—mostly cadets studying—watch me over the tops of their books.

I gather books on wounds and a few on combat. In the history section, I make a stop to leaf through books on Ashtanabo. The A.S.O.P. is carrying too many books as it is, so I tuck a few books under my arm. But no matter how hard I look, I cannot find any books on Lavenai.

One librarian sits at the front desk near the first-floor entrance, her pen scribbling inventory notes into a record book.

"Excuse me," I say.

She jumps and drops her pen. "Oh my, Lady Arris, I didn't see you there." She bows her head and does a small curtsy.

"Sorry to frighten you," I say, bowing my head.

"No worries, my dear! I'm Iris. What can I help you with?" Iris is by far the oldest person I have met on the Imnicus, with lines deep enough to at least have grandchildren.

"Could you direct me to books on Lavenai?"

"Space travel guides are in the section by the wall, dear."

"No, I'm more after their history."

Iris frowns. "I don't believe we have any books on Lavenai's history. You'd have to travel to their capital and search their libraries."

That seems strange. "Wouldn't a planet we have ruled for so long have some sort of book on the Imnicus?"

She chuckles. "Well, twenty-two years is not that long in the grand scheme of things. We are still in the infant stages with Lavenai. As well as this library, believe me. Every day I find a gap in our shelves, it seems."

Twenty-two years. The way Milo and Lleu describe it makes our rule sound ancient.

I get cozy at one of the tables and leaf through the book on wounds. There is a small section on burns, but nothing about blue ones or how they're caused. It seems impossible from what I'm reading, but I know what I saw and how distinct Lleu and Sloane's were.

A V.I.X. unit brings me moon tea in a glass mug. I reach for the book on Ashtanabo. The leather seems to be brand new, though I suppose it makes sense. Natives of Ashtanabo likely already know their own history before ever stepping foot on the Imnicus.

I skim through the table of contents and stop short on a chapter called *Vicars and Proditors*.

A religious group called Vicars formed centuries ago within the snowy Mountains of Eskdale, composed of those who passed down the gift of the crows through generations. In order to keep their powers pure, they only married others of their kind. They shunned those who married outside the bloodline. Over the centuries, the tradition of shunning ended, but they still scrutinized those who watered down the crows.

Vicars were loyal to none except for their own community and closed themselves off from the rest of the Ashtanabo. They never involved themselves in politics, only worship and meditation.

Over the years, a faction of the Vicars split off and formed a group of fighters loyal to the Colum, known as proditors, a name coined by the Vicars themselves. The Vicars chastised proditors for their betrayal of the creed. After some time, the proditors came to accept the term as their own.

I wonder why the proditors chose to break off from the Vicars, but the book doesn't say. Interestingly enough, it seems to imply the proditors' powers are genetic. If that's the case, then why is it that Knox has powers but Milo doesn't? Another question for another time, I suppose.

After spending hours more reading, I leave the library and stop inside one of the public bathrooms to use the mirror. Milo would probably find it improper to use the servant bathrooms, but nobody seems to be around at the moment.

I think more about the proditors and everything I read about their religious background. It makes me snicker slightly. No drinking. No fornication. If any of the proditors still follow those laws, none of them live on the Imnicus. Onyx alone is proof of that.

Voices approach the bathroom door and I panic, running into one of the stalls and locking myself inside. Maybe I do care more about what the servants think of me than I thought. So what? After what the technicians said about me, I haven't been as at ease when any personnel are around, no matter how much I pretend to be.

As two girls barge inside, laughing, I lift the hem of my dress higher, bunching my skirts underneath my arms so they don't see me. Through the crack in the stall, I watch them.

One girl goes up to the sink and dabs her face with a handkerchief. "I'm beat. Gods, if I have to do one more load of laundry, I think I'll fall over. How many more years of service do we have?"

"You have three. I, on the other hand, have four."

"At least we have fun on our days off, I suppose." She quickly turns to the other. "You never told me about how the ball went!"

"I worked myself to the bone, but it was beautiful. As were a few of the men." She winks.

"Tell me!"

I move my head slightly to get a better view.

"Well, all of the Imnicus proditors were there, and they were all dashing, as always. Especially Onyx."

"And the Colum?"

"Sinfully beautiful."

The girl squeals. "I can't believe it! Goodness, I wish he was still single."

The other scoffs. "He might as well be with the way he and Lady Arris bicker. Sometimes I wonder if I should just try my hand at bedding him. I bet he'd cave in an instant."

"But Milo doesn't sleep with servants."

The girl touches up her lipstick. "We'll see about that."

A strange burning spreads over my chest and up my throat. The thought of Milo aroused at the sight of her breasts, the thought of him pleasuring himself with another woman—it brings an ache to my stomach.

After they leave the bathroom giggling, I push open the stall door and splash cold water on my face. *I'm not jealous. I'm not jealous.*

But when I look at my reflection in the mirror, all I can see is the envy housed between my furrowed eyebrows.

Every day for an entire week, I attempt to sneak up on Milo.

I've been successful zero times.

It's as if he has a device implanted into my brain, tracking my every movement. No matter how many corners I hide behind or for how long, he always catches me. I even dressed in the disguise of a soldier and he caught me right away.

Once after he caught me sneaking up on him, he asked me to sit in a meeting with him about how to further aid Lavenai. One commander gave a presentation on the technology developed to help detoxify Lavenai's soil. They believe they can completely filter the planet's farmlands within the decade if their inventions work.

I change my tactics and study his daily routine relentlessly. Which doorways he passes, which stairwell he descends. From what I've gathered, his fatal flaw is that he rarely mixes up his routine.

Every day, after breakfast, he walks the same pattern, talks to the same commanders, and seldom stops for a break. Occasionally he is called off to Ashtanabo on business, but when he gets back to the Imnicus, he always starts exactly where he left off.

Today, I lean over circular railings five stories up in the commander center, looking down at Milo directing commanders and lower-ranking soldiers at their stations.

After today, his rigid schedule will be his downfall.

I'm wearing a soldier's uniform again. There is no way I'll win his game in a gown. While I have a second, I recall my mental map of the south wing and determine where he will go next. I mentally check every corner and room for blind spots for a place I could hide.

That's it.

I take the long way with fewer soldiers. Anyone could mention to Milo that they saw me and ruin my plan.

I stride through the halls until I find a closet with a sliding door on the third floor of the south wing. In fifteen minutes, he will walk past here, and once I succeed, he will have no choice but to train me.

The closet is snug, filled with hanging uniforms and shelves filled with leather boots. A single square light bulb hangs above me, still swaying back and forth from my entrance.

My legs cramp from the tight space. I wish I thought this through and didn't leave so much time before he'd be by. But leaving and coming back will only hinder my plan now.

Five minutes left.

I point and flex my toes to relieve some cramping.

One minute left.

I press my ear to the door and close my eyes until I hear the low-pitched tapping of boots. I turn the settings on the electronic door to manual and rest my hand on the handle.

Ready . . . now!

He takes one step past the door, and I swing the door open and lunge at him, grabbing the back of his collar and yanking him into the closet with me. I accidentally hit the switch and turn the door back to automatic, locking us both inside.

"You've got to be kidding me." Milo looks pissed, rubbing his temples and shaking his head. He's almost chest-to-chest with me from how small the closet is.

I fold my arms, leaning against one of the shelves. "Looks like you'll have to find some time in your busy day to train me after all. You know, if you weren't so focused on work all the time, you may have realized that I've been following you."

"I *did* see you following me. Every day. For a week now. I just didn't expect . . . dammit." Milo reaches for the door handle next to me, his chest pressing against mine.

His warm body brings an unexpected flush to my cheeks. Now that the rush from my victory is simmering down, I'm realizing the position I'm in. That we're both in. He and I are all alone, in a closet, with almost no space between us.

This was a mistake.

"I think it's jammed. What did you do?" Milo hisses, trying to press the control buttons.

"I think I bumped it on the way in."

Milo brings his communicator to his mouth. "Send someone to the location of my communicator. The door is jammed."

"Right away, sir. Wait . . . are you in a closet?" the operator asks back through the device.

"Nevermind that. Just get here quickly." Milo looks down at me. "Happy?"

"If I would have known, I would have done things differently, thank you very much." I turn my head, trying to hide the red in my face. Can he see it? If I try to cover my cheeks more, it may bring me more attention to them. Gods, I hope a technician gets here soon.

"Margot?" he asks, tilting his head.

We stand there for a minute in silence, our breaths the only noise. When I look up at Milo again, he's already studying my face.

Chills domino down my arms, my chest inches from touching his. I've never been so close to him before. At least, not like this.

Milo's breaths grow heavier and his gaze flickers to my mouth.

Warmth fills my lower belly. "Milo—"

Against anything I thought he'd ever do, he leans down . . .

And kisses me.

I freeze for a second. Is this really happening? Is *Milo Arris* kissing me?

For a second, I break away from the kiss before abandoning my apprehension and kissing him back.

His mouth is so warm. So smooth and soft.

Milo holds my waist and the back of my head and presses me into the hanging coats. His kiss turns from teasing to devouring, taking me in as if I'm oxygen.

My skin prickles with both hot and cold energy, and something new is building in my core. I never really knew how much I wanted this until now. Gods, why does he have to be so terrible yet kiss like this?

He drags his tongue over mine as I wrap my arms around his neck. As he presses against me further, I can feel the bulge in his pants against my stomach.

I can't remember anything. How did I get here in this closet with the guy I can't stand? Why did I kiss him back? Why am I enjoying it?

Suddenly, the door slides open. "It took a few minutes. The door controls were jammed, but we got it all taken care—" The technician's eyes widen.

Milo quickly pulls away. The desire falls from his face and he shakes his head slightly, like he's trying to process what he just did. Like he regrets it.

He pushes past the technician into the hallway. A patrolling guard passes by, slowing down slightly with a confused expression.

Milo narrows his eyes. "What are you looking at? Keep moving!" His cape trails behind him as he turns the corner.

"I'm sorry, Columess. I thought he requested us to fix the jam on this door," the technician says.

My face is still beet red. "It's not a problem. Just forget what you saw."

I go in the opposite direction of Milo, even though it's not the most convenient path. My body is still on fire.

What the hell just happened?

Chapter 16

The next few days are rough. Milo went off on business to Ashtanabo, leaving me alone at meals. At least, with him gone, I can use the bed.

The bed that smells like his cologne and makes me dream of nothing but him.

We've hardly spoken at all since the day in the closet. I still can feel the imprint of his lips. The drag of his tongue. The sound of his pleasured moans.

One morning, Knox shows up to my bedroom door holding a stack of exercise clothing.

"What's this?" I ask.

"The Colum sent word from Ashtanabo that you were to be retrained in combat. So, here I am." Knox grins.

Milo is supposed to train me, but I can't tell Knox that. He might ask questions like, *"Why do you want Milo to train you so badly?"* I haven't even told Lleu that Milo and I kissed, but she's not talking to me much lately either. "You mean we're starting today?"

"Not today. *Now.*" Knox shoves the clothing into my chest. "Chop, chop."

After I change clothes, I follow Knox to a large training room filled with exercise equipment and mats. A V.I.X. unit flies around, wiping down seats. Knox disappears into the changing room and emerges in a tank and lounge pants.

"What convinced Milo to let me start training today?" I ask.

Knox shrugs, ruffling his curly golden hair. "Beats me. He just said he owed it to you. He also said you're better off training with a proditor. After all, we are stronger and sharper than normal humans. Now, let's get started."

Knox starts out by teaching me basic strikes and blocks. But when it comes time for me to execute what I've learned, my reflexes are abysmal.

"I thought I was supposed to be a soldier. A spy. Why can't I get the hang of this?"

"A good spy doesn't actively need to fight. You knew the moves, but you didn't use them in practice often."

From the familiarity I feel in muscles, it seems I really knew how to fight to some degree, but I can't execute them in the slightest. He knocks me to the floor—multiple times. Even after a few hours of training, I don't make one ounce of progress. He's not even being rough with me.

After the twentieth time I'm knocked on my ass, he puts his hands on his hips. "I have another idea." Knox bends over and grabs my calves, pulling me toward him.

"I can move myself," I mutter.

He brings his hands toward my temples, but I slap his wrists away. "Knox, no. I don't want you in my head again. The last time was terrifying."

"Milo told me himself to train you using any means necessary. My gifts can enhance your combat. This time, he's okay with it."

"Wait, what do you mean *this time*? You mean he didn't approve of the last time you poked around in my head?"

Knox laughs and rubs the back of his neck. "He was less than pleased and made some fuss about you not being recovered from the attack yet. Not to mention, proditor magic leaves imprints quite easily. But that's exactly why my magic can help you. Imagine having something stronger and more innate to guide you."

I suppose he's right. And if I ever want to find the killer hiding aboard the Imnicus, I'll need to know how to fight when I finally catch him. Time is ticking. I doubt I have much time to learn how to defend myself properly.

"Fine, just do it," I say.

Knox slams his palms against my temples almost like a slap. Just like that, I'm dragged into his world.

But this world is different. This time, instead of him being in my mind, I'm in some small nook of his. The walls are geometric like the north and west wings. The shapes move and morph around me in various shades of black and red.

I turn to see Knox standing behind me in his proditor armor. It reminds me of how it felt the last time he showed me the darker side of his magic. That sinister feeling wraps around my neck like a noose.

Something steps out of Knox. A duplication of him made completely of shadows and ink.

I take a step back. "Knox, what is that?"

"Your new teacher. A lifelong one."

"You're saying that whatever you're about to do to me . . . is permanent?"

"Technically, yes."

"I don't know about this . . . "

"Are you ready?" Knox asks. "And I mean *really* ready? Once you agree, it cannot be taken back."

This is something I know I need to do. Not only will I be able to protect myself, but Lleu. I nod hesitantly.

The shadowy figure takes a step forward. I know no actual harm can come to me here, but I don't want Knox's shadow to touch me.

"Stay still, Margot."

The shadow rushes forward and steps straight inside me. A chill, both nauseating and painful, sears through my body. It's like my flesh is being torn in two and sewn back together. I scream and scream and scream.

Then everything goes still. I'm still in Knox's mind, but my limbs feel different. Half foreign and half mine.

"Did you possess me?" I ask sharply as I study the back of my hands.

"If putting a shard of my motor skills into your body is possession, then yes."

"This is insane." I stretch my fingers, but the end of the motion fans my fingers out more than usual—the way Knox would.

"It's amplified here. Once we're back in the real world, it will only activate at certain times, like when your adrenaline is spiked. You'll still have to train hard, but now it will be easier. *Much* easier."

"Then let's get out of here and go train." I don't want to be in his head another second.

"Careful now. We haven't even gotten to the good part." Knox charges at me.

He swings his fist back as he runs at me, and I want to melt into a puddle on the ground. Though my instinct is to hide, something clicks into me. I stand up straight and quickly veer to the side, blocking the punch as he swings at me.

All at once, it feels like the puzzle has come together, like I've known how to do this forever, yet I know it wouldn't have been possible without Knox's magic.

He turns to look at me. His eyes grin beneath his hood. "Very good, Margot. How did it feel?"

My chest is still tight. "Horrifying, yet also invigorating."

"Good, because I'm upping the stakes." Knox snaps his fingers, and a glitching dagger appears in his hand. "And the pain threshold."

Knox circles me like I'm prey. I don't even have anything to fight him back with. The only way I'm getting out of here is to break the simulation, and to do that, I have no choice but to break him. If he's down for the count, so is this world inside his mind.

Soon his body glitches and it's harder to keep track of him. "Knox, this isn't fair." *Oh gods*, I don't see him anymore.

"Nothing is fair." Knox says near the back of my neck.

That innate fire inside of me lights up, and I spin around quicker than I ever thought possible, grabbing his wrist and twisting his arm behind his back. I don't even think twice about it. I pry the dagger from his glitching gloved hands.

And then I stab him.

Knox somehow howls in pain and laughs at the same time.

Blood runs down my hand, and for a second, I think it's real and fall back. Knox straightens his back, knife still embedded into him. "Well done, Margot. Well done."

The world around us starts to crack like glass, and then all at once, his mental palace shatters.

Static covers my eyes before I'm back on the floor in the training room with one of Knox's hands pressed into my temple.

"Oh my gods, are you all right?" I crawl behind Knox and palm at his back for the dagger, but it's gone. There's no blood either. I sigh in relief.

"Remember, with proditor magic, it's all in your head," Knox says. "The simulations will always seem more realistic than dreams, no matter how bizarre and impossible they are."

"It all felt so real." I stand and start to pace.

Knox pushes himself up to his feet and places a comforting hand on my shoulder. "You did a good job. I mean it. I just hope you don't hate me now."

I straighten my posture. "No, I'm glad you pushed me to fight back."

He raises an eyebrow. "Really?"

"If this is what all soldiers on the Imnicus are subject to, then I should be no different. To refuse training simply because it's hard is what will get me killed by Lavenai. I already came too close once."

"For what it's worth, I know that those Laven terrorists over-powered you to the point that even I would have had difficulty fighting them off."

His words bring me some sense of comfort. They make me feel less weak. "I look forward to our future trainings, Knox."

With Milo gone on Ashtanabo, and Knox and Lleu busy with their duties, I spend more and more time in the library.

But more recently, I've become increasingly distracted while reading. The words jumble around on the pages, and every person or robot that passes knocks me out of concentration. Every time I fall out of focus, I think about the ball. Something about it isn't making sense.

There must have been something that Milo and Aisil missed. Something that could tell us definitively who the murderer is.

My gaze falls on the ceiling at one of the black circular cameras.

Of course, maybe the murder was caught on one of the sur-veillance cameras. But Aisil isn't stupid and would have checked them. Though even if the killer was sneaky and wore a disguise, there could be something in the video Aisil didn't see or that he overlooked.

Still, I try to banish the thought for now and move back to my books, reading more about Ashtanaban technology, the languages in its eight regions, and the many different cultures. It makes me wonder more about Lavenai and what cultures are present on their planet.

But when a V.I.X. unit nearly collides with a passing soldier, it's enough of a distraction to make me slam my book shut.

The cameras have to show something more about the ball. If I ask Aisil or Milo, I'll be dismissed, or rather, reassured. If I want to watch the footage, I'll have to make it happen myself and without prying eyes.

I go to the south wing and pretend to pace aimlessly around that hallway and look out the wide glass windows at the stars. With my training clothes on, people don't seem to notice me. All the while, I'm watching the door to the surveillance room with the corner of my eye.

At one point, the two men leave the room together, heading toward one of the dining halls for lunch. Before the door slides shut, I run to it and stick my foot between the sensor and the frame.

I'm in.

I don't know how long I have. I don't even know how they're permitted to leave this room unattended like this, especially after the Imnicus was just subject to a terrorist attack.

I click through the video feed quickly. To my relief, it seems almost every part of the Imnicus is covered with cameras except for bedrooms, bathrooms, and a select few areas.

The room itself where the murder took place doesn't have a camera inside, but the hallway just outside does. I use the touch-screen to take the recording back to the day of the ball until I see that frightful moment.

The moment I found her.

Remembering how it felt to tug on that ribbon makes me numb, but I push through and go back about an hour. It takes a few adjustments before I see her black curls bouncing as she rounds the halls. When a shadow emerges behind her, my heart pounds.

I'm going to see him. The man responsible for the burns. For the murder.

But then the footage turns to static and fast-forwards to me tugging on the blue ribbon.

It must be a glitch.

I rewind again, but the same thing happens.

I sit back in disbelief. Did someone delete the footage? Did the killer disable the camera? I don't know enough about Imnicus technology or protocol to make the deduction.

And though this information may confirm my theory that the killer works on the Imnicus, I know that I'm at another dead end. I slump in the seat.

But while I'm here, I should take advantage of this rare opportunity. What about if I look at the day of the Laven attack? Maybe there are puzzle pieces that Aisil missed there too. Pieces that could lead Milo to the Laven terrorists.

I search for the date of the invasion and then think back to what I know. It happened in the morning hours, so I scroll all the way up and increase the speed, pulling up multiple cameras all at once from different areas of the west wing as I watch the entire day of the attack go by.

Nothing. There is absolutely nothing. Business continues as usual.

Maybe I got the day wrong.

If the guards are taking their normal hour-long break, I have only thirty minutes left. I skim through the surrounding days, but I find absolutely nothing.

It couldn't have occurred in a blind spot because the invasion sounded huge, yet the footage from the south wing shows that nobody was up in arms. People look calm and collected at every camera angle I can find in every wing.

With only ten minutes until the guards return, I scroll through the day of the invasion once more to search for things I may have overlooked. Again, nothing out of the ordinary.

I slam my hands down onto the desk, causing the footage to jump forward a few minutes onto a camera in the south wing.

The footage shows Milo, Knox, and three officers sweeping through one hallway. Coming from the opposite direction is a guard, but something seems off about this employee. Their gait doesn't match what I usually see when guards pass the Colum.

Normally, when subordinates approach Milo, they stiffen, stop, and give a small bow.

This guard simply steps out of the way then stays in place with a too-bold posture. They don't even bow. Once past Milo and Knox, the mysterious guard speeds away.

Another detail that strikes me as odd is a small red stripe on the guard's right shoulder. No one on the Imnicus has this on their uniform. I make a mental note to ask Lleu about it later.

With only five minutes left, I curl my fist and leave the workspace just as I found it before I head back to my quarters.

Why can't I find footage of the invasion? And how do I question Milo about it without telling him I've been sneaking around?

The invasion happened. I have the scars to prove it.

In order for the Laven to protect their identities, they'd have to erase the footage. But what did Lavenai do to leave no trace of it?

Unlike the day of the murder, there are no gaps or glitches on the invasion day. It's almost like the footage was warped as opposed to erased, as if some kind of magic was used. And there is only one type of being I know that can manipulate things outside of the physical realm.

I seize up at the thought as I walk. Could a proditor really be responsible for the doctored footage?

At first, I pry the thought from my head, but the more I think about it, the more things come together.

If proditor powers can interact with lightbulbs, surely they can interfere with other kinds of technology too. They may not even have to enter the security room to do it. Not to mention, they have enough clearance and power to sneak in terrorists through either of the docking bays.

There are five proditors aboard the Imnicus.

And one of them may have betrayed Milo.

Chapter 17

I knock on Lleu's dorm room door in the east wing late the next night, holding a bouquet of silver flowers behind my back. Ones I had delivered from Ashtanabo. I've decided I won't press her about her burn anymore, but I need her.

Every day since I confronted her, she gets me ready with only the bare necessities of words. I miss confiding in her, and most of all, I hate that she doesn't feel safe around me.

There was a time where she was my resource for everything on the Imnicus and for questions about my past. Without her, I'm forced to use the library or hound the proditors.

And with my suspicion of a proditor being responsible for the attack, I need her more than ever. If my theory has any merit, one of them allowed Lavenai terrorists to dock on the Imnicus and then used the gift of the crows to change the footage of the attack. And if Lavenai got their hands on the allegiance of a proditor, things could change drastically. War could be on the horizon—a war we could lose.

When Lleu answers the door, she looks startled and peers around the halls. "What are you doing here?"

I pull the flowers from behind my back. "I thought you could use some cheering up."

Lleu looks like she's trying not to smile and shakes her head in disbelief. "You didn't have to do that."

"I also wanted to make amends. Know that, if there is ever something you don't want to talk about, I will never press you for it again."

Lleu tears up and shoots forward to hug me. "I'm sorry I was so distant. Just . . . thank you."

I squeeze her tight before backing up. "Milo sent word that he will be in Ashtanabo another day or two. I was wondering, do you want to sleep over in my room?"

"That sounds like it could be fun, but wouldn't you mind?" Lleu asks.

"We could watch something and eat leftover desserts. Besides, we may as well take advantage of the opportunity while Milo's away."

Lleu contemplates before smiling wide. "I would love that."

Soon, Lleu and I are in one of the darkened north wing kitchens, pulling half-eaten pies and cakes out of the fridge.

I set a few on a rolling tray. "Is this enough?"

"Take as many as you want. Nobody will notice." Lleu pulls out a few macaroons. "These will do nicely."

As we leave the kitchen, we are laughing with each other as we watch our backs for the kitchen maids. Running through the halls with her and with the cart full of desserts, I feel almost normal. Like this, we aren't a maid and a Columess, but two friends without a care in the world.

As we turn a corner, my heart drops.

"Where are you two off to all giggly like that?" Onyx folds his arms, but his eyes look amused.

All I can think when I see him is the doctored footage. And if he's the proditor potentially working with Lavenai, it means he's one of my suspects, and one of the last people I want to be around right now.

"It's none of your business, Onyx." Lleu snaps. "Don't you have some servant girl to bed?"

"Ouch." Onyx chuckles. "But you're headed to Milo's room with food and laughter. I have to only assume you're sleeping over, Lleu. Under Milo's nose, I might add."

Lleu looks like she wants to throw a pie square in his face.

I try to soften my expression. "You don't seem like the type to report us. Why don't you just forget what you saw, and we'll call it a night, all right?"

"You're right, I'm not the type," Onyx says.

"Good."

"But I want to join too."

Lleu throws her hands up.

"Onyx, don't be difficult," I say.

"Come on, it could be fun." Onyx paces forward. "I'll even bring drinks. And it's not like I want to sleep in Milo's room. He'd kill me. I just want to hang out for a few hours and forget about work."

"Lleu isn't allowed to see your face," I add. "You'd have to go into the bathroom every time you take a sip."

"Ah, now that's where you're wrong. Lleu is, in fact, the only servant allowed to see us. A lady's maid title is nothing to scoff at."

Even the arbitors aren't allowed to see the proditors' faces. Is Lleu really that high ranking? I look at her.

"It's true," she says sheepishly. "It's also a curse."

"Darling, do you know how many servant girls would beg to be in your position? How many of them whine and groan about me having to blindfold them every time we—"

"That's enough." I take a breath. There's no way he's going to concede. But if he's bringing drinks, maybe I can use him to my advantage. If Onyx is the one who deleted the footage for Lavenai, alcohol could loosen his lips if the conversation ever veers in the direction of the attack. "If you're going to be that persistent, you can join. But only for an hour."

"Deal." Onyx grins. "There are a few things I have to grab. I will be by later."

Lleu and I give each other annoyed glances before heading to my bedroom and setting up. We change into more comfortable clothes, push furniture aside, and turn on the television.

"Gods, why does Onyx always have to butt in?" Lleu mutters.

"Who knows. It could be fun." I set the pies out neatly on the coffee table.

There isn't much time before Onyx shows up, and there are questions I need to ask Lleu outside of the earshot of a proditor. Though I wish I had time to get a few desserts in her first and reel her in more before asking. "Do you know a lot about the military hierarchy on the Imnicus?"

She shrugs. "Mostly."

"What does a red stripe on a uniform mean?"

Her eyes widen as she flips through channels on the television. "Did you see someone like that on the ship?"

"No, I was just in one of the uniform closets and saw one," I lie.

"What were you doing in a closet?" Lleu laughs.

I swallow, her question reminding me of an entirely different closet and of Milo's mouth. I still haven't told her about the kiss, and with Milo and I at each other's throats, she'll be ecstatic, or at least want all the details. "Answer my question and I'll answer yours."

She shoots me a suspicious look. "I believe it marks soldiers still in training. Rookies. It's rare to find one on the Imnicus, as only the best of the best are sent here."

I guess it explains why the soldier in the video seemed so off their game. Still, it's a strange coincidence that it happened on the day of the attack.

Lleu pokes me. "Now, an answer for an answer. What is this about a closet?"

"Well . . . Milo." I can feel my face heating red, not able to tell if it's the memory itself or the shame of who I kissed causing it.

Lleu covers her mouth, like she already knows what I'm about to say. "You two—"

I throw my hands up quickly. "It was just a kiss!"

"Tell me everything!" She grabs my hands. Her curiosity and excitement, at least I think it's excitement, only goes to show how distant Milo and I truly grew apart in our marriage. It somewhat stings. "Did he instigate it? Did you? Was it dark? How did you even find yourself in a closet together?"

"Slow down. One question at a time." I laugh.

Before I can answer any of her questions, the door slides open and two proditors enter. Onyx holds two bottles of liquor in his hands and raises them to the ceiling. "Who's ready to have some fun?"

Lleu whispers harshly to me. "You better tell me later!"

I nod quickly.

Standing next to Onyx is Crux. He rolls his eyes like he never wanted to come in the first place, but somehow, Onyx goaded him into it.

I remember my last interaction with Crux, and a small pin drags down my heart. He didn't seem to like me very much. Somehow, in such a small amount of time, he made me feel so weak. So useless.

This is my first time seeing him in his normal proditor garb. His mask features the design of carbon fiber and he wears three knives on his belt as well as a holstered gun.

"I see you brought company," Lleu says between gritted teeth.

Onyx throws his arm over Crux's shoulder. "Why, of course. Crux is my best friend. We do everything together, and I mean *everything*."

Lleu turns around to me and pretends to gag. I tighten my lips to suppress a laugh.

Onyx and Crux remove the bulk of their disguise and armor until they are down to their gray tanks and lounge pants they wear underneath.

Before Onyx tosses his garb on the bed, he grabs a headband from his belt and pushes back his white-blonde hair.

Somehow, Crux looks more menacing with his mask off. His brown curls only add to the permanently scorned expression his features carry; the shadows cast on his face make him look like he has dark circles. He folds his arms as he follows Onyx into the lounge area.

Onyx sets the bottles on the counter between the pies and then opens a drawer in the area that's filled with shot glasses. I didn't even know those were there.

Lleu dishes out two slices of chocolate pie for her and me and turns on the television to the most recent episode of *Dames of Ashtanabo*.

Onyx fills four shot glasses with a purple liquor. "Come on, Lleu, I'm going to need at least three shots before you force me to watch that."

"You're a guest," Lleu shoots. "Deal with it."

All of us sit on the ground cross-legged around the coffee table and Onyx immediately slides each of us a small glass. "Come on, just one shot to get the night started."

Crux doesn't need any convincing and tosses the liquor in a single swallow.

I look down at the drink, remembering my time at the Jupiter. "I don't know. Remember last time I had a shot?"

"Yes, Margot has a point. We should stick to the pies if we know what's good for us." Lleu takes an extra large bite of her dessert.

Onyx laughs. "Of course I do. You were a beast. So loosen up and who knows what kind of night we will have."

"One where I'm heaving over a toilet, I'm sure." A memory flashes over my mind of Milo holding my hair back and scolding me over accepting drinks from Onyx. But I also remember the dancing, the laughter, and, most importantly, the freedom. If I pace myself, it should be fine.

"Just one," I say sternly and take the shot. It burns horribly, and my head immediately goes fuzzy. I feel Crux's dark gaze on me. He almost seems pissed off at everything I do, which makes me want to do another shot. He's the kind of person you want to tick off more just to wipe that annoying, vindictive look off his face.

Onyx claps and pumps his fists up in the air, then slaps me on the back. "That's the spirit!"

"What the hell." Lleu takes her shot.

Soon, I've had another and then another, and before I know it, Onyx is begging us all to play a game. None of us have the energy to tell him no.

"It's a truth-telling game," Onyx begins. "We go in a circle and have to answer truth-based questions from the other players. If you don't want to answer, or your answer isn't to my liking, you have to drink."

I guess it could be fun, but I could also see it getting messy with someone like Crux playing.

We go in a circle, starting off with easy questions. I find myself lying about my favorite color and my pet peeves, though none of them call me out on it. Not being able to remember such simple facts about myself brings a pang to my chest.

Onyx rattles on about his family history from a question Lleu asked him. "My father temporarily owned a brothel when I was a boy. I never got to see it, of course, but apparently it was the best few months of his life."

"Yes, and the worst few months of your mother's," Crux adds.

Onyx leans on the table toward me. "Well, if you can guess, my parents aren't together anymore."

His father, a proditor, had time to own a brothel?

Onyx points to Lleu. "Your turn. Tell us your most humiliating moment."

She shakes her head. "Gods, no."

"You have to, or else you have to drink."

Lleu leans back on her hands before caving into Onyx's demand. "My father owns a theater in Msanii. I got to perform in a few plays growing up. Anyway, during one of the plays where I was supposed to be lifted into the air like a bird, the hook caught a few layers too deep, exposing my entire backside to the crowd." Lleu covers her face.

Onyx and I both laugh, grabbing our stomachs.

Lleu whips decorative pillows at each of us. "Don't laugh."

"I'm sorry, you're right." I calm my laughing.

"It's just too funny." Onyx pokes her in the side and she slaps his arm.

I look to Crux. "I think it's your turn. Tell us something from when you were a boy."

To my surprise, Onyx frowns.

Crux stares daggers across the table at Onyx, enough that I immediately regret asking.

"You don't have to . . . " I trail off and go silent.

Crux pours himself another shot. "I was once beaten every day for a year in the Vicar temple for scoring low marks on physical exams. I was only five." He drinks again, this time his eyes glaze over slightly. "Happy?"

All of us go completely silent for a solid minute. I look to Onyx, hoping he'll find a way to fix this. *Gods, why did they have to come tonight?*

"I think we could all use another drink," Onyx uncorks another bottle.

The more time I'm with Onyx and Crux, the less I suspect them. Onyx is too naïve and Crux too focused on whatever goes on inside his head.

But then I remember, there are five proditors on the Imnicus, and so far I've only met four of them—Alarik, Knox, Crux and Onyx. Who is number five, and why haven't I encountered him yet?

Regardless of who deleted the footage, even if it isn't a proditor, I should have a backup plan if the Imnicus is ever attacked again. If not a combat plan then an escape one if I ever need to get off the ship quickly. There's no way I'll ever be able to overpower a proditor in a fight to the death, even with Knox's powers.

After two more shots, I am completely loopy and giggly. Crux sits alone on a chair with his arms folded. I can feel his eyes on me. Even with the alcohol, it's hard to ignore.

Things go by in a blur. Lleu puts on some music, and Onyx pulls me to my feet to dance with him. Lleu laughs hysterically as Onyx does his best impression of Milo spinning me at the ball, complete with an over-pronounced frown.

For a while, Lleu wins the argument about the television and we watch two episodes of *Dames of Ashtanabo*. Onyx tries his best to pretend like he doesn't care about it, but soon, he's asking questions every two minutes.

At some point, Lleu, Onyx, and I are sitting on the ground against the couch. I can barely keep my eyes open now.

Onyx has gotten to the point of drunkenness that is making him completely emotional. He hugs me tightly. "I'm so sorry you lost your memories. It's not fair."

Crux throws some blank, wadded up paper at him that Onyx immediately swats away.

"It's horrible, isn't it?" I unexpectedly get choked up and hug him back.

"You three need to sober up," Crux says, "before we start saying things we regret." It seems like he's directing that last part at Onyx.

I get dizzy again and rest my head on Onyx's shoulder. Lleu passes out on the floor, her head near Crux's feet.

"Onyx, we should get back." Crux stands and shakes his shoulder.

"No, go away." Onyx whines.

"Dammit Onyx, you're impossible sometimes." Crux heads to the bed and gets dressed in his proditor armor, preparing to leave. As he stops at the door, he looks over his shoulder and plants one last glare into my soul before disappearing outside.

"Screw him," I say softly, somewhat surprising myself.

"Yeah, you're right." Onyx raises his middle finger toward the now-closed door. "Screw him."

My vision goes blurry and my head falls more before I'm fast asleep.

Chapter 18

"Y ou've got to be kidding me."

My eyes flutter open to a pounding headache and boots in front of my face. My head is on a thigh, and I roll on my back to see Onyx's head tipped back onto the couch, dead asleep.

I shoot up in a panic off Onyx's lap and it all comes back to me. The room is littered with half-eaten pies and empty bottles of liquor. Lleu is still passed out on the floor, feet away.

I slowly turn my head back to the boots and look up. Milo stares down at me with absolute fury in his eyes.

"Shit," I whisper harshly and stand, nearly chest to chest with him.

"Did you have fun while I was away?" Milo's royal attire makes me feel completely out of place in my lounge pants and tank.

Yes, but I can't say that. "You're back early."

"Is that a problem?" I feel his eyes dip to my lips for a second too long, almost making me forget that I'm supposed to be arguing with him.

I pick at my cuticles behind my back. "Not at all."

Of course Milo had to come back early. Anytime I have a second of fun, he's on my heels in an instant. Maybe he sensed it all the way from Ashtanabo. Or maybe Crux contacted him after he left.

I shake Onyx's shoulder with my heel and he groans slightly but stays asleep. When I look over at Lleu, I grow nervous. She could be punished yet again for one of my ideas. But this time, I will make sure that doesn't happen, at least not to Lleu. Onyx can fend for himself for all I care.

Milo steps toward me and gets so close my heart pulsates. *Is he going to kiss me?*

But he simply places his hands gently on my shoulders to move me to the side until he's peering down at Onyx.

After I release a stuck breath, I move to Lleu and gently shake her shoulder. Her eyes flutter open then widen in a panic at seeing Milo. I mouth the words, *Don't worry.*

She nods hesitantly.

"Onyx." Milo bends down and slaps his ring-clad hand against Onyx's face.

Onyx opens his eyes and goes a little pale at the sight of Milo. "Colum, uh, you're back. You see. . ." He forces a chuckle. "It's not what . . . "

Milo punches Onyx in the side the way teenagers would and Onyx hisses, still trying to force a smile.

Onyx slowly falls to his side. "I didn't mean to fall asleep."

Milo grabs his hair and forces him to his feet. "Get the hell out of my room."

Onyx pries himself out of Milo's grip and rushes to the bed, putting on his proditor armor as fast as possible. "I'll see you all later." Then he rushes out, his mask somewhat crooked on his face.

I help Lleu up. She looks nervous, rightfully so, but I know Milo won't rough her up the way he does the proditors. Most of them are basically brothers from what I've witnessed.

"Milo, this was my idea, Onyx excluded," I say. "I won't let you reprimand Lleu for this."

Milo presses his lips together. "I'm not angry at her."

I'm taken aback, enough that I go still for a minute. "What?"

"There were no servants around to humiliate yourself in front of, and I can tell by one look that Onyx intercepted your plans. I'm just simply annoyed."

All things considered, he's actually being . . . nice? "You're serious?"

"Lleu, can you leave us?" Milo asks.

"Yes, Colum." Lleu grabs her lady's maid uniform from the bathroom and rushes out into the hall.

After Lleu leaves, my worry for her completely dissipates, leaving me feeling out of place alone with Milo.

I hug my arms from the draft in the room. "You've been away a for a while now."

"Yeah? Well, I just needed to finish up some business and clear my head."

Right. He thinks the kiss was a mistake. "About the closet—"

"Knox told me you excelled in training," Milo interrupts quickly.

So, he's just going to completely ignore any discussion about it? Pretend it never happened? Fine, two can play at that game. I drop my arms by my sides. "Training that you were supposed to oversee."

"Like I said, I'm too busy to be training you. I figured Knox would be a suitable alternative."

"The deal was that you would train me personally. Not a proditor. Don't tell me you're backing out of your promise now?" I fold my arms.

"What do you want, Margot?" Milo throws his hands up. "Though I trained with the proditors when I was a teenager, I am not nearly as good as they are. Trust me, you're better off with Knox."

"Then train me how to fly a ship." Learning how to fly is next on my list, and he's right that Knox is a more-than adequate fighting teacher. But it doesn't change the fact that I need to have a way off the Imnicus if something ever happens again. I also refuse to let him off the hook. He promised he'd train me and I'm holding him to it.

Milo's face goes blank. "You can't be serious."

"One lesson, that's what I'll compromise for. To teach me the basics."

"And why flying?" Milo raises an eyebrow.

"We live on a floating space vessel. In my opinion, every man and woman on this ship should know how in case of emergencies."

"I'm sure, if anything were to happen, a pilot or proditor would be able to get you off the Imnicus."

"But that wasn't the case during the attack, was it?"

Milo bites his lip. I've got him in a deadlock and have left him without excuses. Even if he tries to get out of this, I'll only push him harder.

"One lesson, and I mean it," he says firmly.

I smile. "When do we start?"

"These buttons turn the engines on, and these levers raise and lower the ship." Milo points to the distinct features of the control panel of his spacious personal ship.

We've been flying for almost an hour around the stationary Imnicus with no traffic. Apparently, a lot of pilots learn to fly in this area during their post-boot camp training. I'm just happy that I get to spend another day not wearing a large gown. Instead, I don a black training uniform.

The outside of the Imnicus is a sight to behold, and something I didn't get a good enough look at last time we flew. It's a silver-white metal with many high points and a half-egg dome in the middle, which I can only assume is the center wing library.

"Are the controls on your ship the same as other ships?" I fiddle with the edges of one of my buttons.

"Not exactly, but they all fly by the same principles." He then rambles about accelerating and landing, much of which goes in one ear and out the other.

If I were ever in an emergency, I doubt I'd remember everything he's saying. In fact, most of what he has taught me has gone completely over my head. This is far more than I could ever absorb in one lesson, and I'm sure he knows it.

From this side of the Imnicus, I have a clear view of Ashtanabo and its green shades. "Do you fly yourself to the planets often?"

The engine thrums when Milo increases our speed. "Sometimes. But my father had me learn for the same reason I'm teaching you—emergencies. I went on to get some advanced training, as there wasn't much for me to do as a teenager, but then I became the Colum quicker than anyone could have anticipated."

"I thought you trained with the proditors?" *The way he describes his adolescence sounds so . . . lonely.*

"I did, but they also train in magic, so I wasn't there for a good chunk of their lessons."

"Did you see your cousin between lessons, I hope?"

Milo shoots me a look. "You know about Knox?"

I didn't expect something like that to be a secret, but they do fight an awful lot. I thought it was brotherly-love, but maybe they're more distant than I thought. "We spoke about it at the ball. He mentioned that your father raised the both of you."

Milo focuses back onto our flight path, tapping controls on the panel. "His parents died around the time my mother disappeared. My father took him in, raising us both. To be honest, we were rivals as children and teenagers. It really wasn't until I became the Colum that he had even an ounce of respect for me."

"What happened? Why are you rivals?"

"Unlike me, both his parents were part of the Vicar bloodline. Not only that, Knox is stronger than most proditors and his enhanced abilities impressed my father, so he invested a lot of time in Knox's training. I competed a lot with Knox, training in the gym and with Crux multiple times a day, but of course, proditors always win."

"And that meant your father had less time for you?"

He coughs and adjusts in his seat. "Enough about me. Let's see what you've learned."

"Oh." I raise my hands and lean away. "I'm fine just watching."

"What kind of teacher would I be if I didn't test my student?" Milo motions to the secondary controls in front of me. "We'll start slow. Turn us back toward the Imnicus."

I hover my fingers above the hundreds of buttons and levers. I know which lever makes the ship go up and down, but right and left are a different story. Still, he's not going to let up, so I take hold of the lever I remember him using.

"No, not that one." Milo unbuckles himself and stands behind me, his arms around the chair and me, pointing to the controls. His cheek is inches from mine, enough that I feel trapped in his body heat. "You need to use this button first to adjust the gears. Then, you can use the lever to turn."

I do what he says, tapping the button, and then holding onto the lever. Slowly, I manage to turn us around without killing the two of us. The Imnicus becomes visible once again, its silver oval exterior glimmering with the stars. I don't know if I'll ever get used to how big it is.

"Good. That was as smooth as I could have hoped from even a cadet." Milo goes back to his seat and flips a few buttons. One of the screens switches from manual to automatic, then the ship self-steers itself toward the Imnicus.

I laugh. "You don't trust me to get us back safely?"

"Maybe in time."

"So, can I assume this means this isn't our last lesson?" I jest.

Milo frowns. "Maybe Crux or Onyx can train you."

The mood immediately goes sour. It's almost hilarious how quickly we can get there. "Maybe I enjoy having you as my trainer. Have you ever thought of that?" I want to take back the words as quickly as I say them.

Milo's ringed fingers pause over the controls and his jaw tightens. "Don't say that."

"Why not?" I unbuckle myself and stand over him. "All you do is avoid me. I am the bane of your existence, aren't I? Here I am being thrown into gowns and lavish meetings, but do you have any idea how alone I feel?"

"Stop!" Milo rises from his chair, almost chest to chest with me now. "Every day for weeks now, I've suffered. When you walk into a room, my chest contracts. Every time Lleu has new dresses delivered to the Imnicus, I can't help but think about how beautiful you'd be in every single one of them. Every time I see you, all I want to do is kiss you. Don't you understand that?"

My bottom lip trembles. "Then, why don't you?"

"Because . . . " Milo closes his eyes quickly, like he's cursing at himself internally. "The girl you were before you lost your memory and the one you are now are not the same person. Truth is, even before you lost your memories, I hated you. In fact, I despised you."

So, it truly was a whirlwind romance we had before we got married. A mistake. "But now?" There is an unquenchable ache in my chest. I'm shaking deep within my core, not from fear, but something much more primal.

Milo takes one of my hands in his. "I'm coming to grips with the fact that I want you, even though everything in this universe is telling me that I shouldn't."

He grabs my waist, pulling me to him, and his lips crash into mine.

It's not like before when we were stuffed inside the cramped closet. I wrap my arms around the back of his neck, barely able to process that we're kissing again, and not just out of some carnal lust. He wants me. *Really* wants me.

Milo backs me up and lifts me by my hips onto a flat portion of the control panel.

His kisses are almost angry, enough to make my mouth sore, but he can't seem to pull away. I should hate him for hating me. But as far as I can tell, I hated him too. Something about remembering that disdain, compared to where we are now, makes my clothes feel tighter. It makes my hands search for the binds of his royal attire even more frantically.

Milo's hands slide under my shirt and rest on my ribs, just under my breasts. My tongue drags against his as I get his cape off and finish the last clasp on his outerwear. He's down to a dark tank before taking a step back to remove that too.

He's beautiful like this, with his toned chest and arms. With the stars in the surrounding windows, it's like he's glistening.

He doesn't bother removing my shirt. Instead, he pushes me onto my back and lifts it over my breasts, kissing across my cleavage and down past my navel by my hipline. He stares up at me, his dark eyes practically begging, as if to say, *Please. Let me.*

I nod. The inside of my thighs feel slicker. I want this more than I think I've wanted anything. The desire radiating off us is all-consuming, and I can't even think straight as he unzips the front of my pants, hooking his fingers in the waistband.

A robotic voice chimes in over the intercom. "Ship docking, T-minus one minute."

My heart drops. Milo rests his head against my stomach for a quick second with the same defeat, then stands to grab his clothes off the floor.

"You should buckle up while we land." His eyes are on my breasts and my abdomen as he slips his tank top back on.

I sit up and shimmy my shirt down. When we get off this ship, will he forget everything? Or will he drag me back to our bedroom where he'll push me into a wall and take the remnants of his hatred out on my body?

Before Milo takes his seat next to me, he leans over and kisses me on the cheek. I turn my head in time to catch a second kiss on my lips.

My heart is pounding as we land. Both of our breaths border on panting. My breasts ache. I expected some of my arousal to wane, but none of it has come even close to dissipating. Milo uses the reflection of the window to fix his hair and I do the same.

When we land, Milo takes my hand and pulls me to the lowering ramp. He stares at me and that's when I know the only thing on his agenda today is taking me back to his quarters and lying me out on his bed.

His thumb runs over my knuckles. "Let's go."

But as the ramp finishes touching down, Commander Aisil appears, his usual soft features drawn into hard lines. "Colum, we have a situation."

"What now, Aisil?" Milo asks impatiently.

He glances briefly my way, hesitating. "A group of Laven terrorists just bombed a production facility in their own city. Nineteen are dead, several dozen more are wounded, sir. Mostly civilians, but twelve of our soldiers were caught in the blast."

"Put the city into lockdown and issue a curfew immediately." Milo pulls on my arm, and we descend the ramp. He glances toward Aisil as we pass. "I trust you can coordinate planet-side for an appropriate response. Enough to send a message, nothing more."

But Aisil steps in front of us, his eyes growing dark. "Sir. Among the dead is a proditor."

Milo's face hardens and the grip on my hand tightens before finally letting go. "Gather the Imnicus proditors. We leave for Lavenai immediately."

"Right away, Colum." Aisil bows and spins away, already issuing commands to his officers.

Milo turns to me and lowers his voice. "Later, all right?"

I nod. "Please, be careful."

Milo nods and rushes off to another ship.

And just like that, any desire I had is now laced with an even deeper hatred of Lavenai.

Chapter 19

I can still feel his lips on my mouth as the warm water in the shower prickles against my skin. All I can imagine is what we would have done if the ship hadn't docked so early. The new places he would have kissed me. The way he would have ruined me right on that control panel.

But then Lavenai had to tear it from me.

The enemy didn't just bomb soldiers and civilians, but proditors too. If the terrorists did something like that, it means things are firing up even more than before. Milo will be more than tense when he returns. Will he come back the same man he was before he kissed me?

A part of me worries about Milo going to Lavenai with the proditors. What if it's a trap? Though, I don't believe all of them are responsible. It's possible none of them are.

And that's when I remember—Milo told Aisil to gather *all* the proditors. That means they should hopefully be gone for the rest of the day, leaving their quarters completely empty. If one of them is involved with Lavenai, this may be my one and only chance to find out.

I finish rinsing the jasmine conditioner out of my hair and rush out of the shower to dry off and dress.

Tracking down the proditors' quarters is harder than I thought. Initially, I believed they lived in the south wing with the soldiers and servants. After a conversation with a few gossipy servants, who didn't even recognize me as their Columess in my casual attire, I learned the proditors have rooms on the border between the north and east wings.

When a maid's back is turned, I swipe her security card off her hip, just in case my ring doesn't work.

The proditors' dormitory hall is dimly lit, causing my eyes to strain. I don't remember this hallway from my time in the surveillance room, which means there are no cameras.

The walls have subtle embossments that are just barely visible, but they are more than just designs. It seems to be telling some kind of story with swirls that represent people, their attention directed to a sea of crows above them. On another wall, there is one giant swirl surrounded by a leafless forest, but instead of crows, there are all sorts of birds—ravens, owls, doves, and finches.

I see a shadow in the corner of my eye, but when I whip around, nothing is there. My palms are sweaty. I know it will be awhile before the proditors return, but I can't shake the sensation of being watched.

There are five doors total in their quarters. I don't even know where to start, so I pick a random door and use the maid's keycard to get in.

It takes only seconds to guess I'm in Onyx's room. There's a pair of lacy female undergarments hanging over a lampshade and a belt tied around the headboard.

I sort through drawers and notebooks. There is a drawer filled with letters from distraught girls. I'm surprised he saves these. Besides fraternizing with too many maids, he comes up clean.

I exit Onyx's room and the door at the head of the hall catches my attention. It's grander than the other four, with triangular embossments. If I had to guess, it's Knox's room. He is a higher station than the rest and Milo's right-hand man. I hesitate before entering. As Milo's cousin, he shouldn't even be a suspect, but I have to check.

Knox's bedroom is almost as big as the Colum's. The bed alone seems too large for just a single man. Unlike Onyx's, Knox's room is clean and organized. Every shirt ironed and folded. He's even lined up the items on his bedside table parallel to one another. If I'm not careful, he may suspect someone moved his things.

I comb through his drawers, searching for anything I can get my hands on, but come across nothing except clothes and toiletries.

I get on my knees and look under his bed. On the floor, all by itself, sits a singular wooden box. I drag the box toward me, careful to memorize its exact placement.

The top of the box has a heart jaggedly carved into it with a slice down the middle. Something from a scorned lover?

As I crack open the box, I feel something akin to whispers in my ears, making me shake my head. I'm being overly paranoid, I know it. There's a chill in the air as I lift the lid all the way off and stare at the item inside.

It's a necklace. But not just any necklace. It's the symbol of the Laven terrorists. I saw its design in one of the meetings Milo let me sit in on.

Why does Knox have this? My heart pounds. Could it really be him after all? There's no way. His uncle was like a father to him.

I hold the necklace up at eye level and the whispers return as it spins, making me slap at my ear.

Milo and I are closer now. I should keep this and let him know my suspicions. Maybe he knows why Knox has something like this and it's all just a big misunderstanding. But why is a broken heart carved into the box? Nothing feels right.

I slip the necklace into my pocket and put the box back exactly how I found it. After I do one last sweep of the room to make sure everything is back in its place, I slip back outside and secure the door.

As I step out of the hallway of the proditor quarters and into the main walkway, I almost collide with another chest.

I take a step back and lower my head. "I'm so sorry."

When I look back up, Crux is staring at me, his eyes narrowed. "What were you doing in our quarters?"

Oh gods, I don't even know what to say. *Think, Margot. Think.* "I just wanted to see if Milo took Knox with him to Lavenai. If he stayed back, I was going to see if he could give me more training."

Crux still looks as suspicious as ever. "Training, you say?"

I nod. "I see you didn't go to Lavenai with them."

"I found it wise to stay back. This is the Imnicus after all. We need proditors to protect it." Why is Crux so terrifying? And even more so, why does it feel like he hates me as much as Milo once did? If not more?

I press my lips tightly together. "If you don't need anything else, I'll be getting back now."

"By all means." Crux motions past him to the direction of my room.

I rush by, probably faster than I should. Every time I'm around him, my skin crawls. Even his beauty doesn't mask how horrible I feel every time he's near.

And when I check over my shoulder before I turn the corner, I see him still watching me.

As I slip on my nightgown, I still envision Crux's suspicious glare in my mind. The way he let me go so easily was even more unsettling. I expected him to question me more to see if I was really snooping. But he simply stepped aside. Somehow that feels worse.

I feel a shiver along my arms before I banish his face out of my head for good.

Milo's bed is soft under my muscles, and it's much better than sleeping in the cold, hard bathtub. The sheets still smell like him, and when I turn the lights out, I pretend like he is really here.

Just thinking about his fierce kisses makes me want to slip a hand up my nightgown, but I grip the comforter instead. I'll save it for when he gets back, though I don't want to. What will Lleu think when I tell her? Will I tell her? Of course I will. Milo and I are already married. It's not like we have to keep any kind of romantic relationship a secret. So why does it feel so forbidden?

I doze off into some light phase of sleep. There're flashes of Milo's face and body in my dreams and how good it felt to see his hardened face turn into one of desperation.

Hours of waking and dozing off have passed, but I'm still dreaming of him, enough that I can feel his lips against the back of my neck and his hands on my hips.

It isn't until his hands move to my waist that I jolt awake and realize the dream hasn't changed.

I reach back and feel the side of his face. "Milo, you're back already?"

He makes a soft shushing sound into my skin. "We can talk about that later. Right now, I just want to hold you."

I roll over and capture his lips, my hips already lazily grinding against him. I tangle my fingers into his raven hair.

Milo's chest is already bare, and he's down to his boxers. His hands explore my body with need, like he's angry that he has to choose no more than two spots at a time.

He's grabbing my breasts, holding my bottom, rubbing my thighs. "I want you, Margot. I *need* you."

"Then take me." My heart is palpating from his words and from his touch.

"I want the cries you stifle at night, the pains that I've caused you." Milo hikes the hem of my dress up my thighs and lifts it over my head, then kisses my breasts tenderly.

"Milo . . . " My eyes roll back.

"I wanted you in that closet. I shouldn't have called the technicians. The gods know I didn't want to. I should have taken you right then and there. I should have kissed you more. Touched you." He captures my lips again then rests his forehead against mine. I can feel his hungry stare in the darkness as he slides his hand down the band of my underwear.

I moan into his mouth as he moves his fingers in slow circles. It wasn't too long ago that I hated him. That I even fantasized about leaving the Imnicus forever and starting a new life by myself away from him. But somehow, in such a short amount of time, he became my dream.

He places open-mouthed kisses on my neck while his fingers make their way lower and plunge inside me. The sensation of two fingers filling me up is overwhelming. I move my hips to the rhythm of his hand. A part of me is still trying to convince myself I hate him, but it doesn't work.

"I need all of you," I whisper.

Milo sucks in a breath. "You're ready for me?"

I nod. Part of me is nervous for what it may feel like. Because of my amnesia, I may as well still be a virgin. Every kiss feels new and every movement of his hands is unfamiliar. As far as my body is concerned, this is my first time.

Milo tugs his boxers off while I peel off my panties.

He hovers over me, hands on either side of my head, his dark hair hanging down. "Don't forget to breathe."

I open my legs more as his length finds my entrance. I stifle a cry as he presses in slowly, but soon everything relaxes and I'm filled with him. Our mouths collide again as he moves his hips rhythmically.

As I relax more, I want him to go faster. In fact, I crave it. It only takes the frantic roll of my hips for him to get the picture. He rests his forearms next to my head and pounds into me.

My head tips back into the mattress. Everything is building so quickly. I'm losing control of myself with ripples of pleasure vibrating all the way down to my toes. My body starts to tense up.

Milo's breaths are unsteady, his groans uneven and almost whispery. Even in the dim light, I can see the sweat that glistens on his shoulders. The pulse beating on the sides of his neck.

It hits me all at once—the bowing of my body, the gripping of the sheets, the moans. I can feel myself clenching around him.

His head falls slightly as he groans deep, his forehead falling against mine as his thrusts stutter until they go stagnant.

Everything is silent between us, only our breaths audible. Milo Arris bedded me, and the worst part is, I enjoyed every second of it. I lift my head and peck his lips.

Milo rolls off me onto his side and pulls me into his chest, his fingers caressing my scalp. "Sleep now, Margot."

My eyes grow heavier in his warm embrace, and I curl into him. "Trying to get rid of me already?"

His voice is sleepier than mine while he kisses my forehead. "You're not going anywhere."

Chapter 20

With my eyes still closed, I pat the bed around me in search of Milo.

He is nowhere to be found. The sheets are wrinkled where his body once lay. It's too early for him to be up, even compared to his normal diligent routine. The bathroom lights are off, and I don't hear the shower running either.

My breath quickens when I remember the lines we crossed. How there's no going back to who we were before. For the first time since the attack, I feel like his wife. Well, maybe not his wife, but his lover, and that's a good place to start.

Despite this, more happened yesterday besides Milo bedding me. He caught me so off guard when he climbed into bed that I completely forgot about the necklace in Knox's room. Considering Lavenai's attack, this isn't the kind of conversation I can simply put off until I find a good opening. He could be in danger. I need to grab the necklace and find him.

I open the wardrobe to grab the necklace, which I hid in a spare pair of heels. I reach inside the shoes and my heart drops. No,

I know this is where I put it. I check the other heel just in case I miscalculated, but it isn't in there either. This isn't right, but maybe I'm mistaken and threw it in the hamper by accident. '

I grab the day-old pants out of the hamper and stuff my fingers in every pocket. I throw every item of clothing out to ensure it didn't fall deeper into the hamper. Then, I check beneath the bed and wardrobe.

No. No. No! Am I going crazy or something? Or is my amnesia starting to get the best of my short-term memory too? How could I have lost it already?

Take a deep breath. At the end of the day, it doesn't matter that I misplaced it. I know what I saw and I can still tell Milo. He'll believe me now more than ever.

I throw on a day dress and rush out into the hallway in search of Milo. It's too early to rely on his normal routine to find him. I search the north wing for any signs of him and ask a passing humanoid if he's seen him, but the humanoid simply shrugs.

In one of the more unused halls of the north wing, there's an open door. I peek inside to find a drawing room fit with luxurious furniture and a holographic fireplace as the only source of light. Above the fireplace is a portrait.

I step inside and approach the portrait. It must be four times my height from top to bottom.

The man appears to be in his early forties with white, long hair that continues well past his shoulders. His jaw and cheekbones remind me of Milo, but he has those same overly-confident eyes as Knox. The plaque beneath his photo reads, *Colum Balistar Arris.*

The overhead lights suddenly turn on, making me flinch. I spin to face the door and Knox stands there with his arms folded. "Looking for something?"

"Knox, you scared the heavens out of me." I place a hand to my chest before my fingers go cold. I'm not sure if I can trust him until I talk with Milo, and though being with him usually makes me feel like I can finally relax, this time I am filled with unease.

Knox takes a step inside and lowers his hood before strapping his mask to his belt. Then the doors click shut behind him. "You're up early."

"So are you." I try not to let the doors shutting get to me. "I was just looking for Milo and got a little sidetracked." I motion to the portrait.

"Ah, yes. Uncle Balistar." Knox walks deeper into the room and stands at my side to admire the portrait with me. "There's not a day that goes by that I don't think of him. The day he died changed everything for me and not for the better."

I swallow. "You must have loved him very much." The last two words have a shaky edge to them, and I pray that Knox did not notice. "I should probably get back to my room." I don't even wait for a response as I step away from him.

A hand grabs my wrist, followed by something cold and metal being forced into my bound hand. It's the Laven necklace, tucked into my hand. The sight of it makes me completely numb.

"You were in my room, Columess." Knox presses his forearm against my collarbone and quickly presses my back into the wall hard. So hard, it's difficult to take a full breath.

I grunt as I try to push him off, but I don't scream. I don't even say anything at first, because what can I say?

Knox. Humorous and at-ease Knox who would never hurt me. The one who seems to understand me even more than Milo—a Laven?

"How long?" I finally ask as I pry at his arm. "How long have you worked for Lavenai?"

That makes Knox laugh until he loses his trademark smile all at once. "You think I'm in allegiance with Lavenai? Not even close, but nice guess."

He's not working for them? Then why trap me for digging around his room? Why risk me telling Milo how he manhandled me? Unless this is all a test, but by the look in his eyes, I know this is real. I feel it deep in my bones.

In my panic, I land a solid kick to his shin.

Knox hisses and stumbles back. I take the opening and charge for the doors, nearly tripping over the hem of my dress. When I get to the door, I press the button to open it.

Access denied.

"No!" I try to override the control panel with my ring. Knox is recovering and fast walking toward me, laughing deep within his chest.

Access denied.

"Dammit! Milo!" I pound on the door ferociously with the side of my fist, shouting for anyone who may hear. "Lleu!"

Knox pulls off his gloves. I feel nauseated and weak. No, he wouldn't use his magic on me like he does on criminals. Would he?

Black smoke twirls between his fingers and a thin layer of water pools at my ankles.

"I thought you couldn't do anything unless you touched my skin." I say the words in the same tone as a beg.

"Most proditors can't. But as you may have already gathered, I was Balistar's favorite, and all for good reason."

Sure, he may be causing me to hallucinate, but he's not fully in my head yet. I can still get out of this.

That is, until he gains on me, swiping his fingers over the back of my neck. My legs weaken. "Stop, Knox, please!" I fall to the ground on my side.

I pull myself forward with my arms, trying to get as far away as possible. But I know it's no use, and even he knows it as he follows behind at an insulting pace.

"Margot, has your rendezvous with Milo taught you the difference between pleasure and pain?"

He knows Milo and I slept together? I suppose if he snuck into my room after Milo left to retrieve the necklace, he saw my naked body beneath the sheet sheets. Still, it's sick.

"I've always found them the same. The screams, the pained gasp a woman makes when she's overwhelmed with agony."

And then I realize . . . the burns on Lleu and Sloane, the dead servant . . .

"You . . . you're the killer!" I yell.

All he does is smile.

He's close enough now that I twist my body and lunge for his ankles.

Knox springs back before I can grab him and laughs. "Nice try, Little Fennec." He rushes at me and tries to grab my wrists.

I slap at him, avoiding touching his skin at all costs, that is until he takes a fistful of my hair and arches my neck back. I cry out from the pain.

He places his thumb on my neck, tracing my windpipe ever so delicately, making me shudder. *No, gods, no.*

All it takes is a single blink for the room to change completely. Smoke fills every corner from wall to ceiling.

My bottom lip trembles. "What are you going to do? Kill me? Torture me?"

Knox pins my wrists to the ground and brings his face close enough that I can feel his breath on my mouth. "All I want is to have a little fun."

In another blink, he's gone.

The paralysis leaves my legs, and I shoot up in a panic. The only thing worse than him trapping me is not knowing where he is in this proditor trance.

I can't see a single thing. What will happen if I take a wrong step? Will I fall down a never-ending hole? Will I encounter a monster straight from a nightmare?

There's a ticking feeling right behind my ear. The hair on the back of my neck stands on end, and for just a second, I can't move.

"Now run, Little Fennec."

Crows explode from the ground, enough for me to scream and run regardless of what awaits me in the smoke.

Nothing you see is real. Nothing is real.

No matter how many times I repeat that mantra, I know what I feel. I know that, even though I may be safe from death in this mental prison, Knox still has free rein over my body in the real world. I need to escape and fight him off.

An arrow flies past me, narrowly missing my cheek.

He's hunting me.

Even though I know the arrows cannot truly kill me, I'm not ready to find out what will happen if one pierces my flesh.

I see a sparkling light far off in the smoke. There is chattering and laughter, like there is some kind of crowd overhead. I rush toward it until I finally emerge from the smoke, completely winded.

I'm in the ballroom now, but one filled with people, decorated just like that day at the ball. Men and women chat away, drinking champagne and dancing. The guests wear formal attire and masquerade masks over their eyes. Every color is more vivid than the real world, but I don't let myself get distracted. I need to find a way out, if that's even possible.

When I look up at the balcony, I gasp in horror.

Knox balances in a squat on the railing, a bow and arrow in his hands, aimed and ready. He winks at me before releasing the string.

I lunge to the side just in time.

Behind me, a woman screams and falls over. The arrow sticks out of her chest.

She's not real, she's not real.

I pull myself over to her. No blood seeps from her chest, but there's terror in her eyes. An unadulterated fear.

None of the other guests are bothered in the slightest, and a new song begins. Everyone changes partners and dances.

Knox slips off the railing and heads to the curved stairs with the bow in his hand and his eyes pinned on me. A man in the crowd reaches forward and grabs my hand, pulling me into a dance.

"No, let go!" I shout at him, but my words go in one ear and out the other.

When Knox is nearing the end of the stairs, a large crow flies overhead and lands on his shoulder.

I shimmy out of the man's grasp and head toward the large double doors of the ballroom. They automatically open for me. I run out of the crowded ballroom and rest against the wall for a second to take a breather. But I know there isn't any time to rest; Knox could be on me any second now. I have to keep going.

But when I look at the hall, I almost faint.

There is no end. The hallway is infinite.

I spin to go back into the ballroom, but the door no longer exists.

"Shit." I lean my head against the wall. It can't be over like this. Rain drips from the hallway ceiling, droplets falling down my face and soaking my dress. "Knox, let me out of here!"

I turn to look back at the endless hallway, and my jaw trembles as a set of eyes gazes down at me.

"Let you go? Now, why would I do that?" Knox smiles.

I jab at his face, but he catches my punch and pins me between the wall and his body.

"If you're going to kill me, just do it already!" I'm crying now. I'd rather die than suffer in a proditor entrancement. Though, if the murdered girl is any evidence, Knox's version of killing is sicker and slow. One that is painful enough to satisfy his sadistic desires.

My muscles lose all tone and I fall. Knox catches me and then lowers my body to the ground with him. He sets me between his legs, wrapping his arms around my abdomen and letting my head rest back on his shoulder.

"Milo would never let me live if I killed you." Knox scoffs. "That idiot, going and falling in love with a spy."

I try to speak, but no words come out. How could he keep me alive and expect me not to tell Milo?

He tucks my hair behind my ears so he can get a better look at me. "You were so close, Lady Arris. So close to finding out the true secret. You had some things right, though. I killed that girl and burned Sloane and Lleu, among others. It was all for you, though."

For me?

"Since the moment I first saw you, all I've wanted was to spill your blood. To feel it dripping between my fingers as the light fades from your eyes. One day I will. Until then, I have to find other . . . more unique ways to control the urge."

He's a psychopath. One in love with death and pain themselves.

He continues on, "The necklace isn't mine, as you presumed. It was a souvenir. One I stole off the body of a Laven rebel."

Rebel. It rings differently than Milo's word—terrorists.

"But enough of my rambling," Knox says. "It's time for you to start over."

He cradles my head, resting his thumbs against my temples. "When you awaken in your soft bed, you'll forget you ever suspected a thing. You'll forget about the murder, and anything you've investigated will burn away."

I fight it, battling the pecking of crows. Their beaks chip away at every neuron, swallow every memory or suspicion until their hunger is met.

Then there's only blackness.

Chapter 21

With my eyes still closed, I pat the bed around me in search of Milo.

Once I find his chest, flashes of the scene from last night make my breath quicken. Half asleep, he wraps me tightly in his arms. His warmth wards off the cool draft from the vents. There's a soft, purple glow that leaks inside the room from a passing ship. His lips press against my forehead and the tips of his fingers brush down my spine.

There is a nagging feeling on the back of my head. There was something I was supposed to tell him before, but I cannot for the life of me remember what it was. If it was that important, though, I'm sure I'll remember later.

"Did you sleep well?" he whispers.

I nod. I slept so well that I hardly want to get out of bed. Not only that, but my body is completely sore and my energy wiped. My back aches and my head is pounding. Even my collarbones throb.

"Don't you have your duties?" I ask. It must be late morning right about now. Normally, he's already in the south wing this time of day.

"Aisil is taking care of it." He kisses me gently and circles my hips with his thumbs.

My breath hitches when his lips trail down my neck and then my torso. I feel the inclination to close my legs once his mouth is at the skin right above my still-oversensitive bud. "You're going to kiss me there?"

Milo nods. "You'll like it. Trust me." He kisses it once then flicks his tongue slowly.

My head falls back. *Mother of the Stars.*

He holds onto my thighs as he works and my body is already shuddering. All this time, I saw him as nothing but a grueling leader who hardly tolerated being married to me. Now, I'm starting to see the little reasons that must have made me fall for him. For once, his features look somewhat happy and relaxed, and his hair falls in a way that makes him look airy and youthful.

Soon, I'm crying out his name while his fingers dig into my hips and his groans reverberate throughout my pelvis.

Everything feels so right. The Colum, the Imnicus, Lleu, and even the proditors.

This is my home.

The jade tub that I once called my bed is now filled to the brim with water and bubbles. My head rests against Milo's chest. The silence that once filled the air around us with disdain now holds nothing but peace. Peace that could last forever if we allowed it.

He lathers jasmine soap on my back, his movements as delicate as a painter's. The warm water aids in relaxing my aching muscles. Even with everything we did together, I wouldn't have expected it to leave me this sore. Maybe I'm getting sick.

It must be late afternoon now and Milo still hasn't shown any signs of going back to work. We've spent the entire morning kissing and making love on the bed, on the floor, and in the lounge area. The servants have dropped all our meals off in front of the bedroom door at Milo's request.

I rest my chin on my knee. "Are you sure you don't need to monitor things in the south wing?"

Milo holds me tighter. "Aisil is taking care of everything, and anything he can't do, the arbitors can. At least for one day."

There was a time where Milo wouldn't spare me a single hour, and now he's giving me much more than that. After the bombing on Lavenai, I would have expected him to be completely swamped, but maybe it's more under control than I realize.

"Does Aisil know *why* you're taking the day off?" I ask.

I feel him smile into the back of my head. "You mean does he know that married people are doing married people things? Perhaps. More likely, he probably thinks I caught some kind of sickness on Lavenai."

I make designs in the bubbles with my fingers as I rest against him. There is so much I want to learn about Milo. What he likes and dislikes. The things he thinks about on the rare occasion he gets a break. "If you weren't the Colum, what would you do?"

"I'm not sure." Milo shrugs.

"It could be anything in the world. Just think of something."

He moves my hair off my shoulder. "My mother used to make pottery. She was good at it, too. All our vases and plates were hers. She even made them for our neighbors. I suppose I've always taken an interest in it since then. Once every few years, I find time to fly to Ashtanabo in disguise and take a class or two. Any time I do, I remember my mother more vividly."

It's the first time he's spoken of his mother. In the past, he's shut down or changed the subject. Even now, I find myself holding my breath, nervous that he'll find something else to talk about.

"May I ask what happened to her?" I turn in time to see Milo's throat bob.

He doesn't speak for a second and holds me tighter. "It happened shortly after the proditors broke off from the Vicars. Some say she ran away to avoid the conflict. Others say the Vicars took her. I searched high and low through Ashtanabo once I became the Colum, but every trail came up cold."

"I'm so sorry," I say, but I keep my words short. As much as I want to ask him more about her, it would only upset him. "You didn't have time to do pottery while you were a teenager?"

"My father didn't like the reminder. Not only that, I've been on the throne a decade now. It doesn't leave much time for fun."

I do some mental math. "You were only seventeen when you became the Colum?"

Milo nods.

"You were so young." What a burden for someone to carry. To rule two worlds when his life hadn't even started yet. And as an only child, he had no choice but to take it.

"Monicas held my hand for the first year or two until he thought I was mature enough to handle it on my own. I mostly faked my competence until it felt like second nature, much like my father did. Of course, the majority of my work is calming the relations between Lavenai and Ashtanabo. Sometimes I wish everything could be as it once was, but Lavenai will never have that."

"Was anyone taken into custody yesterday?"

"It took a while for the guards to get everyone under control and all the bodies accounted for. The entire capital had to be put on lockdown. Events like that tend to have chain reactions." Milo kisses my cheek. "And even though we didn't apprehend anyone yet, it wasn't all for nothing. We came across a map detailing the entrances to the terrorist organization's underground bases."

I jolt up. "Wait, you know where my attackers are hiding out now? Then what are you doing here? Why aren't you arresting them right this minute?"

"It's not that easy. We don't know what they are capable of. They could be crazy enough to blow up their entire base, sinking parts of the capital into the ground. I don't want to risk any of my subjects' lives, even the ones on Lavenai."

"Then, we should plan. If there are things I can do, politicians I can meet with, proditors I can direct, or anything to help speed up the process, I will do it. Let me help you in any way I can as the Columess. "

Milo doesn't speak for a minute, searching my face, then darting his eyes between me and the corners of the bathroom. "How about as a spy?"

I raise my eyebrows. "What do you mean?"

"Knox has had nothing but good things to say about your training progress. Maybe with a little more, you'll be ready. Between your days as a spy and the combat abilities he's gifted you, I think it could work."

"You would let me do something like that?" I'm so used to the old Milo. The one who used to not even let me leave my bedroom unattended. The one who barely let me go to Ashtanabo, let alone Lavenai.

"You've done nothing but impress me."

I wrap my arms around him, water spilling out from the sides of the tub as I squeeze him with all my might. "Thank you."

We talk for sometime more, his fingers brushing my upper thighs beneath the water until they eventually move between my legs, into purposeful strokes. When I can't take it anymore, I face him, and once we're joined together, my hips move in sync with his, our moans echoing throughout the bathroom.

I know that, in the end, I'm not only going to Lavenai for Milo, but also for myself.

Chapter 22

"There she is." Onyx claps as I enter the proditor training room in exercise clothes.

Crux is doing pull-ups on a bar, his thick brunette waves leaping with every rep. Alarik places his weights back on the rack. Onyx is lying on the floor as if he was just doing crunches.

It's been too long since I've seen Alarik, though Lleu is always finding ways to bring him up when I give her updates about my relationship with Milo.

It's funny that a beautiful girl like her, who talks almost constantly, is too nervous to exchange more than surface level conversations with him. I thought it may be because Alarik's a proditor, but that doesn't stop her in the slightest from mouthing off to Onyx.

Crux, on the other hand, is somebody I could go without seeing ever again. Honestly, if I would have known he was going to be here today, I may have settled for Knox's mind-bending training sessions instead. But Milo thought it may be helpful to train with more proditors than just Knox.

If I can hold my own, even a little, against one of them, I'll be more than ready to face normal humans. That's how I'll know I'm ready to complete Milo's mission.

"Crux, get over here!" Onyx waves him over but Crux ignores him. Onyx scratches the back of his neck. "Just give me a minute." He rushes over to his friend and leans on a nearby piece of equipment, their conversation inaudible.

I stride over to the workout bench Alarik's sitting on. "Long time no see. How have you been?" I ask.

Alarik wipes his face with a rag. "Well enough."

I take in the bags under his eyes. "Is everything all right?"

"No, I'm doing fine, I promise." He forces a half smile.

I frown at the obvious lie.

Compared to the other proditors, Alarik has always felt a bit out of place. Too soft for the roles the proditors usually fill. It's a great honor, sure, but Alarik hasn't struck me as the type to seek out highly coveted positions either. But maybe that's because he's already in one.

"Milo seems to be softening a bit. Maybe he'll give you some time off," I say.

Alarik shoots me a look. "Define softening."

"I don't know . . . things are better between him and I."

I expect him to be happy or even surprised, but his face doesn't move. "You two made up?"

"It's strange, but honestly, it feels like I can breathe again. Like I'm finally becoming part of the Imnicus the way I once was."

His lips form into a straight line. "That's good to hear, Margot."

Does Alarik not like me either? Does he find me as repulsive as Crux does, enough that he doesn't want my relationship with Milo to be anything more than professional? Did I really use to be that horrible?

Onyx shouts over to us. "Crux is ready! *Finally.*"

"That's our cue," Alarik says, brushing past me. "Good luck today."

Good luck? I want to ask what he means, but once I see Crux, I know I don't have to. Crux is already staring at me like he's going to put me through hell.

And when I realize Crux is the one leading the session for all of us, I want to run.

"Let's start with some stretches," Crux says.

I'm able to go deeper into the stretches than the three of them, making me feel a little more confident. I laugh at Onyx, who struggles to even touch his toes while I'm able to bend over and hug my legs, to which Onyx makes an innuendo and Alarik punches him in the arm.

"Pushups next." Crux eyes me in the mirror with an almost challenging look.

You're on, I think to myself, wishing his powers meant he could read minds, just this once.

But I'm overzealous, not pacing myself like I should. Crux finishes his pushups first and stands, watching the three of us finish our reps. Once I'm at the fifteenth pushup, Onyx and Alarik are already done.

Dammit. My arms shake horribly under my own weight.

Crux walks behind me and places his hands on my hips, adjusting them back into proper alignment. "Time is ticking, Margot."

"I'm almost done," I grit the words through my teeth.

On number eighteen, Crux puts his foot on my back to add more weight. "Last two."

My arms are like jelly, shaking like crazy. I finish the eighteenth one, but halfway through the nineteenth, my arms give out, making me fall flat on my chest.

I want to curse at myself for failing. For letting Crux win. But there is nothing I can do but lie there with my cheek pressed to the mat.

"You did good, Margot!" Onyx yells, but his smile is uneasy.

Crux kneels down next to me and lowers his voice so only I can hear. "Just as weak as I expected."

Asshole.

Alarik comes over and helps me to my feet. I shake my arms out, trying to bring life back into them. Throwing punches is going to be even harder now, even though, by Crux's definition, this was supposed to be a light warmup.

"Time for sparring," Crux says. "Alarik and Onyx, you're up."

Alarik and Onyx get into position on the mat. Crux sits far away from me, thankfully. I don't even want to look at him right now.

"Want to make bets this time?" Onyx asks.

Alarik scoffs. "You're only saying that because you won the last three fights."

"Maybe you'll get lucky."

"How about this: If I win, you stop bringing girls back to your room for the next week. I can hardly sleep, for goodness' sake."

"Jealous of my success, Alarik?" Onyx puts his fists up. "Anyway, it's not much of a bet. I can hook up anywhere."

When Alarik and Onyx start fighting, my body slowly stiffens. They beat down on each other like ruthless animals, and soon I'll be next. Proditor fighting is meticulous, calculating, yet gruesome. Onyx's punches are quick, but Alarik's fighting is organized yet unpredictable.

Finally, after five whole minutes, Alarik wins and Onyx has a busted lip.

"Damn you," Onyx wipes the blood off on his shoulder.

"Better luck next time," Alarik jeers.

"I'll go next," Crux says to Alarik, peeling off his tank and throwing it to the side.

While Alarik looked as confident as ever fighting Onyx, a thin layer of anxiety seeps over his face at the prospect of fighting Crux. "I'm ready when you are."

The two men fight, giving me insight to Crux's fighting style, which incorporates strong punches and well-timed kicks. He's ruthless, even in sparring.

For a second, it seems like Alarik has the upper hand, but then Crux spins, slamming his elbow hard into Alarik's shoulder.

Alarik falls over, gritting his teeth. "Dammit, Crux, the point is to spar, not to disable each other."

"If you treat every match like the real thing, you'll never lose." Crux looks to me. "I won, which means you're next."

I stay put on the floor with panicked eyes. There's no way I can fight Crux. "I think it's best if I sit back and study your techniques."

Crux ignores me, grabbing my wrist and yanking me to my feet. "Don't be afraid. I know how fragile you are, so don't worry. I won't shatter you, at least not this time."

I gulp. Not even Alarik could beat him. But with Knox's shadow, maybe I have a chance. But then that begs the real question—can Knox beat Crux? If he can, maybe I'll make it through this. Or maybe, and more realistically, Onyx will be carrying me back to my room and stacking ice packs on my muscles.

I stand across from Crux. He paces while keeping his eyes on me, as if thinking up a strategy. The fact that he thinks he needs a strategy against me is confusing, to say the least. With his confidence, I would have thought he could beat me while simultaneously reading a book.

"You've got this, Margot!" Onyx cheers for me on the sidelines.

I force a smile. *Gods, this is going to hurt, isn't it?*

I know Crux won't let me out of this, so I have no choice but to consider this a real fight.

At that thought, my adrenaline rises, and then I can feel it. Knox's shadow. His energy builds inside me, making my muscles feel like they are not my own.

The reason I cannot win against Knox is because he knows what moves he himself would do, therefore he is able to accurately predict what I will throw at him. Crux doesn't. Maybe, just maybe, I have the upper hand.

I lift my fists like Knox would, waiting for Crux to make the first move.

Crux charges at me, swinging a fist in my direction. I duck just in time and then use his weight against him, pushing him behind me and making him stumble, almost tripping him into the deadlift equipment.

When he turns around, he looks absolutely furious.

"Don't get too confident," Alarik warns. "Keep him in your eyeline."

I take the advice, noticing how Crux uses pacing to his advantage to make it harder to track when he is going to strike. When he swings again, I narrowly block it.

Fighting him is more than my heaving lungs can take. Still, I can't seem to land any punches. Instead, I continue to use his moves to my advantage. When he swings extra hard, I step back quickly, more than needed, making him lose his balance.

I take the opening and kick him, my barefoot landing right in his side. He snarls and falls onto the mat.

"Attagirl, Margot!" Onyx jumps before locking eyes with Crux and simmers down.

Crux pushes himself up off the mat and shakes out his wrists as if he's warding off my touch. "I guess I've been bested." Crux extends his hands for me to shake it—a truce.

Something about it feels good. Powerful even. Crux has been nothing but horrible to me since the ball. I wonder how we handled each other before I lost my memories. What did I do to him to make him hate me so much?

I shake his hand back, but as I do, he pulls me into him, his head near my ear. "Those crows protecting you aren't really yours. Without them, you'd be nothing but a weak little girl with nothing but a Columess title getting you by in life." His grip is harsh.

My arm shakes from the pain. "I don't have crows. I'm just borrowing Knox's shadow."

Crux breathes a small laugh from his nostrils. "That's what you think."

I don't have Vicar or proditor blood. According to the texts, it isn't even possible for me to have them. He leaves me standing on the mat alone with a sore wrist and more questions than ever.

Chapter 23

Early one morning, I lie naked on Milo's chest, soaking in his warmth before another day of hellish training starts. As I learned the hard way, having a portion of Knox's fighting abilities doesn't mean I win every match. Sometimes Onyx gets me in the stomach. Crux has won more often than not. Alarik refuses to hit a woman, even in training, so he works on a different kind of combat with me.

"I'm so sore." I groan and flick Milo's shoulder jokingly, "And you're not helping any."

Milo strokes my back. "You're only experiencing a tenth of what proditors have to go through in their training. Count yourself lucky."

"I don't even want to go today."

"You don't have to. Knox is back from Ashtanabo and you will be training with him one-on-one. Besides, I need my proditors back. We are on the horizon of a war, after all."

Knox is back? I haven't seen him since before the Lavenai bombing, which was well over a week ago.

"Do you want to sit in and watch?" A part of me is asking only because I don't want this moment to end in a few short minutes when Milo starts his vigorous daily routine and I train most of the day.

"I need to finalize the details with the arbitors before you leave for Lavenai."

I laugh. "You make it sound like some sort of vacation."

"Maybe after this, we can enjoy one. I want to take you to the springs in the northern cities of Ashtanabo. It's beautiful there."

"Have you ever been on leave since you took the throne?"

"Well . . . not exactly. Any time I do, I get bombarded with communications. That's why this mission is so important—if we can subdue your attackers, and these terrorists are finally out of my hair, maybe I can finally relax for once."

"That's what I'll think about during training and the mission then." Knowing that successfully completing this mission means giving Milo a much-needed break makes me actually excited to train with Knox today.

An hour later, I sit in the proditor training room, alone. Knox still hasn't arrived, which is strange. It's not like him to be so late.

While I wait, I stretch my arms and legs and practice a few backbends Alarik recommended. As I stand to do arm circles, the doors slide open.

Knox enters in his proditor armor, and when his eyes lock onto me, they look different. I can't even put a finger on it.

"How was Ashtanabo?" I ask.

Knox strips off his mask. "Invigorating."

Once I see the emotion on his face, I frown. Anguish with a dash of annoyance? Coldness mixed with grief? No, neither of those seems right.

"Are you okay?" I ask. "You seem . . . off."

"Just a little familial bickering is all." Knox pulls a pair of training clothes out of one of the gray lockers.

"You were just with Milo?" I ask because I find it strange. Milo saw me off to train with Knox, and then he sought him out for a discussion?

Knox nods. "It was brief. He pulled me to the side, reprimanded me for something he understands nothing about. Sometimes he can be oh so very—"

"Himself," I answer quickly. Though it's been a while since I saw that side of Milo. The one who chastised every subordinate, never smiled, and focused on nothing but work.

"Exactly." He chuckles. "You're very perceptive, you know."

I smile back at him. "Perks of having you as my trainer. You can't hide things from me anymore. Besides, you're not just Milo's cousin. By law, you're my cousin too. And it's my duty to know all about my family's quirks."

My words lighten his face up slightly. "You're right about that." He holds his training clothes up in one hand. "I'm going to change before we begin."

As Knox disappears into the locker room, I think of what Milo could have scolded Knox about. Whatever it was, it was enough to make him late to training. I've heard that he and Crux like to spend their leave in unsavory clubs on Ashtanabo. Then again, Knox has a history of being rebellious. It could have been about any number of things.

When Knox emerges from the back, he wears lounge pants and a tank, his feet bare and ready for the mat. "I understand you've been training with the other proditors."

I tie my hair back. "Yes. I did all right at first, but the more I fight them, the worse I seem to get. Guess I just had some beginner's luck."

"Well now, there's your problem," Knox says. "Proditors are trained to memorize fighting styles and use them against opponents. That's what's happening. No matter how much of my ability you have, you're still sixty percent yourself and inadvertently creating your own style. So, today, we'll focus on moves that aren't innate to either of us. Next time, you'll catch them completely off guard. I assure you."

"I sure hope so." I laugh. "I don't know if I can handle being thrown across the room again."

Knox studies my body, his gaze raking across my upper arms. "On the bright side, it seems like you've gotten stronger too."

Months ago, I was almost skin and bone from the coma and recovery process, but now my muscles are toned in a way that even surprises me. Though, I'm galaxies away from being as sculpted as any of the proditors.

"Should we start?" I ask.

To my surprise, Knox's eyes are still lingering on my body, enough that I instinctively cross my arms over my sports bra, which finally takes him out of the trance.

Knox rubs the back of his neck. "Today, we'll work on defensive moves. Ways to use your opponent's strength against them. Turn around."

"All right." I turn my back to him to start the training. He's quiet for a second behind me, and only the sound of his breathing keeps me aware of his presence. I don't know what he's waiting for or if he is gauging how to best teach me.

It isn't until I hear him take a few steps toward me that I release a stuck breath. His arms wrap around my torso, one just below my collarbone and the other against my abdomen, and if we weren't training, I would find it strangely intimate. Though, so is Crux picking me up by my waist and then throwing me across the mat.

"Try to resist me." His hold tightens in a way that I know we've begun, yet his voice is softer than I'd expect for a training session.

I anticipated Knox would give me more direction before throwing me right into it, but I can guess what he is trying to show me. I'll do it by instinct, get it wrong the first time, maybe learn some practical experience along the way, and then he'll show me all the ways to exploit my weaknesses and how to avoid it. Or at least that's how Alarik trains me.

I try to shimmy out of his grasp by using my elbows and shoulders. When that doesn't work, I ram back into him with my body, but he stays put like an indestructible pillar.

"I don't think I'm getting it," I say.

Knox is quiet for a second before speaking. "Then we'll move on."

"Wait, aren't you going to teach me the correct way?"

"At the end. Right now, it's time for phase two."

"Phase two? I don't—"

Knox intentionally falls to the side, bringing me with him, our bodies colliding with the mat. A dark shiver runs up my spine, and for once, I have no idea what's going on or what he expects me to do. We've never trained like this before.

"This isn't helpful." I try to pry his arm off, but it only makes him hold me tighter.

"Just trust me, Margot. Try to get out of it and you'll see."

I muster up enough strength to elbow him in the stomach, making him grunt and his grip loosen. As I slip out from his grasp and crawl away, a sense of panic washes over me. I know that this is only a simulation, but something dark is scraping down the back of my brain that's trying to convince me otherwise. Something Instinctual. Primal.

Knox clutches his side as he laughs. "See, I knew you had it in you. But can you do it a second time?"

I crawl faster at his words. "I need a minute."

His hand takes hold of my ankle, trying to pull me back.

"Knox, wait!"

"There will be no breaks during an actual fight. It's best if you learn that now." He yanks my leg, making my torso hit the ground.

My adrenaline kicks in as Knox crawls over me. I roll on to my back and aim my foot at his crotch, not caring if it's a cheap move. But when I kick, he moves his pelvis, narrowly evading it.

"You're fighting dirty now, like a real proditor would." Knox wastes no time sitting on my abdomen in a straddle.

I know we're only training. I know this isn't real, so why does it feel like I'm fighting for my life? Is it true that proditor training is so intense that you're not sure if you'll make it through alive?

I try to scoot backward on elbows, but he pinches my hips between his knees. There's only one more thing I can do, so I throw my fist at his neck.

Which I immediately regret.

He grabs my wrist mid punch and then captures the other, pinning them far above my head into the mat.

"Knox, you won." I say, unable to even hide the panic in my voice. "Let's start over, all right? Show me what I did wrong."

"Would a Laven let you go? Do you understand the gravity of being in a situation like that? Maybe I need to show you." He moves both his hands to my neck.

This can't be happening. "Stop!"

In an instant, my air is cut off. I claw at him. My heart beats violently in my chest. This isn't him. This isn't my friend—the man who tells me jokes and has guided me through training. So why? Why is he doing this? In what world does he think this is helping me?

And what's worse is he doesn't look the same either. There's a darkness pooling beneath his eyes. His breaths grow deeper before his lips part.

"Knox!" I gasp.

He stares layers beneath my eyes as if searching for something only he knows is there.

"Please . . ." I squeak out. Everything is getting blurrier and my head feels fuzzy. If this is a test, I'm failing miserably. But maybe he's right because if he were a Laven, I would already be dead.

As my feet and hands go numb, my survival reflexes kick into full gear. *Focus, Margot. If you were Knox, what would he do?* I search my mind for the knowledge he embedded in me. If he could get out of this, it means so can I.

With seconds remaining before I lose consciousness, I position my forearms over his.

His eyebrows arch in surprise as I quickly push his forearms down, making him lose his grip on my neck. I take in a sweet, heaving breath, but there is no time to enjoy it.

Before Knox has another second to think, I arch my lower body and flip him onto his back until I'm sitting on top of him.

I can't move for a second as I pant, catching my breath. There is a shake to my teeth, arms, and legs. A part of me feels crazy for thinking Knox was actually trying to hurt me, but the other part tells me he already did. Not even Crux has tried to choke me out before, and out of all the proditors, he seems like the one most likely to.

"That was outstanding." Knox grins.

I huff in disbelief before losing control of my emotions and slapping his chest a few times as hard as I can. "What the hell were you thinking?"

"You did great, even better than I could have hoped."

Is he serious right now? Does he not see a single thing wrong with what just happened? "You could have killed me!"

"Come on, at the most, you would have passed out. I had to see what you were capable of in a real fight. We can't exactly send our Columess on a mission to Lavenai without having the utmost confidence that she'll come back alive, now can we?"

My body moves with the rise and fall of his torso. His breaths are so deep, as if he were the one who was just strangled half to death.

"You're going to teach me the moves," I demand. "Then, and only then, will we try the techniques. Got it?"

"Where's the fun in that?" Knox rests his hands behind his head.

"It's not supposed to be fun." The delighted look on his face is enough for me to push myself off him. "Now, will you teach me properly? No unexpected moves, no real life simulations. Just normal training, the way we always have done." My next word sounds on the edge of desperation. "Please?"

Knox sits up, frowning. "If that's what you want."

After taking a breather, we continue the session. This time, he teaches me a few new methods to escape various holds, but every time he touches me, there's a dark electricity that makes my muscles twitch. At any moment, he could change his mind and take me by surprise.

When we move on to combat, it makes me wish I was fighting Crux again.

Knox uses an extravagant force to take me down time and time again. Whereas Alarik is unpredictable, Onyx is quick, and Crux is strong; Knox is all of those things combined into one lethal force.

When there's less than an hour left, I lie on the mat with my arms spread out. I stare at the white panels of the ceiling. My body is completely battered and my lungs are on the edge of breaking. I didn't realize how long it would take my body to catch up after Knox choked me.

"Come on, Columess, get up." Knox nudges my side with his bare foot.

I stare up at him, studying his face. It's as wickedly charming as always. But now all I see are those unforgiving eyes.

Then I realize, I'm not just scared of him.

I fear him.

I haven't felt this unsettled since I found . . . Gods, *why can't I remember?* I found something horrible during the ball, but what was it?

"Let's call it a day. I'm beat," I say.

Knox folds his arms. "Don't tell me you're giving up?"

It takes all my effort to push myself up onto my sore hip. "I can hardly stand straight."

"Nonsense. Get a drink of water and let's do this."

I throw my hands up. "No, Knox. I'm not training anymore today. I need to rest."

"Do you want to get killed out there? Your life depends on this."

I push myself onto wobbling legs and take a swig of water from my canister. "None of it will matter if you leave me too broken to go to Lavenai."

Knox scoffs.

A deep rage explodes in me. I storm up to him until my face is just inches from his chin. "I am your Columess, and when I say we're done, it means just that. We're done."

I've never spoken to Knox this way. In fact, I've never spoken to anyone on the Imnicus like this, including Milo, who has pissed me off more times than I can count.

Knox's stare hardens, and I can't tell if my legs are shaking from the training or from his intimidating height.

He takes a step back and strides toward the locker room. "I'll see you tomorrow."

I don't even say goodbye to him and limp back to my quarters, my muscles aching and my stomach growling. Every step hurts horribly. All I can think of as I walk are flashes of Knox's face. How it feels like he's completely changed, or am I wrong? Has he always been like this and I'm just now seeing it?

When I get into the bathroom and strip out of my clothes, one look in the mirror leaves me gasping. There are bruises everywhere from my neck, all the way down to my thighs, and crusted blood under my nose. I didn't even realize I was bleeding.

I still have a handful of sessions left with Knox before I'm ready to leave for Lavenai. I gulp thinking about those days and the way he'll push me to my limits again and again.

I crawl into the tub completely naked and lie on my side, not caring how cold the jade is on my skin. Shaking turns into sobbing, and I wish for nothing more than to blink and for all of this to simply be a nightmare.

I ask the staff to deliver my lunch and dinner to my room. Lleu comes around mid afternoon to do a treatment on my hair, but I speak through the intercom and send her away. I can't let her see me like this.

I haven't even been able to put on clothes. When I tried to put a simple nightgown on earlier, the fibers brushed against my bruises. The only thing I can tolerate is a thin top sheet wrapped around my shoulders. Even sitting is hard, so I stand and look out the window, gazing at the twinkling stars to distract me.

But it feels impossible. All I can think about is what I did to Knox to deserve this.

Maybe he really did push me because he cares about my survival. He wants me to make it back alive from Lavenai so badly, he's willing to go to extreme lengths to make me into a competent fighter.

But nothing explains that look in his eyes.

When the bedroom doors slide open, I physically cringe. A part of me hoped Milo would get swamped on Ashtanabo and he'd have to stay overnight. How am I supposed to hide something like this from him?

"How was training today?" Milo's soothing voice vibrates across the room.

Tortuous. Horrible. Almost Deadly. "Good. I learned a lot." Still counting the stars, I adjust my blanket higher, covering the bruises that cover my neck.

Behind me, I hear Milo stripping off his royal attire, then his footsteps walking up the stairs of the lounge area. To my relief, both his palms press onto the glass instead of me as he boxes me in. I can feel his breath on the top of my scalp.

"I missed you." He presses his lips to my temple. His body heat is so warm and inviting, almost making me forget about today. The way Knox beat and bruised me in every way imaginable. He tugs at the edge of the sheet. "Nothing on, Columess?"

He wraps his arms around me, and I cry out, howling in pain. "Please, stop!"

He immediately backs away, and in the reflection of the window, I see him put his hands up. "Margot, what in the world—"

I can barely hold back the tears as I turn toward him.

His face goes cold, and he grips the sheet again.

"Please, Milo. Don't!"

He ignores me, ripping it effortlessly in a single stroke.

Immediately, I crouch on the ground, wrapping my arms around my body, shielding it the best I can, even though I know it's useless. The bruises are everywhere.

"Show me." Milo says firmly, any ounce of lust that was there previously now completely gone. His next words are shakier. "Stand up, please. Let me see you."

Reluctantly, I rise, lowering my arms to my side. I'm shaking and the tears I held back are falling. As they do, all I can hear is Crux's voice in my head.

Weak.

Milo presses his fingers to his mouth as his gaze rakes up my thighs. He steps forward and holds my chin, lifting it to see my neck. The motion makes me wince.

He circles behind me and I can hear his angry breaths as he sees my back. "Knox did this to you?"

"Milo, it's not what you think. With the mission coming up, he wanted me to be ready for whatever Lavenai may throw my way."

A dark silence trails over the room. Milo grabs the sheet from the ground and hands it back to me. "I'll be back later."

"Wait—" I reach a hand out to grab his arm but miss it.

Before I know it, he's dressed and heading to the door. As he goes to leave, he pauses at the threshold. "And Margot, I will personally be at the rest of your trainings."

As the door shuts, I fall to my knees.

I think back to my trainings with the other proditors. How Milo has had no problem letting them rough me up. But this was different. I know it. Milo knows it.

Knox knows it.

Chapter 24

The next morning, the west wing swarms with robots, servants, and humanoids alike finishing last-minute cleaning and setup. Lleu picked out a long-sleeved dress for me that covers all my bruises. The only downside is the fabric rubs against them unless I stay perfectly still.

The arbitors are coming today to discuss my mission to Lavenai before I depart. Apparently, even as the Colum, Milo has to get their approval on certain matters, but this is one I'm sure they'll accept.

By the time Milo and I enter the conference room, Knox has already arrived and is standing by a wall near two guards. Just seeing him makes my chest tighten.

His eyes lock with mine and I almost wince. But then I see something that surprises me.

He has a black eye.

"Did you sleep well?" Knox asks Milo with narrowed eyes.

Milo keeps his face completely neutral. "Like a baby."

At any other meeting, I would have made an effort to talk to Knox, joking around and laughing. Now, things are deathly silent as the men refuse to exchange another word with each other.

Somehow, losing his friendship hurts even worse than the wounds he gave me. He was one of the first people on the Imnicus to make me feel truly comfortable again. Maybe even the first one to make me genuinely laugh.

I hear the arbitors' voices and footsteps coming down the hall. I'm somewhat relieved that I have an excuse to sit far away from Knox.

As the arbitors enter, Monicas opens his arms to Milo, like he wants a hug. "Colum, a pleasure to see you again, as always."

Milo doesn't make any moves to embrace Monicas. Instead, he extends his hand. "Thank you for coming all this way."

Monicas clears his throat and abandons the hug in favor of a handshake. "Why, of course! I'd never pass up a trip to the Imnicus. In fact, we should have meals together more often."

Milo motions to the long conference table. "Why don't you all take a seat?"

To my relief, Anya and Lady Bruis are nowhere to be seen. On top of dealing with the awkward tension around Knox, they're the last people I need to worry about right now.

I stifle any hisses of pain as I take a seat on Milo's right at the head of the table. The thought of sitting so long is agonizing. But I am the Columess, so I muster the strength to endure it.

Monicas gets sidetracked right from the beginning, bringing up old meeting notes about Laven factory production. Arbitors

Lorne and Bruis listen intently, adding their own points on the matter.

Milo puts a hand up. "Sorry to interrupt, but we should speak about the Laven terrorists, if at all possible."

"Yes, right." Monicas straightens his posture and grabs a cookie from the tray in front of him. "The terrorist base lies beneath Merth in West Beteny, the capital of Lavenai. A very strategic play from them, as we can't very well bomb through the city. There are, as you presented to us, fifteen entrances concealed within various businesses. Do you propose a full scale assault? Kick the hornet's nest and chase the pests through their own tunnels?"

"It isn't that simple. Those tunnels are robust, and there may be natural paths not listed." Milo says. "If we attempt access, or even let slip that we know more than we let on, then they may flee. Our preliminary search has been cautious, but we've found no hints of entrances within the businesses themselves yet. If they really are located where the map says, they're hidden well."

"And interrogating these business owners with your . . ." Monicas glances toward Knox. "Special talents is out?"

"As soon as proditors start pulling business owners, we lose all manner of surprise."

"A spy then? Someone to slip in and discover the truth behind these hidden entrances?"

Milo smiles and Monicas sits back, pleased with himself for coming to such a conclusion.

"Precisely, Arbitor. Now that we know the locations, we can send in an agent. Ideally, they'll find us the information we need to move forward."

Monicas glances around at the other two arbitors. "This plan is sound so far, and I trust you've thought more upon this than you've let on. Plans tend to fall apart in the execution stage, after all. Do you have anyone in mind to infiltrate?"

Milo straightens his posture. "I do have someone. I will be sending Lady Arris."

Monicas's smile falls. "Are you mad?"

Milo places his hand on mine. "Before the attack, Margot was our best agent. I know things have changed, but for the past few weeks, the proditors have been retraining her in combat. She may have lost her memories, but she hasn't lost her talent. She can hold her own now, and I have confidence in her abilities."

"This is absurd. We have our first Columess under the Arris Reign and you want to risk her life?" Monicas clutches at his temple, searching for words. He sets the cookie back upon the table, like he lost his appetite. "Heavens, Colum, this is your wife we're speaking about."

Arbitor Bruis clears his throat. "Monicas, before you veto this mission, we should consider it more deeply. Margot is so young and docile, nobody on Lavenai would suspect her, nor do they know what she looks like."

"Moreover, she will be wearing a disguise," Milo adds. "Ideally, once she is in their base, she'll hack into their electronic records and steal information on the identity of each and every member of the organization. If we know the key leaders, we'll be able to pick them off from above ground. With Lavenai's surveillance system in place, we can track their every movement. If we strike at the head of the organization, the whole beast will fall. Why risk an assault when we can snuff out the flame from the top?"

A sharp idea, in theory. But in the end, Monicas has to approve it. If he doesn't, Milo will never truly be able to relax knowing my attackers are still out there. On top of that, I have my own vendetta against the terrorists, and maybe if we can question a few, we'll find a way to restore my memories.

By the wall, Knox stands at attention with his hands behind his back. His focus darts between each arbitor speaking before his vindictive gaze settles on me. The blood rushes out of my face, the devil himself glaring back.

I quickly break myself out of his line of sight and focus back on the meeting. The arbitors are still arguing.

"I don't distrust the validity of your plan, Colum," Monicas says, "I just falter over the thought of Lady Arris alone on the planet. They crippled her memory during the last encounter, and I shudder at the thought of throwing her into the lion's den."

"Arbitor Monicas." I leap in before Milo can respond. "Ignore my role in this mission. Would you approve it, knowing we sent the most capable agent to accomplish this task?"

"I—" he says, glancing at the table top before him. "I suppose I would have no choice. It is a sound option, and one with the highest chance of success."

"Then I do not see the issue here. I wouldn't have agreed if I didn't find myself capable. Do you think I'm capable?"

Monicas stutters. "Yes—of course, Columess! Why, I would never dare insult you by questioning your abilities."

"Then it's settled. I'm the most qualified for this mission, and I doubt anyone else would have the level of success I will. Do not see me as a frail Columess, but a confident spy, capable of ending this conflict once and for all."

Arbitor Monicas is at a loss for words. I see Milo in the corner of my eye, stifling a laugh.

"Yes, Lady Arris. You're right, I'm sorry if I implied in any way that I question your competency." Monicas looks at Milo. "You have my full approval to begin the mission as soon as you're ready. All in agreement?"

"Aye," Arbitor Bruis says.

Arbitor Lorne takes a sigh of relief. "Aye."

Monicas takes a bite of his cookie, talking it with his mouth full. "It's settled. Margot, the three of us wish you the best of luck." He raises his glass. "To Arris Reign."

I wake up to Milo's warm mouth on my forehead. His raven hair brushes the sides of my face before he places a gentle kiss on my lips. The aroma of a delicious breakfast wafts into my nostrils from the lounge area.

Then reality hits me like a ton of bricks.

Today is the day of my mission to Lavenai. The one where I'm expected to infiltrate an underground base of a terrorist organization. Where I'll possibly encounter the same people that left me scarred and broken, devoid of memories. Even though I've practiced countless hours in combat, stealth, and technology, only now am I questioning whether I believe myself to be ready.

The breakfast's scent quickly turns sour. I sit up, taking a deep breath.

Milo stays on his side, running his fingers along my arm. "You're nervous."

"Is it that obvious?"

"It's like you've pulled into yourself."

"I don't think I really processed what I'd be doing until just now." I rub my hands over my face.

"If I believed there was even a one percent chance you wouldn't make it, I wouldn't be sending you. You can take my word on that."

"No matter how much training a soldier has, it really never prepares them for the real thing, does it?"

Milo shakes his head. "I'm afraid not."

I wish I shared half the amount of confidence in myself that Milo has in me.

"There is something I want to give you before you leave," he says.

"Milo, you didn't need to get me anything."

"Come on, trust me." Milo pulls me out of bed, leading me up to the lounge area.

A box made of rippled brass sits on one of the chairs. I don't know what it is, but I already know it's too much. "Are you serious? This is too lavish."

"What's the point of being a Colum if I can't spoil my wife on occasion? Though I don't think you'll find this gift lavish. Come on, open it up."

I run my hands over the brass before lifting the lid. As I do, Milo wraps his hands around my waist from behind, staring into the box with me.

Inside sits two folded items of black clothing. I take the jacket and lift it up. It's similar to the attire of a soldier but with a few impractical differences, like the silver that lines that collar. Gems sit across the shoulders' boning, and two circular chains hang down each of the upper arms.

The Ashtanaban insignia is on the breast pocket with five crows in a line at the top, their arms outspread and stiff like ships flying straight up. The center point is a stem with growing leaves and budding flowers.

"It's an Ashtanaban uniform. The same ones the other spies wear to formal meetings with commanders. It's more fitting of a gift for when you return, but I'm impatient."

Something about this gift makes everything feel even more real. Something to celebrate the relearning of my abilities. I bring the stiff coat fabric to my chest, looking at my reflection in the window. The black fabric layers in an overlapped triangular pattern that resembles scales.

I turn around and hug Milo tightly. "You have no idea how much this means to me . . . Thank you."

Milo squeezes me back. "You deserve this more than anyone I know."

After I force down some breakfast, Milo and I get dressed and head to the docking bay.

The cool draft hits my neck and makes my skin prickle. His gift tempered my nerves but not fully. Not only that, but the person flying me to Lavenai today is none other than Knox himself, per Arbitor Monicas's request. It was enough to quell the arbitors' worries about sending the Columess into a terrorist base. Knox is the most talented of the proditors, therefore he's the best person to send in case something really did go wrong. His skills in flying and magic are completely unmatched.

However, knowing he'll be with me is almost worse than the mission itself.

We approach a smaller ship where Knox stands at the top of the ramp with folded arms. "It's about time you two showed up."

Alarik stands slightly behind him on the ramp, giving Milo a slight nod. Seeing him, and knowing I won't be alone with Knox after all, makes me release a breath I didn't realize I was holding.

Milo bites. "Did the technicians finish their inspections?"

"Like clockwork," Knox says.

At my side, I hold a bag containing a wig, a hat, and an empty flash drive. Lleu made the hat for me, and she said it was for good luck. It will also ensure that the brunette wig stays secure. "I'm ready if you are."

Knox nods. "Let's not prolong this mission anymore than we have to. Let's go."

"Take this." Milo pulls out a holstered gun and hands it to me. "Hide it and only use it if absolutely necessary."

"Thank you." I really hope I never have to use it. Part of me wonders if he's giving me this for the mission or because of Knox. "When I get back, we should do something special."

Milo smiles and gives me a peck on the lips. "Maybe that trip to the northern cities?" He puts a hand on my waist.

"Margot!" Knox shouts from the ramp. "We don't have all day."

"Right . . . uh . . . coming!"

I give Milo another kiss before running up the ramp to meet Knox.

As the ramp closes, I wave goodbye to Milo until I can no longer see him.

Inside the ship, everything is quiet and cold. This is the first time I've been so close to Knox since that day, and even though I've trained with him since then, Milo was always there too.

But Alarik's here, presumably to keep an eye on Knox. Though, when I look to the back of the small ship, I realize that we're not the only three on the ship.

There's another proditor whom I don't recognize, and that's when I remember that there are five of them. He's the one I haven't met yet.

"Get comfortable." Knox moves to the front of the ship and powers on the controls. "The journey will be well over an hour."

"In a ship this size? Probably two," Alarik counters, removing his mask.

Knox smirks. "Not when I'm in control."

Alarik shakes his head as he takes a seat. "If we hit an asteroid, I'm blaming you."

I sit by Alarik and the new proditor. I study the man's mask, embossed with kaleidoscope-like designs. Unlike Alarik and Knox, he keeps it on, like he's not used to letting anyone, including the Columess, see him without it.

Alarik looks between me and the man before a stark realization passes over his face. "I'm sorry, I should have introduced you. Margot, this is Dune Catawnee."

Dune sits very properly compared to the other proditors, with his hands resting on his kneecaps and his back straight, almost like he's in a constant state of meditation. "It's nice to see you again, Columess."

"Nice to meet you too." It's been almost six months now since I woke up from the attack. Shouldn't I have bumped into him at least once? "Are you involved in the mission at all today?"

"No. Just hitching a ride."

Alarik interrupts. "That's not all true. The mission wouldn't have been possible without your investigation."

My lips part. "Are you the one who found the base entrances?"

"No," Dune says. "I was simply the proditor who led the scouting missions, as well as some of the interrogations. The person who gave us that information is someone else entirely."

"Is there more trouble on Lavenai?" I ask.

Dune glances at me, enough that I can clearly see his tan skin and dark features hidden beneath his mask. "You could say that."

As the ship takes off, Dune relaxes his posture and closes his eyes, resting into the seat for some kind of power nap. Alarik pulls out a small book and gets comfortable.

As we enter Lavenai's purple atmosphere over an hour later, I am filled with both anticipation and dread. When we get close enough to the ground to see the city of Merth more clearly, my mouth gapes.

I knew Lavenai wasn't nearly as luxurious as Ashtanabo.

But this is worse than anyone could have prepared me for.

Chapter 25

If Ashtanabo is green thanks to its lush flora and vine-covered houses, then Lavenai is purple because of its horrific level of pollution. The clouds—that aren't really clouds—part for our ship, and it isn't until we're closer to the ground that I can make out anything.

The skyscraper city comes into view, and then the hundreds of factories that surround it. Dark purple smoke puffs out of their industrial chimneys.

Every building is more run down than the last as we fly over Merth. Still, colorful neon lights line almost every building, though some flicker like the bulbs need to be changed. It's easy to see what Lavenai once was before the power plant explosion. I can see why it was enough to start a war.

Something about it makes my heart stir, though it also feels familiar. I wonder if I was posted here before I started working on the Imnicus.

Knox lands the ship on a beach just outside the city, making Dune stir from his nap. Alarik closes his book and stretches.

After powering down the ship, Knox stands and makes his way to Dune, Alarik, and me. Knox rests his elbow on the back of my seat as I unbuckle myself. I feel his eyes on the back of my head as I grab my bag and fish out my disguise.

"I see you finally met Dune," Knox says, his voice bordering on the end of taunting.

"Yes, Alarik introduced us." I look at Dune to give him a kind nod.

Knox stays put, leaning against my chair. I try to ignore him as I put on my disguise.

"You know, in proditor circles, Dune is known as the torturer." Knox paces to the closed ramp.

"Don't scare her, Knox." Alarik bites.

I look to Dune. Though tall and tough like any other proditor, there is something serious about him that the other proditors don't have. He carries himself like he's the oldest of the five, or at least the wisest.

Knox hits the button on the ramp, opening it until it touches down on the sand. The second the air wafts in, I begin to cough.

"It's unbreathable." I cover my nose and mouth with my forearm, my throat as dry as bones.

Knox takes a thin respirator out of one of the ship's compartments and shoves it into my chest. "You can take it off inside buildings. Most have built-in airlocks."

I quickly put it on, yet I can still smell the smoky stench of the city. This planet is almost unlivable.

Dune steps onto the ramp. "Don't wait up for me. I'll be more than a few days."

"Wasn't planning on it," Knox teases.

Dune treks out onto the sand, avoiding empty metal cans and debris under his steps.

Knox and I stand on the ramp together. Even with Alarik watching us from behind, it still feels like it's just the two of us, which is enough for me to keep him in the corner of my eye.

"Stop looking at me like that. I'm not going to hurt you." Knox thrusts a data pad into my hand that's preset to a destination a few blocks away.

"I still don't understand . . . " I shouldn't be bringing this up right now. Nothing explains that day, but still I have to know. "What changed between us?"

"Well, for one, you tattled to Milo. Made me look like some kind of monster."

I bite down on my lip. "You know that's not what happened. Milo saw my body and made his own judgments."

"Do I make you nervous now, Margot?" Knox takes a step forward, making me stand on the edge of the ramp. It's not a far drop, but it would still hurt.

I swallow. "Not in the slightest, Proditor Knox."

Knox purses his lips. "So formal now—friend."

If I stay here another minute, I will lose all composure. I brush past him and head down the ramp, my shoes meeting the sand.

"Margot."

I look over my shoulder. Knox looks like a prince of darkness in his uniform, with the dark purple sky and blackened water behind him.

"Once you're inside their base, and those doors lock shut behind you, there is no saving you."

I push down the building fear his words bring and trek across the litter-filled beach, refusing to look back at him. Whatever has changed in Knox shakes me to my core. Every word and every touch has become coated in poison.

Once my feet find a sidewalk, the city air tastes bitter, even with the mask. As I see the first Laven citizen, I try to put a handle on what I'm feeling. I thought I'd be mad or angry seeing even a single one of them. Instead, I feel a deep sadness. A sort of grief for their planet.

There are factory workers in green jumpsuits walking home from their shifts. A woman and her young daughter enter a grocery store that has Ashtanaban soldiers guarding the doors and scanning ration cards. A teenage boy passes me with a crate full of junk wire and computer parts.

Everyone—man, woman, and child—wears respirators, and the few that don't lie on sidewalks with metal cups in front of them, some of them looking on the brink of death.

This is horrible. In fact, I feel a primal level of anger, but I'm not sure who or what it's directed at. The Ashtanaban worker who exploded the plant? Lavenai for not accepting Ashtanabo's help and keeping themselves stuck in this mess?

Or is it Ashtanabo itself and the nagging feeling that they could be doing more?

But maybe Milo really is doing all he can do where an entire planet is concerned. Most Laven are not overly thin, but that doesn't make me feel any better. There are still dark circles under most of their eyes and their jaws are thin and narrow.

A glossy layer on the concrete streets reflects the neon lights. To my surprise, the streets themselves are clean enough to lick, but the sidewalks and alleys are filled with litter.

I follow the datapad until it beeps in front of a shop with a pink neon sign that reads, *Bevs and Shrooms*.

Once I'm inside and the doors closes, I remove my mask and inhale a deep cleansing breath, promising myself to never take clean air for granted again.

The shop has a few patrons but is mostly empty. Everything from the tables to the walls looks completely worn down.

An old bartender stands behind the counter, his face covered in stubble. "Take a seat anywhere, young lady." Different-colored mushrooms brew in large jars behind the counter.

I climb onto one of the barstools and lay my mask on the counter. "Thank you."

"Now, what can I get for you?"

"Um . . ." I default to my favorite drinks on the Imnicus. "Do you have moon tea?"

He laughs as do a few other patrons in earshot. "Oh, that's a good one, miss. You must be all the rage around the boys with that sense of humor."

Shit. So moon tea is a strictly Ashtanaban drink then. I laugh with them to mask my panic, realizing I've made a potentially critical error. "Just give me what's most popular."

"Shroom juice it is." He pulls a pre-made drink from the glass fridge behind him, pours it into a cup, then tops it off with a glittery, powdered garnish. Sediment sits at the bottom. I hold back my aversion to the brew.

"Thank you."

I expect him to walk away so I can start figuring out where this supposed secret entrance is within this shop, but the man doesn't stop watching me. He has an excited smile on his face, waiting for me to try the drink.

I force a smile and bring the juice to my lips. To my relief, the drink is sweet. Not the murky water I was expecting. "It's delicious."

"Glad to hear it. Now, enjoy." The man takes a rag and heads into the main dining area to wipe down tables and converse with patrons.

Nothing in this shop looks like it could have any kind of secret-base entrance, unless it's in the back. But any comings and goings from the employee-only section of a shop wouldn't go unnoticed from Dune's scouting efforts. They'd keep their entrances just barely out of sight, unnoticed, but not suspicious either.

I leave my drink at the counter and head into the ladies' bathroom. While I search the stalls one-by-one, I cross my fingers that nobody walks in. I press against walls for weak spots and check behind the toilets for any clues.

The datapad says the base is in this shop somewhere, yet it's nowhere to be found. I start to feel anxious again. What if I can't find the entrance? Somehow that feels worse than narrowly escaping death in the terrorist underground. Everyone would be so disappointed. Milo would be disappointed.

How did Milo first learn of these secret entrances in the first place? Did some other spy come across the map? Did they interrogate a fugitive for it? I lean my weight on the leaky sink and stare into the mirror. The brunette wig washes out my skin, making me look as pale as one of the Laven.

I go to turn around, and my shoulder accidentally brushes the light switch, leaving me in total darkness. "Dammit."

As I fumble to turn the lights back on, I look back to the mirror. In the darkness, there is a small, red light blinking on its top corner.

I slowly walk through the dark toward it. As I do, I hear faint, inaudible whispers, making me rub my ear. I reach around the mirror's edges to find the source of the light. My heart stops as my fingers brush over a button.

I press it.

The privy lights turn a deep red. I fall back and narrowly avoid hitting my head on the tiled wall. A holographic scanner shoots from within the mirror and moves across my face.

Oh no, face detection? This isn't something we prepared for. If the terrorists get my face, they'll know we're on to them. Nobody prepared me for what to do in a situation like this. I need to get out of here, and fast.

I rush to the door, but before I can unlock it, an automated voice speaks. The words send an aching shiver up my spine.

Access granted. Welcome back.

Chapter 26

Access granted?

Welcome . . . back?

The tiled panels of the wall jut out slightly behind me, then lift, revealing a titanium blast door, which slides open soon after.

This isn't right. It shouldn't have let me in, unless the terrorists' technology is really that bad.

Or this is a trap. Why else would my face scan automatically? After all, I am the Columess. They could have gotten an image of me and put it into their system. For all I know, if I enter through the door, there could be a group waiting for me downstairs, ready to strike and use me as a hostage against Milo.

Regardless, I need to do this. I can't go back to the Imnicus empty-handed. I don't think I could face Milo without getting him what he needs—the faces of every single terrorist. The people who erased my memories and made my life hell.

I curl my fists and ignore the possibilities as I step over the threshold. The titanium door shuts behind me before another one opens farther down the dark, musty hallway. After going through the second doorway and climbing down a ladder, I find myself surrounded by white brick walls.

The base is enormous, and now I see why Milo was so concerned about an underground bombing. The hallways are three times my height and wide enough to fit a vehicle.

As I turn down one of the halls, I hear the echo of voices and laughter. I quickly find a smaller hallway and press my back into the wall, then I peek around the corner at the source of the noise.

A few of the terrorists walk in a group, all wearing black training outfits. They talk and laugh together like this is any other day. They don't look at all as I expected. I assumed the terrorists would be primarily men in their thirties with hardened stares or maniacal expressions. But these people are as young as me, if not younger.

Still, I feel angry watching them prance around their base as if they didn't destroy every part of me. It makes the scar on my back burn. I hold back the temptation to jump out from the shadows and beat every last one of them senseless.

After the hallway clears, I sneak out of my hiding spot. I need to find a better way of blending in, so I search for anything that could work while avoiding new groups of terrorists that roam the halls.

Finally, I find a closet filled with jackets with the terrorist insignia—a leafless tree with plentiful branches. My skin crawls as I sort through the racks and find one in my size to slip on.

For a solid hour, I search the base, passing the occasional person who pays me no mind. Some even say hello in passing, and I force myself to say it back but only to blend in. The words feel like poison on my tongue.

There are dorms, recreational rooms, and even a school. Do children live here? Are they born into this life or kidnapped into it? Both possibilities make me even more bitter.

At last, I stumble upon a large, empty computer room with a long, U-shaped table in the center. I always thought Lavenai's terrorists would be sloppier, living in near filth. But everything is so clean and meticulously organized. Not even a wire is out of place.

I quickly sit down at one of the computers. It's only a matter of time before someone will come in here and start asking questions. I need to work quickly. I fish out the flash drive and plug it into the round port, then use the touchscreen to sort through the files. But everything is locked behind a PIN, even the one I need most, titled *Organization Census*.

Damn. Without a PIN, it will be impossible to access the file. I can already see Milo's disappointed face. He'll lie and say I tried my best, and I can't have that. I ball up my fists and start to guess, typing in any and every number combination.

4747. Incorrect. 0001. Of course not, that'd be too easy. I try a few more.

Without thinking, I type in 5826.

It works. My fingers stiffen and hover over the touch screen.

How could this be? The odds of it matching my old tablet's passcode seem like an anomaly, but when I typed it, it felt so familiar. So natural.

I shake my head. There's no time to think. I need to get these files before I'm found out. After dragging the organization census onto the flash drive, I swipe a few others over that Milo may find useful.

Within one of the folders, I see a document titled *Deceased Members* and hover my finger over it.

"You're working during lunch?" an older female voice says from behind.

My bones weld together.

I need to stay calm and act natural. Panicking or being rash will get me in all sorts of trouble. I don't turn to face the woman as I speak. "I'm just catching up."

I hear the woman walk closer before stopping. She just stands there, just out of sight. Her breathing becomes deep enough to be audible, and I know right then and there, I've been caught.

Which means I don't have a second to lose.

With all my force, I stand and kick my chair into her. She tumbles to the ground as I pull the flash drive from the computer just as the transfer completes.

The middle-aged woman's tight silver-gray bun loosens from her fall. She pushes herself upright as I run around her toward the door.

She grabs my ankle, tripping me. As I try to get up, my wig catches under my hand, ripping it off my head.

The woman takes a step back with a look of horror on her face. "Margot . . . It's you."

She knows who I am? It's probably as I expected before. The terrorists know my name and have records of my face, I'm sure. In fact, this woman has probably known this entire time that I've been sneaking around the base. This is a trap, just one they didn't expect me to trip so soon.

I move to charge out of the room, but something stops me. She doesn't look angry. No, she looks sad. Her eyes become glassy and a tear runs down her face. "It's really you. Margot, I can't believe it."

I reach into my bag and pull out the gun Milo sent with me. "Normally I don't care when people use my first name, but to scum like you, I am Lady Arris."

"Arris?" Her eyes widen. "Oh gods, Margot, what did they do to you?"

I add more purpose to my stance. "You mean what *you* did to me? My lost memories, the sleepless nights your organization has caused me. All of you deserve what's coming. The Colum will make sure of it." My voice is on the verge of a sob.

The woman doesn't retaliate or lunge at me. She simply shakes her head.

I should be running, but I stay still. Why won't I just turn around and leave? She's practically letting me. *Go! Go while you still can!*

The woman pulls a small pill-like item from her belt and throws it at the ground, making a smoke cloud appear around both of us.

She emerges from the smoke, hunched low, trying to tackle me to the ground. Knox's shadow takes over, and I drop the gun, sidestepping easily, using both arms to carry her momentum past me and making her stumble into the mainframe.

Despite her age, the woman is nimble. She falls into a roll and is back on her feet before I can regain my own footing to escape. But she doesn't immediately lunge back for an attack and instead reaches for a small amber jar on her belt. She uncorks the top, and I lunge to stop her from using whatever is inside. I'm too slow, and a puff of white powder blasts into my nose.

I wheeze as powder fills my lungs, making me stumble back. Even through the heaving, I feel my heel bump into the gun, and I manage to pluck it from the ground, pointing it at the woman before she can close the distance. Whatever was in that powder makes Knox's shadow weaken almost completely. If she tries to fight me again, I'm left only to my innate abilities.

"Don't take a step closer," I say, resting my finger upon the trigger.

This time, she raises her hands in defeat. "Go, Margot, I won't try to stop you."

I back up toward the door, still aiming. "What did you do?"

"In a few hours' time, you'll see."

Did she poison me? I don't have time for more questions. I sprint out of the room before she changes her mind.

Another fit of coughing takes over while I retrace my steps, staying as hidden as I can from any other terrorists. I lean against a corner, almost gagging. What is this stuff? The taste of blood and metal flows down the back of my throat.

Once I'm back in the bathroom at Bevs and Shrooms, I wheeze into the sink. I cup water into my hands and drink it, though it doesn't help much in clearing my lungs. Then, all at once, the fit stops completely. In fact, it ceases too fast for my comfort, like it was never there at all.

I splash water on my face, ignoring the whispers in my head.

On my way back to Knox's ship, I check over my shoulders every few steps, worried the woman has changed her mind. I try not to think of her words or anything that happened before she showed up. She's probably just trying to get in my head.

As I step onto the sandy beach, the ramp lowers. Knox emerges from the ship, a smile in his eyes, making my muscles tense. I should tell him about the powder and facial recognition. Maybe even how my passcode worked. Ashtanabo's safety could be on the line.

"Did you get it?" Knox asks as I walk up the ramp, shortness in his voice.

"Knox, something strange happened—"

"I said, did you get it?"

I press my lips together and pull the flash drive from my pocket. "Yes, but—"

Knox swipes it from my hand and tucks it into a small compartment of his belt. "You did well, Margot. I know Milo will reward you greatly." He places his gloved hand on the small of my back and guides me back into his ship.

I want to tell him about the woman, but something tells me to keep it to myself. With their files in our possession, none of that matters now. The terrorists will be taken down in time, and Milo can finally have some peace.

Chapter 27

When we land in the docking bay, Milo is already waiting for us. I run down the ramp to him and wrap my arms behind his neck.

He kisses me and then looks over at Knox and Alarik standing on the ramp.

Knox nods at him. *She did it.*

"I haven't stopped thinking about you," he says, tracing my cheekbone.

I break away from the embrace, placing my hands on his forearms. "There were a few close calls."

"But no one suspected anything?" he asks.

"Not a thing," I lie. I'm not ready to tell him about the woman or the chilling words she left me with. Just like with Knox, something tells me to wait.

"And you found the entrance all right?"

I nod, lips pressed in a straight line. "It took some searching, but I found it."

"All that matters is that you're back here with me." He presses his lips to mine again.

Knox descends the ramp, rolling his eyes. As he passes Milo, he slaps him on the back. "Get a room."

Milo rolls his eyes before whisking me away.

We take the long way back to our bedroom. I can't help but feel happy, almost giddy, on top of a huge sense of accomplishment. I just infiltrated a base and propelled Milo toward stopping the terrorists. He's never been this close until now.

But there's still that nagging feeling in my chest. One that wants to tell Milo about the woman. Then there's the other part warring in me, almost begging me to hold off.

"What was it like? The inside, I mean," Milo asks.

"Huge, like a skyscraper turned on its side. I see why you were so worried about them potentially bombing from underground."

Milo tugs at the hem of the Laven jacket, inscribed with the terrorist insignia. "It's so strange seeing you dressed like one of them."

I peer down at the clothing. "It was stupid for me to walk through the city with it on." Like my formal Ashtanaban uniform, I doubt it's common for Laven terrorists to wear their garb in public.

Still, Milo passes no judgment on me. "We'll give it to the south wing for safekeeping. It could prove useful in future missions."

Once we're back in our bedroom, it doesn't take long for Milo's lips to find mine. His hands caresses my thighs and my breasts before he strips off the Laven uniform and has me trapped between his firm naked body and a wall.

Everything about him feels so right. So raw. And once our bodies meld together, we're moving quickly and desperately, trying to take more of one another in. Every touch, every lick, every moan brings me close to unraveling.

And when I do, Milo snakes his fingers up the back of my neck and into my hair, gripping the blonde strands. He brings my forehead to his, even as my neck tries to arch from the pleasure.

"I love you . . . I love you." Milo's voice is jagged and restless, chasing his own pleasure as he brings me through mine. He breaks, his hips stuttering.

He doesn't just want my body, he wants *me*. The girl who made his reign as the Colum so much more complicated. The girl who defied him at every turn. The girl who once wished he would simply disappear. And now we are here, our bodies and souls bound together by constellations, binding us for the rest of our lives.

"I love you too," I whisper against his lips.

Deep into the night, Milo is sound asleep, his arm resting across my torso. He looks so peaceful and so happy. I can't help but smile.

Because I'm happy too. The happiest I've been in months.

It's only a matter of time before the Laven terrorists are unable to leave their base without being immediately detected and arrested. Soon, the attack will be nothing but a distant memory, and I can move on, with or without my memories. As long as I have Milo, I don't need my past. I can make new memories with him.

My temples start to ache and my throat constricts. It's not very surprising. The pollution on Lavenai was horrible, and besides that mushroom drink at the bar and some water from the faucet, I haven't had anything to drink since breakfast.

I shimmy from under Milo's arm and tiptoe out of bed, wrapping a robe around myself and tying it tightly around my waist. In the lounge area, I pour myself a glass of water from the pitcher and stare out into the stars.

The dull ache throbs across the band of my forehead, then a sharpness forms beneath my eyes. I finish the water and pour myself another glass, then rub the back of my neck.

The pain simmers down, which I can only assume is from the fight. I did hit the ground hard during the mission. It's highly likely I pulled something.

All at once, pain explodes across my skull, like a dozen knives jabbing into my brain all at once. I grab my head, falling onto my knees.

It's horrible, as if I'm dying. Somehow, I've managed not to scream yet, even though it only seems to get worse.

Then I have no choice as an invisible knife-like sensation spins in my mind as if it's a key.

I scream bloody murder.

My fingers turn into claws at my side and my neck curls backward.

I hear Milo shoot out of the bed and rush into the lounge area. Then he's in front of me, cupping my face, almost gripping it, in horror. "Margot? What's wrong? Margot!"

And just like that, reels of film run through my mind and the pieces of the puzzle finally come together. The pain exposes every secret and every blank is filled in.

You've been betrayed, I tell myself.

My memories befriend me—and then become my mortal enemies.

Chapter 28

Past: Lavenai

"**I**s this all?" I sift through one of the under-packed cases on the truck, ignoring the stench of the musty alley. Every few seconds, I gaze over my shoulders and up the sides of the building to quadruple-check that there are no cameras.

The dealer folds his arms. "I assure you, everything is there."

Just like all of Joriel Sinclair's goons, there's an air of dishonesty to every one of his words. But that's just how things are on Lavenai: those with money scamming those who can hardly scrape by.

Lucinda won't like this at all.

My cousin, Dimitri, steps to the case and takes his own look through it, counting the day-old bread and somewhat-fresh vegetables. He tightens his fists. "This is half of what you gave us last week, and you know it. What's your game, huh? To rip us off and think we wouldn't notice?"

Dimitri tries to take a step forward at the man, but I quickly grab his arm and pull him back. "Dimitri, let him speak."

The man tilts his head and smiles. "Unfortunately for you two, Sinclair's cost has gone up. The soil is worse this time of year."

"Bullshit," Dimitri says, and he's right. The soil on Lavenai is bad all times of the year. The only way anyone can get anything to grow is in greenhouses using imported soil from Ashtanabo, unless they're trying to grow mushrooms.

This time, Dimitri lunges forward. Immediately, the man pulls out a contraband gun, pointing it straight at my cousin's chest. I grab Dimitri's arm and hold it tighter this time.

"I wouldn't do that if I were you," the man sneers. "One-hundred boxes just like that one for ten-thousand geeds. That is Joriel's offer."

"We don't want trouble," I say. "We just want what Joriel promised us."

As if Joriel doesn't eat like a king every night on his throne of debauchery at his brothel while women sit on his lap and feed him grapes and caress his unblemished skin. He eats foods and enjoys luxuries that most Laven can't even dream of obtaining.

Still, I know it isn't Joriel that is scamming us this time. He's known Lucinda since he was a child, even though he's just as horrible as every other crime lord. Sinclair's brothel and the rebellion have a bit of a symbiotic relationship. We get to keep one of the confidential sixteen entrances of our base in the basement of his club and in return, we provide him assassins and spies to use when he pleases.

This man, on the other hand, is underpacking boxes and overcharging us to make a profit of his own right under Joriel's nose.

The man doesn't lower his weapon. "No deal."

We need this food. It's been weeks since we've gotten a shipment, and our rebellion has many mouths to feed. There's no way we can walk away from this empty-handed, but we also can't give him even a geed more. I inspect the gun closely from feet away, and then I see it. I tap my thumb once against Dimitri's arm and then another two quick taps.

Dimitri's cheeks rise in a smile beneath the respirator. "I think you may want to reconsider."

I let go of Dimitri and let him rush forward at the man. The man panics, pulling back the trigger multiple times, but no bullets exit. Dimitri pries the gun from his hand and knocks him to the ground.

"You'll pay for that!" the man screams.

Dimitri kicks the man in the stomach and then roughly digs the sole of his boot on the side of the man's head, keeping him on the ground. "Perhaps we'll tell Joriel about your little side business using his merchandise. I'm sure he'd love to know all about that."

The man's eyes widen. "I don't know what you're talking about!"

"Since the boxes are underfilled, we'll pay you five-thousand," I say. "If you don't accept, we'll make sure Joriel himself knows we turned down the deal, something we've never done. He'll ask why, and we'll tell him about the quality of the boxes. In the end, it will all lead back to you."

It doesn't take much more convincing for the man to frantically accept and thank the heavens he did.

As we drive away from the meeting spot, my stomach growls. In the rebellion, we don't go hungry as often as most Laven do. But there are times like this when food is in shorter supply and we find ourselves skipping meals for sometimes weeks.

We pass through the dining district where all the restaurants advertise similar deals—different ways to cook and brew mushrooms. It's the only food that grows on Lavenai since Balistar Arris took over, so Sinclair's cases are valuable. A lot of them contain food smuggled in from Ashtanabo.

Sure, Ashtanabo gives everyone on Lavenai rations, but only to keep the Laven people strong enough to man their factories and take on the brunt of the pollution. Those rations don't come to the rebellion, for obvious reasons, leaving us to fend for ourselves in a world that can barely sustain a crop.

"How did you know the gun was unloaded, by the way?" Dimitri asks, signaling to his arm where I had tapped him.

"It wasn't. The safety was on."

Dimitri scoffs.

I laugh and shake my head. "I may be smart, but I'm not strong like you."

Dimitri is one of the most skilled assassins in the rebellion. It's something I could never stomach doing. Spying and stealing is one thing, but killing? Count me out.

"Still, Lucinda won't be happy we risked our lives to get the cases," I say.

"And that's why we won't tell her." Dimitri smiles, but then he goes solemn. "I know you don't like it when I ask, but are you nervous?"

My jaw twitches. "What about?"

"Don't play dumb. The Imnicus mission. It's less than a week away, and you never bring it up."

I don't respond as I watch the road. I never bring it up because nobody could possibly understand how I feel. But after everything Lavenai has been put through, being nervous is the least of my worries. I want to break Lavenai free from the Arris reign, even if I have to give my life.

It's been twenty-two years since Balistar Arris and the proditors occupied Lavenai. Twenty-two years since he murdered Ashtanabo *and* Lavenai's Colums for the throne. He even betrayed the Vicars and turned many of them into his regime of proditors. Vicars don't involve themselves in politics or war; they only use their magic for worship. The Vicars called Balistar's faction proditors, meaning traitors. Balistar took a liking to the name and adopted it himself, forsaking religion, and became destructive in the name of reformation.

Lavenai was no match for the proditors. Once they had the population in submission and took away our ability to fight back with space navels, they didn't even need to touch our planet to take our energy and resources. From there, it was easy to conquer. All they had to do was inject portions of their dark power into magnetic temple points stationed among Ashtanabo. Lavenai's life force was sucked out and placed into their formerly desolate planet.

Much of Lavenai accepted a liberator from the plagues and desolation, but some of us stayed resolved to fight back against our oppressors. It was a weak force at first, striking against propaganda centers and supply depots, but after a key member of our rebellion was killed at the hands of a proditor a few years back, our efforts increased tenfold.

Our original plans of attack have always been an uphill battle, but there was always an avenue that would buy us a rare advantage. A plan that involved one of us going to the Imnicus itself and infiltrating their ranks. To bring an end to the Arris reign, we would need to be strategic.

If successful, we could assassinate the Colum, ending the reign of terror.

But Balistar Arris was smart. He didn't set up a dictatorship when he took over. He set up a hierarchy to ensure that, even if his heir died, there would always be someone to take his place and keep Lavenai chained forever.

So it falls to me to infiltrate an impenetrable space station in search of a weakness to exploit. Information can win wars, after all. Assuming I survive long enough to find it.

Dimitri continues, "You know, Lucinda wouldn't let you go if she thought you wouldn't make it back."

"I know." Yet there's an ache in my belly, just like anytime I think about the Imnicus mission, so I try to keep it out of my mind. But sometimes it's unavoidable, like now when Dimitri brings it up or during the countless planning meetings we've had every week for years.

The worst thought is losing Dimitri, or rather, him losing me. I'm his only blood relative still alive as he is mine. In fact, I see him more like a brother than a cousin. To leave him alone—I don't want to face it. But I will go to the Imnicus to avenge my aunt, uncle, and parents' deaths.

"Listen, if I don't make it back—"

"Stop," he interrupts. "It won't be the end. I know it. You'll gain intel, steal a thing or two. Next thing you know, you'll be in an escape pod and back to causing chaos with me."

I smile. "Yes. You're right."

Deep down, I know the price of failure. The strongest of the proditors live on the Imnicus, and if I'm captured, my fate will be worse than death.

Lucinda paces in the middle of the U-shaped table with holographic images surrounding her. An ivory pendant holds silver-gray bangs off her delicate cheeks. Even in her forties, she still has this girlish air to her features. She is fierce and has committed her life to the cause more than anyone I know.

Because unlike all of us, Lucinda Demille-Watts actually met Balistar Arris.

He was apparently unassuming at first, someone she thought was a simple business contact for her organization's new endeavors. But it was all a front, and not long after, Balistar attacked Lavenai.

Shortly after, she met my and Dimitri's parents, and they all worked tirelessly to make this base their own and recruit members.

Of course, Lucinda was the only one of them to make it through that idea alive.

"Before we get started, do you three have any questions?" Lucinda asks, her hands laced behind her back.

"Have you confirmed the ship at the Ashtanaban docking bay will depart tomorrow for the Imnicus?" Oliver, another assassin, asks.

Lucinda smiles. "I guess we'll get right into it then. Yes, the ship is still planning on making the journey to the Imnicus. Dimitri, have you still been tracking that rookie guard?"

Dimitri flips through a small notebook scrawled in indecipherable handwriting. "Yes. She's shifted some of her routines, but her usual walking route remains the same. She'll be passing through the textile district around eleven."

"Good." Lucinda taps her fingers on the table. "No oversights, no emotions, no unnecessary items. One hair out of place could mean the end." Lucinda eyes all of us. "That doesn't just apply to Margot once she's on the Imnicus. It also applies to everything before then. Got it?"

We nod in tandem.

Lucinda was reluctant to send me from the beginning, considering the risk. Everything about the Imnicus is mysterious to

Lavenai. From what we know, the Colum and military personnel live aboard. That's all.

I don't know if I plan on staying under the guise of a guard the entire time, considering the knowledge involved. My best bet is to become a newly hired servant or maid. They have to have them. I can't imagine a man as ruthless as the Colum doing his own laundry.

After the meeting, Lucinda calls me into her office. I sit with her in the room made of glass walls, overlooking one of the larger hallway systems. She likes keeping an eye on us, even when she's deep in her work. Many of us in the rebellion are in our twenties and thirties with some even younger. Children of older members, or orphans whose parents were killed by proditors or the war. She unofficially adopted many of us after the takeover happened.

We sit at a small table in the corner on green velvet chairs. She pours me tea from her favorite black teapot. It's geometric and asymmetrical and very Ashtanaban. Of course, the only way to get something like that is to get in good graces with a crime lord or smuggler, of which Lucinda knows many.

"How are you handling things?" Lucinda asks.

"Exactly the way I need to."

"Remember, if you say the word, we can call everything off. With the danger involved, nobody would blame you."

I fiddle with a chip in the teacup. "To abandon this mission would be to betray Lavenai."

Lucinda shakes her head. "The same cut-and-dry mindset your father had. You know, I didn't train you to be a mindless sleeper agent."

I pause in the middle of my sip. "Do we have sleeper agents?"

"And the ability to miss the point like your mother." She undoes the clip from her hair, letting her bangs hang free. Her shoulders relax into the chair.

I take a deep breath. "You know, I've never even seen photographs, but somehow I dream of them all the time."

"That's important." Lucinda takes a sip of her tea. "To have something you're fighting for. Of course we want to save Lavenai more than anything, but what Balistar took from us makes this personal. Anytime you feel like you can't do it, think of them."

I smile, placing my hand on the back of hers. "Is that what you do when you feel weak? You think of *him*?" I don't say her husband's name. His name brings Lucinda more pain than Balistar's name ever will.

Lucinda stares at the table. "There's never been a day that I haven't."

Chapter 29

Past

I check my watch, tapping my foot. Water drips from the ceiling of the musty basement in the abandoned building. *What's taking them so long?*

Even if Dimitri and Oliver get here in the next five minutes, that leaves me less than thirty minutes to change into the guard's armor, get to the docking bay, and board the ship. *Gods, I hope they are both all right.*

Finally, the door whips open and two sets of boots thump down the concrete steps. A large bag hangs over Dimitri's shoulder; one large enough for a body.

"How did it go?" I ask.

Oliver's eyes are glassed over. "She defended herself till the end."

Dimitri's face is pale. I know he kills people all the time on missions, but they're rarely ever women.

The boys set the bag on the ground and drag the body out. She's still dressed in the uniform, her face covered with the helmet. I kneel next to her, and as I slide the helmet off, Dimitri turns his head, pretending to notice something behind him.

Before I cover her face with a handkerchief, I see the swirls of purple and green on the side of her neck from where they injected the toxin.

Once she's undressed, Oliver kisses his little finger and momentarily places it on her temple, a sign of finality in Ashtanaban culture. I assist him in sliding her back into the body bag. Dimitri holds the uniform in one arm and the helmet in the other.

"No cameras saw you?" I ask.

Dimitri shakes his head and hands over the suit. "Get dressed. We're already behind schedule."

Behind an old shower curtain, I change into the dark gray suit, ignoring that a dead girl wore them just minutes earlier. After I apply the top portion, I go to take off my necklace, but the clasp gets stuck and I know we're running out of time. I tuck it down my uniform and make a mental note to dispose of it later.

"How do I look?" I spin as if I'm going to a ball.

Oliver sneers. "Like royalty."

I roll my eyes.

Dimitri carries the last piece of the uniform over to me—the guard's circular helmet, consisting of convex triangle shapes with two mesh gaps for vision.

He secures it on my head. "Ready?"

"As ready as I'll ever be."

"Let me show you how to use this. We don't have long." He takes my forearm and presses a button on the slim, metal wrist piece. "This is your interface. Our sources tell us that the wristband will get you into secure areas of the Imnicus just by tapping it to doorways."

Dimitri places his hand on my shoulder then slides my rebellion-assigned tablet into my pouch. "Take this in case you need to send a distress signal. We can't save you, but at least we will know if something happens."

"Nothing will happen." I hug my cousin tightly.

"Now go. We will watch you from vantage points."

As I walk down one of the many streets of Lavenai covered in neon lights, I try to block out the sounds of the jumbotrons playing advertisements and spewing new laws decreed by Ashtanabo's arbitors.

Even before the occupation, Lavenai's technology was highly advanced. Ashtanabo ensures our high-tech remains, which makes it easier for them to observe defective citizens. Nearly every street, shop, and attraction has cameras and microphones. We have a whole rebellion scavenger unit assigned purely to find surveillance blind spots.

Thin, overworked citizens pass me. Those who can afford it wear thin respirators to protect their lungs from the harsh pollution. Their eyes are dark and sunken, faces overly defined.

As I turn a corner, only a block away from my destination, my chest tightens.

A figure stands on top of a three-story building, inspecting the crowds who walk even faster in his presence. His hood and mask conceal his identity, and his cape moves with the light gusts of wind.

A proditor.

Proditors wear their masks for the same reasons an executioner does. Not too long ago, a proditor tortured and killed a shopkeeper for suspicion of working with our rebellion. He had no association with us, but one sarcastic joke about knowing us was picked up on surveillance. That joke cost him his life.

A rare survivor of their torture lives alone in the crime district. He's mute now. Some say the proditors made him feel like he had died, only to reveal it was a mind trick, bringing him back to torture him once again—a hundred times.

To my relief, the proditor's gaze doesn't touch me and instead washes over other parts of the crowd. Still, I grip the long gun closer to my chest.

I bite my lip hard enough to stop the thought. *There's no time to get scared now. I need to keep going.*

As I near the Ashtanaban docking bay, my muscles tighten. The surrounding electrical fences are high, and there are cameras seemingly everywhere. Other guards approach the heavily guarded entrance, and I stay close to them. We all tap our wrists to the security sensor one at a time as we pass inside.

The transportation ship to the Imnicus is grand and massive. A brass-like color with purple streams of energy runs vertically through it. It's fancier and more luxurious than any building in Lavenai.

As I near it, a bell rings and guards form a line to board. I find a place behind another female guard, studying everything about her uniform and demeanor. Her posture is rigid, so I adjust mine to match it as I wait.

That's when I notice something strange. On my uniform is a red stripe on the right shoulder, but on hers, there is none.

I raise my chin to see the other guards in front of her and begin to panic.

Nobody has the red stripe—except me.

Why is there one on my suit? Is it a sign of rank? I know the guard we took out is due to be transferred to the Imnicus today, but I don't know if this stripe affects anything. Was she supposed to change into something else before boarding?

I should excuse myself to use a privy then escape back to the base. Before I can shift to leave, the gates to the docks slam shut. The lines move and two high-ranking officers scan the identification codes of every guard before they are allowed to ascend the ramp.

If you're caught, your fate will be worse than death.

I have no choice but to go forward. I'll need to lie, cheat, and manipulate to get through this.

As my turn nears, my adrenaline spikes even higher.

"Next," an officer calls.

I step up, parroting the posture of the guard walking parallel to me.

The middle-aged officer looks at me sternly. "Arm."

I raise my arm straight in front of me. He waves his wand over my wrist.

No manifest record, the robotic voice on the wand says.

My knees are on the verge of buckling.

Frustrated, he tries again, and it gives the same error message. "What's your number?" A hint of suspicion lies in his voice.

Oh gods, what number did Dimitri say in his meetings? "808," I say the words quickly to keep him from hearing the shake in my voice.

The officer snatches a tablet from behind him, grumbling words under his breath. He types in my number and brings up a holographic profile of 808. A virtual image of her appears on the screen.

Another officer steps over. "Is there a problem here?"

The first one continues to sort through files in the tablet. "I can't find her manifest in the record. It's quite strange, really."

The other one points to the red stripe on my shoulder. "Oh, are you a rookie?"

I grip my gun tighter. Without hesitation, I nod.

"Commander Aisil mentioned that a few rookies would join us over the upcoming weeks."

The first officer's shoulder's relax. "Well, that explains it then. The Imnicus often forgets to enter them into our manifest. Move along now."

I nod and quickly ascend the ramp, biting into my lower lip. How could her record not be on the official manifest? Isn't that what Dimitri used to track which guard to assassinate?

There's no time to overthink it. The inside is filled with rows of leather seats. I find a seat as far away from others as possible. The last thing I need is to start casual conversations with one of the guards. The risk of slipping up is too great.

The guards chatter with one another until the last one gets settled and the ramp shuts.

A robotic voice plays on the intercom, *Welcome to Imnicus Transport. On arrival, please report to your assigned postings.*

That will be the most complicated part of the mission. I had thought switching disguises when I got there to a maid would be the best option. But now that I know 808 is expected to start rookie service, I know I need to keep with it. She looks similar enough to me that I can pass as her and say that I dyed my hair recently.

As the ship ascends, I think about how rare this is. How many Laven have had the chance to fly in a ship since Balistar's rule began?

When the nose of the ship aims for the sky, I brace myself for an impact that never comes, and soon we leave Lavenai's atmosphere.

I peer out the window at Lavenai and its purple glow. It would be beautiful if I didn't know why it was that color.

The ship adjusts its angle. Next thing I know, it shoots like lightning toward our destination. Guards murmur to each other, unfazed by the view and speed, taking their freedom for granted.

An hour later, the ship slows, and as it does, I see what I've only seen on clear nights.

The green glow of Ashtanabo chants of its planet's prosperity. A place where flora and food grow easily. The sight of it makes my stomach sour knowing it's only that way from stealing Lavenai's life force.

As we approach the outer edge of Ashtanabo's atmosphere, something massive comes into view. It's silver and metal, like the outworking of a ship or space station, but it has peaks, reminding me of a castle.

"Docking in T-minus one minute," the intercom says.

Guards stretch their necks. Others unbuckle their seatbelts.

I shove my awe and anger to the back of my mind. This isn't a time to gawk. I need to focus.

When the ship lands in the docking bay, reality hits me hard. From this point on, I'm completely on my own.

Chapter 30

Past

I descend the ramp in an organized line with the others and into the enormous docking bay with my mouth gaped. Between the ship-entrance to the Imnicus and outer space, there is an invisible shield to keep in the oxygen. The view makes me feel like I'm actually standing in space, gazing at the stars.

It's a challenge to keep my posture inline with the others as we pass by over a hundred ships of different shapes, sizes, and uses. Some ships seem to be for intergalactic combat, others for transportation or even taking joyrides.

As we reach the docking bay's exit, Imnicus officers scan the lines of new guards before they can step into the hallways on the Imnicus. Considering how the docking bay is built, this doesn't seem routine. Unless they suspect there is an intruder.

The thought makes me shrink back, but I have no choice but to keep moving forward. There is no way they suspect I'm here, not so soon. And they'd send a proditor, not some officer, if they suspected anything.

They choose random people to scan and let others through without inspection. I do my best to predict how to avoid being scanned again. I turn my head to a guard next to me and pretend to listen into his casual conversation with another guard. The ruse works, and I pass through without being pulled to the side.

Finally, we exit into the white-walled hallways, and I can't help but smile beneath my helmet.

I'm on the Imnicus.

This plan has been in the works for years, and now I can do what I need to do for Lucinda, for the rebellion, and for Lavenai.

I slow my steps until I trickle behind the rest of the group, then I slip into a nearby one-room privy. After shutting the door, I set the gun on the sink and free myself from the helmet. A small laugh escapes me, and I examine my reflection in the mirror. The formerly tight bun high on my head has loosened, and strands of sweaty hair frame my face. Mentally, I'm exhausted, but there is no time to rest until I find where 808 is supposed to be. I splash my face with water before replacing the helmet.

At the end of the hallway, there is a pair of sliding doors with the words *Imnicus: South* overhead. I expect the doors to slide open on their own, but they don't. On the right side of the door, there is a scanner. I tap my wrist to it, but it doesn't budge.

"Level three door. Access denied," an automated voice says. *"Level one employees must use the A terminal entrance."*

Level one. It's not much clearance, but it will do for now.

When I find the correct walkway, it leads me to a command center filled with military personnel sitting behind computers on a large tiered platform. With Lavenai forbidden from using spacecraft, I'm surprised by the amount of officers. Ashtanabo has beaten us completely into submission in terms of aviation. We are prisoners living behind the cool steel bars of a polluted atmosphere. But I suppose we are not the only two planets in the galaxy.

Once I find myself in the east wing of the Imnicus, I finally start seeing servants. Some are cleaning, and others are gossiping as they walk together to their next task.

A female officer approaches me. I notice a gun strapped to her waist belt. "Are you our new arrival, rookie?"

I straighten up. "Correct."

"Red stripes stay in the military dorms."

"I'm so sorry. The Imnicus is so big, and I got a little lost."

"No worries, right this way."

I follow her down to the correct dorms and she opens the door into my new room. It's more than anything I've had for myself, though I'm sure an Ashtanaban would call it small. It has a bed, desk, and dresser. More importantly, I will have the room all to myself.

"Report to the dining hall in an hour." The woman spins on her heels stiffly and marches down the hall.

A month passes, and nobody on the Imnicus has caught on. I've eaten meals and attended trainings, but no one has noticed that I'm a Laven. Somehow, I've managed not to bump into the Colum. My trainers say he's been away on business in Ashtanabo.

I don't know how I would react if I ever did see him. Would I have to hold back the urge to lunge at him or gouge his eyes out for what his father did to my parents? With my Imnicus-issued gun, it would be so easy to kill him, but I know Lucinda explicitly told me not to.

While out of my dorm, I rarely remove my helmet. I don't want anyone to get to know me too well. The only time people see my face is at meals, and I always pretend to have my nose stuck in some book.

On more than a few occasions, I've been invited to after-shift parties, but I decline every time. The less connections, the fewer questions I have to answer about myself. One slipup about my backstory could get me executed.

Still, I wish I could be part of it. But I'm not here to make friends or live out my fantasies about what a normal life would look like.

It only takes a few additional weeks for me to receive level two security clearance.

It changes the game completely. I'm able to open doors to rooms I wasn't allowed in previously and pretend to inspect them, all the while trying to find hints of anything Lucinda could use against the Colum.

I don't want to transfer any information on my flash drive until I know a ship is leaving for Lavenai. The ships on the Imnicus fly to Ashtanabo all the time, but the Laven-bound ones leave once every month or two, at least for the guards.

Today, I am assigned to patrol a circular hallway. It's tedious work, but it gives me a chance to keep memorizing the halls of the Imnicus.

I wonder how Dimitri is doing. Maybe he's taken on more freelance missions for crime lords, or maybe he finally had the guts to ask out the girl he likes in the rebellion. I miss him and Lucinda every day. I wish I could use the tablet for more than a final distress signal and update them, but the Imnicus would immediately pick up the transmission.

Lost in my thoughts, I don't process the footsteps heading in my direction.

That is until I see him.

I nearly trip over my own feet as I come to a halt and step out of the way. The man who leads the group of three officers and a proditor is none other than Milo Arris, the Colum.

My heart thumps as I watch him. I've seen very few photos of him, but I'd never forget a face like that. His raven hair and sharp features may even be handsome if he wasn't as evil as his father. Or if he wasn't the reason Lucinda has to keep the rebellion stronger than ever as he continues his father's legacy.

He wears a cape with his dark armor-like uniform. It's a cultural symbol on Ashtanabo to signify power and authority. Proditors sometimes wear them, as well as arbitors and other political leaders.

I study the proditor with him next and his dark eyes, and I'm more fearful of him than the Colum. Proditors are loyal yet prideful in their roles. After all, they could destroy the Colum and take control of the Imnicus if they desired.

I try to make my stance more confident and keep my chin high as they pass.

The Colum gives me a hardened stare, but I keep my posture confident and collected, thankful for the helmet protecting my cracking expression. It feels like his eyes are on me for a lifetime.

Soon, he concentrates back on the path in front of him, and once he's past, I zip down the opposite hallway, releasing a breath of relief.

My fear quickly turns to anger. He lives here in luxury, protected in space. No matter how much Lavens rebel against the guards on land, there's no way we could ever hurt him without a fleet of ships. I'm no assassin, but if I were, I'd take the Colum out and I'd make it hurt.

Lucinda is right though. If Milo died, someone else would simply take his place and Lavenai may be even worse off. All things considered, Milo is still a better Colum than Balistar, and we know that an arbitor taking his place would be even worse.

During one of the military personnel meetings, an officer passes out a sign-up sheet for those who want an extension of their Imnicus training, meaning that those who don't take it will be sent back to Lavenai.

I don't sign my name and pass it on to the next person. The ship leaves tomorrow, and who knows when another one will transfer us back.

This is my chance to transfer data onto my flash drive. If I don't do so tonight, I may not have another shot if I ever want to see the rebellion again.

Once my shift ends for the day, I trek back out in the direction of the south wing. Even though everyone is on different sleeping and eating schedules, the Imnicus most respects the time zone of Ashtanabo's capital, meaning the lights are dimmed in most hallways.

I startle when one of the bulbs starts to flicker. I didn't think anything on the Imnicus, even a simple lightbulb, was capable of malfunctioning on such an advanced spacecraft. I ignore it and find the computer room.

After scanning my wristband, I flip the lights on, illuminating the rows of computers. This room is used for research by soldiers still in training. The computers contain information about Ashtanabo and the Imnicus, and though it's not confidential information to Ashtanaban trainees, it is to Lavens. Anytime I researched here, I fought the urge to drag files to my flash drive and run.

I approach one of the computers and plug in my flash drive. After a check of my surroundings and noting no cameras, I access the files with my security clearance and release a breathy laugh. Everywhere I search, there are manifest logs, employee records, and even a map of the Imnicus itself.

I drag the Imnicus map over to the folder of my flash drive. As I do, every monitor goes as black as night, leaving me in complete darkness.

The room glows red as sirens begin to blare.

Shit, shit, shit. If I can get back to my dorm undetected, I can still salvage this. This could be a coincidence. I don't know that the sirens are going off because of me.

I rush to the exit, but before I reach it, the doors slam shut and lock.

I pound my fist on the door and frantically tap my wrist to the security sensor.

Access denied.

Access denied.

Access denied.

I spin to find something in the computer room to pry the door open. My vision blurs and my ears ring, like standing up too fast after a nap. I rub my temple, trying to ignore it. But when the ringing increases to a violently high pitch, I know that what's happening to me has to be as a result of poison or . . .

I cover my ears, but it only gets worse, like a thousand knives stabbing into my skull. I lose my balance and fall on my side.

What . . . What's happening to me?

I curl up in a fetal position. The ringing is so shattering that I can't hear my own screaming.

As the world grows blurrier, a pair of boots steps out from behind one of the pillars.

No . . .

All at once, the pain releases and a black static coats my vision, the room falling away.

Chapter 31

Past

My wrists sting and my head pounds. There's a faint buzz in my ears, and when I open my eyes, I jolt enough to rattle the chains holding my arms above my head.

I'm in a sterile white cell with lights so bright I want to close my eyes again. I'm kneeling on the ground, my ankles also in chains.

No. Gods, please no.

I think I'm going to be sick. After everything, I failed. Failed the rebellion, Lucinda and Dimitri, and even myself.

But it's not over yet. I'm still alive, which means they want information. All I have left is my resilience and my refusal to spit out the truth, no matter what they throw at me.

If training has taught me anything, it's that the next few hours or days of my life will not be pleasant. I think back to the rumors of the proditors' torture tactics. If the proditors on land are as bad as I've heard, then the Imnicus proditors are so much worse. Unless I escape, I will be a lobotomized shell of myself if they don't end up killing me.

I lift off my knees and balance on the balls of my feet to give the chains more lag. It enables me to bring my head toward my hand and reach for the sole bobby pin that should still be in my hair.

To my relief, I am able to grab it between my thumb and middle finger. I bend my wrist to try and fit it in the manual override lock. I curse to myself. The angle burns horribly, but I have to try . . . I have to . . .

"That won't work."

Without warning, the chains zip higher, pulling me up to the point where I have to stand on my tiptoes just to breathe. Pain blazes through my shoulders, making me yell out. I grind my teeth together, doing anything to distract myself.

"You made it farther than anyone ever has."

The voice comes from behind me. Someone has been in here watching me this entire time as I struggled to escape. He was probably holding back laughter.

Footsteps come closer until the man is standing close enough for me to feel his body heat on my back. If this is a proditor, the pain in my shoulders is a mercy.

"Margot Tavish, is it?" I can feel his breath on the back of my skull as he speaks, which means he isn't wearing a mask. Whoever this is, he isn't a proditor, but maybe a commander sent me to warm me up before the real horrors begin.

But the real question is, how does he know my name?

"You may as well get it over with," I say. "Beat me, torture me, I don't care."

I can hear him turn on his heels and start walking again.

My body goes numb when I see him. The last person I expected to be interrogating me in an Imnicus holding cell.

Milo Arris himself.

He's holding my tablet in his ring-clad hands, and on it, there is a small label with my name. The only reason I put that on in the first place was because Dimitri kept taking the wrong one. I don't keep a lot of sensitive documents on it. But there is one. One that could end the rebellion completely. One I didn't even consider deleting when Dimitri handed me my tablet.

The file that holds the locations of fifteen of the sixteen rebellion base entrances.

"There's no need to hold back or lie. For instance, I know you're part of the rebellion." The Colum walks forward, his expression too calm. Too merciful. He reaches for my collarbone and grabs my pendant. "I guess we can't be on our best game all the time. Truthfully, if you weren't wearing this, I may have dropped the matter of data transferring entirely and blamed it on you being a rookie."

I should have taken it off before I left for the mission. Gods, why didn't I?

The only solace I have is the fact that my tablet is still locked with a password-protected pin, and unless he finds a way to get me to speak, the rebellion will stay safe.

The Colum takes a deep breath and paces with hands behind his back. "You're probably wondering why I had a proditor following you too. Oh, you didn't know? You may have made it far, but it was pure luck and happenstance. The second I laid eyes on you, I knew you didn't belong. Even for a rookie, your walk was different. Foolishly defiant. Very Laven."

I remember the flickering light as I entered the computer room. I hadn't thought much of it at the time. If I had known a proditor was following me, I would have booked it right back to the dorm and chosen to go back to the rebellion empty-handed.

Nothing I say can help me now. All I have to do is wait and endure. I will never betray the rebellion. The Colum will have to take an arm and a leg.

No oversights, no emotions, no unnecessary items. One hair out of place could mean the end, Lucinda had said, and how right she had been.

"Well, then." He taps the tablet against his opposite palm. "Give me the code and I'll see that you're returned to Lavenai unharmed."

"Do what you need to do." My throat bobs. "You may as well kill me."

His eyes rake over my body before finding my eyes again. "Oh, I won't kill you. But after I'm finished with you, you'll wish I had. Your body is strong, which means you'll last longer than most of the traitors I have to deal with. In times like these, it's almost a curse."

The Colum sets the tablet down and strides toward me until he's almost chest to chest. He looks down at me with a small smile on his face, watching me struggle to breathe from holding myself up on my toes.

I spit on his face.

He frowns, wiping the saliva off his cheek, before slowly moving his hand behind my head and gripping my hair. He yanks it hard, forcing my head at an uncomfortable angle. "You'll regret that."

I go to spit on him again, just to get one last jab in before it all starts. But before I can, there's a painful blow to my head before everything goes dark again.

Dimitri once told me light could be found even in the darkest places.

After that day, after everything I was put through, I knew for certain he was wrong.

As my eyes flutter open, I stare up at the dim lights on the ceiling in the dark-gray room. My wrists and ankles are bound to a medical table.

I flinch to the hiss of a door. Whoever entered, I cannot see them, even as I strain my head.

As footsteps near the table, the lights start to flicker. Chills shoot through my bones. I turn my head to my left to catch a glimpse, but all I see are grotesque instruments hanging on the wall. My body feels overly sensitive as I imagine what it would be like to feel blades and needles on my skin.

No amount of training can really prepare you for torture.

The flickering of the lights becomes worse until they go out completely, leaving me in complete darkness. My breath shakes as

I wait for whatever is going to come. The things they will do to me to make me submit.

I shimmy against the bindings, trying to find any weakness in the leather restraints. The lights turn back on all at once, and sitting on the edge of the table near my legs is a proditor.

As a child, the teenagers would tell Dimitri and me scary stories about the proditors. *Don't touch my stuff or I will tell Proditor Brawns to punish you*, they had said.

Rumors are always flooding around Lavenai about proditor tactics used to gain information. Some say they can read minds. Others say they can step into your thoughts and memories to twist them into nightmares.

The proditor palms his mask and removes it, placing it on my stomach. My jaw tightens as he smiles at me wickedly. His hood falls off his curly golden-blonde hair.

All I have against a proditor is the illusion of strength. "I—I thought it was against protocol to show your face," I say.

He smiles at my shaky voice. "There's no need to protect my identity when you won't be around long enough to tell the tale of the man who broke you."

I close my eyes for a second and try to collect myself before speaking again. "Isn't it cruel to hurt a woman?"

"You say that as if women are weak, but no, your kind is far from it. That's why you're the most fun. You last so long. So stubborn, so cruel, even up until your last breath." This proditor speaks like he enjoys the pain more than the result, making him more dangerous than even the worst proditors. He leans forward and runs his gloved fingers down my face, then tucks stray strands behind my ear. "Is that what you want, Margot? Do you want to have fun with me?"

I shake my head. My bottom lip trembles.

The golden-haired proditor chuckles and sits up, peeling off his gloves.

No, no, no.

He reaches forward and presses his thumbs into my temples.

I can still hear everything in the room, but my brain immediately dissociates. My body feels like it's on a bed of pillows, falling into a blissful sleep filled with sweet dreams.

Then there's pain. Horrible pain. Crows peck at my eyes and skin while I lie there, helpless to defend myself. They rip me to shreds as they caw. Tears run down my face, but no matter how hard I try, I cannot scream.

Already, I feel myself breaking, as if I'm about to turn a corner into death, but I know that's a pipe dream. Death is a mercy. Death doesn't exist here, at least not yet. It's what makes proditor powers even more cruel.

All at once, the pain ceases and the room comes back into focus. Mere minutes may have passed, but it feels like it's been hours. Sweat beads on my skin, and I can't seem to catch my breath.

The proditor brushes his hands together. "It doesn't have to be this way, you know. Tell us the code, and Milo will even send you back to Lavenai. Not every screw will be in place, of course." He pauses, as if considering something. "Though, if I can be honest,

I hope you don't give in, at least not this easily. I want you to put up a fight. In fact, I'd even enjoy it."

I pant. "I will never betray Lavenai or the rebellion."

He smirks. "I'm glad to hear it. Now, where were we?" He wraps one hand around my neck and places the other over my nose and mouth. He squeezes.

I buckle against my restraints and try to fight him off. My lungs scream and tears run down my eyes and onto his hands. Any cry or shriek is muffled. *Please*, my eyes beg.

Once more, the doors hiss open. "Knox, that's enough for now."

Knox frowns. "Oh, come on now, we were just getting to the good part."

The Colum paces to the end of the table where I can see him. Knox is still squeezing my neck.

"I said stop. She's no use to us dead. Save it for later," the Colum says.

Knox rolls his eyes. "If you say so."

I gasp for air, and when I look down at my hands. My nail beds are blue. No matter how bad the Colum is, Knox is so much worse. He craves causing others pain. Quenches his thirst with it. It has to be against some kind of code.

"I'll assume she hasn't said a word yet," the Colum asks.

Knox pats my abdomen, making my muscles tense under his touch. "No. She's stubborn as ever."

"Unbind her." The Colum paces over to the side of the table.

Knox undoes my restraints, and before I can even consider fighting one of them, the Colum shoves me off the table.

I land on the ground with a thud, my shoulder on the brink of dislocating. I try to crawl away, but the Colum grabs my hair and drags me to the more open area of the room and throws me again.

Does he really expect me to take all of this willingly? I push up onto my side and look at him like he's a rotten, spoiled child. I think of how he wouldn't even be here if it weren't for his father. How, if his father hadn't killed millions, he would have less than I do.

The oxygen-deprived thought makes me grin, even though I know I shouldn't.

The Colum takes a step forward with curled fists, like he's been given that look before. "Wipe that smile off your face before I do."

Before he or Knox can grab me, I spring to my feet and sock the Colum in his jaw. Knox lunges forward and twists my hair around his hand and pulls me back before I can strike again.

It feels so good to see the blood trailing down the corners of the Colum's mouth. He holds one side of his jaw as steps toward me. I fall back farther into Knox's chest.

To my surprise, he doesn't strike me back. Instead, he swipes the blood off his face and wipes it off on Knox's uniform. He turns around and heads for the door, tapping his ring to the security sensor.

Without looking back, he voices a command that makes my knees want to buckle. "Knox, you and the others will work in shifts. I want a proditor with her every hour of the day. You can use any method you wish to get that code, but leave her alive and her mind intact enough to answer. If any of you kill her, I'll slit your throat myself."

I can feel Knox's grin against my scalp. "Of course, Colum."

Chapter 32

Past

One after the other, Imnicus proditors are sent to break me into submission. Somehow, I manage to keep the code safe. Though, I admit there are times where I am weak enough to submit, but I'm too battered to find the words. When my mind is at its lowest, ready to give in, my body does not cooperate, too broken to even move my lips. There's something about proditor torment that lacerates the mind so greatly. I can temporarily fall out of their spell and dissociate into a world of my own.

Dimitri and I are children again, running through one of the Laven mushroom fields, passing farmers and women collecting the harvest in metal-woven baskets. One farmer chases the two of us out of the fields with his shovel while we laugh and escape. Then, Lucinda appears at the field's edge with folded arms. She scolds us before bringing us back to the rebel base and washes us up for dinner.

Each time I regain consciousness, it's in the blissful rest between proditor shifts. Blissful to my body, but a secondary torture to my mind as I wait for the new set of hands upon my skin that force me back into that mental prison.

Each proditor has a different method of torment, and it does not take me long to learn them intimately. Some stick completely to mental simulations and others use more traditional methods. One likes to throw me off buildings. Another likes to project the illusion of bugs crawling up my nose and inside my ears.

Knox likes pain. Real flesh and blood pain.

As Knox begins a torture too horrible to recall, I slip back into the recesses of my mind. Dimitri and I sit under my comforter with a flashlight, reading a picture book I received for my birthday. We quietly snicker at the silly doodles and quickly turn the flashlight off anytime we think Lucinda may be checking on us.

I come out of this memory to Knox staring down at me, his smile wide. My breathing is ragged as my body twitches.

As the door hisses open, I bite down. There are only so many times I can do this before I give up the code without even realizing it.

"You're getting awfully close to breaking Milo's rule," a new voice says to Knox. "You're going to leave her brain-dead."

"Relax, Alarik, I know what I'm doing." Knox peers down at me again. "I'll see you in a few hours."

After Knox leaves the room, I lie there in anticipation of the new proditor, Alarik, and wait for it to start all over again. Though other proditors have taken more than one shift, this proditor hasn't been in to see me yet.

I feel my lips moving by themselves to speak. I think I'm begging him, but everything feels so muddy that I don't even know what is reality anymore.

Alarik says nothing and undoes the bindings of the table. I'm too weak to even contemplate trying to overpower him. He slides his arms underneath me and picks me up bridal style and heads toward one of the empty walls.

None of the other proditors have . . . *touched me*. Would this one? Is that his method of torture? Why else would he bring me to a wall but to give him better access?

I whimper against his chest and close my eyes. Maybe I can find that world again with Dimitri before he starts. I can pretend like this isn't happening at all.

But once we reach the wall, Alarik presses his own back to it and slides down to sit with me in his arms. He undoes the top part of his armor and presses my cheek against the skin of his chest. "This will save your mind. Now, sleep while you can. I'll keep an eye on the door."

Is this proditor . . . helping me? I'm still too out of it to question why. Already, a blanket of comfort washes over me. Before I can muster up enough strength to even find words, I'm asleep. It's a sweet, restful sleep too, one that he must be using his crows to make possible.

Even in my dreams, I can sense my brain rewiring back to how it was before I was captured. Every image is sweet and free of pain. If I could stay here forever, I would.

Once I awaken, I feel completely different. I don't feel the imprints of the crows leftover from before and can think cogent thoughts. Whatever this proditor did, he saved parts of me that were mere hours from tumbling off the cliff.

I look up at him, where he rests his head against the wall with his eyes pinned on the door. When he looks down at me, I hold my breath.

"There isn't much time left before my shift is over," Alarik says.

I part my lips in disbelief. With everything I know about the proditors, what this one is doing would be considered treason. "I don't understand . . . Why are you helping me?"

"I'm not doing this for you. I'm doing it for me." I can tell he wants to say more, but he holds it back. Whatever personal reasons he has are his business, but I can't help but wonder.

Despite how much Alarik has helped me, the time until his next shift will be hell. Without him, I was at risk of either going irreversibly mad or caving enough to spill rebellion secrets.

Alarik carries me back to the table and instructs me to sit up while he gives me water and disinfects wounds. He pulls an energy bar out of his pocket and I nibble on it the best I can, though I still don't have much of an appetite.

When it's almost time for him to go, he helps me lie back and begins to strap me back in. Even with how gentle he is, the sound of every click shoots panic through my limbs.

"Thank you." I mutter the only words I'm able to bring myself to say, and I mean every word of it.

"I'll bring more water later. In the meantime, do what you can to endure it."

And I do, every grueling, horrible second of it.

By the time Alarik comes back, gods know how many hours later, I'm back to not being able to speak or move. But like before, he lets me sleep in his arms. With him, I even feel safe enough to let down my guard and relax my muscles. When I'm done sleeping, he brings me to the table and helps me sit upright to assist me in drinking water.

I take a gulp of the water and then take a deep breath. "Will they kill me soon?"

"It's hard to say. You've lasted far longer than anyone expected, even without my help." He avoids looking at me.

So, it's a no. The Colum will keep torturing me for years if it means getting what he wants. "If I'm still alive in ten hours, will you . . ."

I don't even have to finish the sentence for him to place a hand on my shoulder. My heart shatters at his refusal to answer the question. Though, I remember what the Colum said—if any of the proditors kill me, he'll kill them.

"Drink some more before I go." Alarik raises the canister to my mouth.

"What's this?" a voice says. We didn't even hear him come in.

Alarik pushes me down onto the table hard enough for me to grunt.

"Are you . . . helping her?" he says, trudging up to Alarik.

"Of course not, Crux." Alarik laughs nervously and shakes his head. "It's that bastard Knox. He's so hard on her that she's practically half-dead when it's time for my shift. It's a waste of time when she's barely alive."

My heart pounds as Crux folds his arms. "That's true. Knox has been particularly harsh."

"You see my point, then." Alarik attaches the canister to his utility belt. "She's all yours."

"You still have five minutes left."

Alarik goes still. "There's not much I can do in five minutes."

"Sure you can." Crux pulls a knife from his belt. "Let's work together."

The proditors have done a lot to me, but knives have never been a part of this yet. Alarik never locked me back into the restraints, so I try to roll off.

Crux grabs me and hauls my wrists over my head, pinning them hard enough to nearly shatter my bones, using his own grip instead of the restraints to keep me subdued. Alarik tries to play the part by grabbing my ankles roughly and locking them into the restraints. But I can see his hesitancy, which means Crux can too.

"Alarik, Alarik," Crux taunts. "Going soft again, I see?"

"I already told you. It's not like that."

"I haven't seen this look in your eye since the first time Balistar made you kill." Crux motions to a clear bottle of liquid over on the counter. "Grab that and bring it over here. Unless, of course, you want me to tell Milo what I saw."

"Don't bring Balistar into this." Alarik tightens his fists. He reluctantly walks over and grabs the liquid. When he comes back over to the table, he slams the bottle down by my head.

Crux leers at Alarik. "Unsheathe one of your daggers. You know what to do. Just like how I taught you." He bends down close to me. "I enjoy showing you Laven how weak you truly are."

Alarik moves up to one of my restrained arms and lays the blade on my skin.

"What are you waiting for? Do it." Crux keeps my wrists restrained with his gloved hands. I now see why he didn't put them back in the restraints. Like this, the blade has better access to the more sensitive parts of my arm.

My breaths grow heavier and more uneven as I wait. Alarik is probably thinking of a way out of this, or a way to make it less painful, or . . .

The blade slices once, carefully and controlled, hitting nerves I didn't know were there. It's not enough to make me scream, but my body jolts, and because Alarik healed my mind already, I can't even fall into some dissociative trance.

"Oh, Alarik, she didn't even make a peep," Crux says. "This time, press deeper, and . . . actually—"

Crux yanks Alarik's hood down and throws his mask to the floor, exposing his dark auburn hair and pale skin. "I want her to see your face while you do it."

Alarik's face is a mixture of sweet and hardened. He looks completely torn up, no matter how hard he's trying to hide it. I can't bear to look at him. I close my eyes and turn my head away.

"No, sweetheart. You don't get the mercy of looking away." Crux lets go of my wrists for a second and grabs my head to face it toward Alarik. He slaps the side of my face to make my eyes open. "You're going to look at him. Know that your weakness caused this."

Alarik's skin has dropped a few shades lighter and my heart shatters.

"Now, don't stall, Alarik. And do it correctly this time or I'll make you do her thighs too."

Alarik's jaw tenses, and he positions the knife on the side of my arm. The pressure is deeper this time, just shy of pressing into muscle, making me grit my teeth. I can't imagine what it will feel like when he—

A sharp slice.

I scream, my entire body writhing.

"Ten more," Crux instructs him and transfers both of my wrists to one hand so he can keep readjusting my head to look at Alarik.

Alarik's bottom lip trembles as he works. The slices are controlled, drawing little blood but finding every little nerve.

Crux rolls his eyes as I scream, so he covers my mouth. I sob into his hand.

By the time the tenth slice is complete, my face is stained with tears. Something about watching Alarik's face makes it ten times worse. Seeing the reluctance in his expression but feeling the skill at which he works makes me almost hate him too.

Crux lets go of my wrists, but I leave my arms in place above my head, worried that if I move the pain will reignite.

"I trained you well." Crux pats Alarik on the back. "These cuts are perfect for what's next."

Alarik's eyes widen, pleading at Crux. "You've proved your point. There is no need."

What's next . . .

Crux shakes off his hood but leaves his mask on. He grabs the bottle next to me and pops the lid off with his thumb.

Alcohol.

No.

He pours the liquid up and down the cuts. I shriek loud enough for half the Imnicus to hear. My eyes practically bulge out of my head. The liquid stings as if thousands of hornets were attacking my skin.

Crux rolls his eyes once again.

It's enough that my mind can no longer quantify the pain and I black out.

I don't know how much time passes after that. It could be minutes, hours, maybe even days. It isn't until ring-adorned knuckles stroke my cheek that I realize I'm on the floor.

"I see you barely obeyed my instructions to keep her alive," the Colum says.

I'm facedown on folded knees with one of my cheeks pressed to the ground. I'm so tired. All I want is sleep, and besides my two naps with Alarik, I haven't slept at all. Even the times I've blacked out or dissociated, I know it wasn't truly sleep.

I start to fall into a dream, too weak to be scared of whatever may be coming. Maybe Crux was right . . . *I'm weak, I'm weak, I'm weak.*

I'm jolted back into reality by a hand yanking me onto my knees by my hair. I yelp, but only out of habit. I could fall asleep right here, even as my follicles are being pulled by Knox holding me up.

The Colum paces in front of me. "How much more must I do for you to break?"

Knox suddenly lets go of me and I barely catch myself. My palms hit the ground and my arms shake for a moment before they give out and my chest is on the floor again.

"Look at you. You can't even hold yourself up anymore," the Colum says.

Once again, I attempt to lift myself, but instead I fall onto my side on the cold floor.

"Just tell me the code and all of this could go away." He squats and rubs my back, the way Lucinda would when I'd wake up with bad dreams.

If I don't die or escape soon, this could go on and on for weeks. Maybe even months or years. I try once more to push myself up, gasping through the pain.

When I hear Crux's laughter behind me, I realize that all the proditors are in the room.

I clench my jaw. To give up would be to prove that Crux was right. That I truly am as weak as he says.

Even if I don't survive, I need to die well.

I continue to push until I'm high enough to meet the Colum's gaze. He's hard to read—a mixture of anger and intrigue.

My lips curl, and I smile as wide as I can. A fit of laughter overtakes me that I can't seem to control, and honestly, I don't want to.

The Colum's face falls.

I make my laugh seem directed at him, and when I do find that place where I'm genuinely laughing at him, it overtakes me to the point where it hurts.

"Stop it."

I don't stop. It's as if someone else has taken over my body. I cackle to the point of needing to cradle my abdomen.

"I said stop!"

Knox kicks my lower back, making me howl and fall to my side. Still, I feel giddy and absolutely delusional.

"Milo, she's delirious. Clearly, her mind broke long ago. It's time to end this," Knox says.

"Crux. Make her sleep," the Colum orders.

A hand strokes the back of my neck, propelling me into a strange place between sleep and reality. A place where I still know where I am, but I feel no pain. It's like lying on a cloud of cotton. Still, I can hear the conversation going on around me.

"All of you leave. Knox, stay."

The other proditors walk past me toward the door, one intentionally stepping on my hand, breaking my fingers, though no pain comes through the trance.

And once they're gone, Knox starts off the conversation eagerly. "Milo, let me end her."

"No, this is the closest we've ever been to finding where the rebellion is hiding."

"She's never going to tell us anything. Let me do us all a favor."

"Your thirst for blood is clouding your judgment. We have her tablet and that's not something to take lightly."

"A tablet she's never going to open." Knox's voice grows increasingly more frustrated. "You promised I could have her if she didn't talk."

"And we don't know that she won't." The Colum pauses for a minute. "There may be another way."

"Which is?"

"The more we push, the more she holds her ground. We need a new approach. She needs to give us the code willingly and unknowingly. The only way to do that is to make her forget who she is."

Knox pauses. "It's been years since we've erased a memory. How would that unlock the tablet? She would forget everything."

"Proditor magic can keep other types of memory intact, right?"

"You ask as if you don't know the answer." Knox grumbles. "I know what you're planning, and I don't like it. Too much could go wrong and the arbitors would never approve."

"They don't have to know. We'll find a cover story that will be believable enough to tell her and to tell them. Maybe some kind of attack to explain her wounds and memory loss. We'll blame it on the rebels. Maybe we can even get her to hate them."

"But once we get what we need, can I still have her?"

The Colum sighs. "If it stops you from picking off my servants like flies. We'll work out the details later, but I want it done immediately."

"As you wish. But, just to keep things clear between us, I don't support any of this."

I stir at their words but can't seem to find the emotions I need to feel.

The Colum strides to leave, but before he does, he leaves Knox with a last command: "Have your last bit of fun with her, then deliver her to the medical bay in a proditor-induced coma. Until we determine a backstory, I don't want anyone except humanoids taking care of her. We'll wake her when we iron out the details."

"Whatever you say, Milo."

After the doors hiss shut, I feel a thumb stroking the back of my neck, lulling me out of sleep. The excruciating pain returns through every wound as Knox pushes me on my back. I can feel movement on my collarbone over the chain of my necklace. Then, I feel a tug as he rips it off my neck.

When I open my eyes, I see him inspecting the rebellion necklace, and he places it on the back of his knuckles, moving it around like it's some kind of party trick. "It's been a pleasure, but our time together is coming to a close. Terrible, I know. But don't worry, before long, we'll be right back where we started." He throws the necklace in the air and catches it, then tucks it into one of the compartments of his utility belt. "Until then, I'll keep this as a souvenir. A memento to commemorate this moment."

When he flips me onto my stomach, I grimace at the sight of the blood-smeared floor. My blood.

I shiver when I hear a knife unsheathe.

"I know you heard our conversation. I know you think this will be a reprieve for you. You won't even remember anything we did to you. But it's not fair that all I get is a measly necklace to remember this by." Knox cuts down the fabric of my tank top. "Every time you see this scar, you'll be reminded of my touch. Even with no memory, it'll feel fresh with each passing glance."

He moves my hair off my back, then runs his fingers down my bare spine like it's some clean canvas. "Goodnight, Margot. Don't be scared. When the time is right, you'll be mine again."

He places the tip of the blade into my shoulder and starts dragging it slowly across my back in a long, horrendous line. I scream in such agony that my throat dries up and I lose my voice completely. Blood drips down my waist and pools onto the floor.

And when he touches the back of my neck again, I feel something like flames ripping through my mind. I see the reels of my life and the fire that follows it.

Dimitri disappears.

Lucinda vanishes.

The Lavenai rebellion no longer exists.

My mind goes empty as the flames burn up everything I am.

Chapter 33

Present

My fit of screaming ceases, but I can't seem to catch my breath.

No, no, this can't be happening. Just minutes ago, I thought I knew the truth. Milo was my husband. I was Ashtanaban and worked for the Imnicus. We were supposed to finally start our lives together. He was the only family I knew.

Now, I know it was all a lie.

I was a rebel set on taking Milo down. For heaven's sake, his father personally saw to my parents' execution. After the proditors publicly tortured them, he had them hung in the center of town and made an example of them to scare off any other forming rebellions. Their bodies hung from streetlights for a week.

Everything Milo said about the power plant explosion was a lie. It was Balistar's vendetta and disdain for Lavenai that caused the takeover. Ruling over Ashtanabo wasn't enough. He had to have control of us too, because without Lavenai's energy, Ashtanabo would still be desolate.

When I look up at my reflection in the window of the lounge area, I see my bloodshot eyes and sweat-coated face. Something about Knox erasing my memory suppressed the imprint of the proditors' tortures. Now, I remember it like it happened yesterday. Every unspeakable mental and physical horror.

Another face stares at the window's reflection with his eyes locked on mine. He sits relaxed in one of the chairs, now dressed in his normal attire.

He knew. The second he saw me screaming, he knew I got my memories back.

In our bedroom—no—*his* bedroom, the lights are still dimmed. I can barely make out his expression. He looks as vile as the first time I met him. The first day I *actually* met him.

My body pumps full of adrenaline. He made me feel safe. He even protected me from Knox. But now I question every one of his intentions. Did he protect me from Knox because he loved me? Or did he do it because he wasn't done getting as many rebellion secrets out of me as possible?

That woman who sprayed the powder at me—Lucinda. She's the only mother figure I've ever known because of Balistar. When I showed up to the base for Milo's mission, she knew they had wiped my memory. Her quick thinking both spared and condemned me. It was hyssopite she threw at me—a rare herb and the only antidote to proditor entrancement.

Milo stands and walks over until he's right behind me. "Now you know the truth."

"You . . . you lied to me!" I gather my strength and spin around, throwing my legs out and tripping him to the ground.

He lands on his back with a thud and a grunt.

I may have regained my old memories, but my new ones still remain. I still have Knox's combat abilities, and if I must use them against Milo to escape, so be it. The rebellion is in danger, and I need to warn them as quickly as possible.

Everything Milo has done has been calculated. He has known about the fifteen locations ever since I unlocked my tablet for him without a second thought. But once he and Dune found the entrances, they realized the only way to get in was with facial recognition, as the doors are virtually impenetrable. It explains his change of heart in letting me train. One minute, it was a bother, or he didn't want me knowing combat. The next minute, he made it his mission to get me strong enough to infiltrate the rebellion.

I straddle him, and as I go to swing at him, I suddenly go weak. He catches my wrist and grabs my waist, forcing me under him.

As he holds me down, a necklace slips out from under his top. This is the first I've seen it, as if he put it on to protect himself while he waited for my screaming to stop. I've seen necklaces like it before. Many crime lords wear them in case proditors ever come their way. The pendant is silver and looks like a cage, and inside it are hyssopite buds so fragrant, I can smell them.

Since my combat abilities are from the crows, the hyssopite turns me back into the girl I once was. A girl who may be good at spying but is truly awful at combat.

I struggle against his hold, but his strength is too much. With my memories back, he should kill me, but instead he just waits for me to tire.

"Are you done?" he asks, his voice hardened.

"My title, the attack, Knox's intentions . . . All of it was just one big lie. Even us—"

"No!" Milo's grip tightens. "Not us."

I force a laugh. "Who would have thought, huh? That the Colum went soft and fell for a Laven spy. Do you think that somehow makes everything better? Does it change what you did to me? You had me *tortured*, Milo!"

Milo's lips move but no words come out. He releases my wrists and climbs off me. Immediately, I crawl backward until my back presses into the cold window.

He stays sitting on the ground with his forearm resting on his knee. "I meant what I said. That I loved you. Every kiss, every touch. Even under different circumstances, I would have wanted that. I never knew I wanted anything more than my title until I fell for you."

"You don't torture someone and then pretend to be their husband. You *broke* me. Knox broke me. You two were family. I trusted you!"

Staring at Milo is like looking at two different men at once. My first love, yet at the same time, the man I've sworn my whole life to take down. It hurts so badly and I can hardly take it. Just seeing him makes scenes of the torture flicker over my vision. Every scar on my body is because of his orders.

Milo tries to reach forward to cradle my jaw, but I quickly turn my head.

"Don't you realize it? That there is no way I could ever love you?" Tears spill down my face as I say the words, because I know I don't mean them. If only one thing was true about the way I feel, it's that I really did fall for him, wholly and completely.

But I know who I am. A rebel. My life's goal has been to stop Milo Arris, and I will. If I ever get off the Imnicus, I will never stop fighting him, and I will always choose Lavenai.

Milo's face hardens. "If I could go back in time and do things differently, I would."

He was only six when Lavenai surrendered to Balistar. I imagine him playing with Knox in the back of a ship, docked in the middle of Merth, while my parents were slaughtered mere feet away.

I shake my head in disbelief. "You can take it all back. You can make this right. Stop stealing Lavenai's life force. Destroy the proditor temple points. Stop outsourcing all your factories to Lavenai and polluting our atmosphere."

"I meant if I could take back torturing you, I would. The Arris Reign ensures that Ashtanabo can thrive the way Lavenai once did. If it weren't for my father betraying the Vicars, Ashtanabo may not even exist anymore. My father did what he did to Lavenai because your Colum refused to help us. This is rectification."

I can't believe what I'm hearing, but why would Milo believe anything different? He's been brainwashed by Balistar Arris since birth.

What else has he lied about?

I taste bile on my tongue as I think about the one person I thought was on my side without fail. "Lleu? What role does she play in this?"

Milo looks even more reluctant. "She's an actress from Msanii. A prominent one. That's why I couldn't have her attend the ball. People may have recognized her."

Somehow, that reality hurts the most. She was more than a maid—she was my best friend. But our friendship was just another role for her.

But now it makes sense why she wouldn't tell me about her burn. If I had suspected Knox of hurting servants, it would have ruined Milo's entire plan. She knew that. It's why, when I found my necklace in Knox's room, he had to erase some of my memories again.

The floor of my reality caves under me.

If I didn't need to save the rebellion, I would beg Milo to kill me. I can't go on knowing that everyone I thought was a friend was simply playing a part. What remains is the aftermath of torture and a broken mind, only held together by the merciful reprieves that Alarik gave me.

"What are you going to do with me?" I ask.

Milo stands next to where I'm sitting and stares out the window at the galaxy. "I'm not sure. I can't execute you because the arbitors would ask questions, but you can't prance around the Imnicus as my wife either. And even I'm not cruel enough to wipe your memories again or to force you to love me."

"Do something for me," I say. "Don't harm any of the rebels yet. Give them a warning before you put their names and faces in the camera database."

"Don't be ridiculous. You signed their death warrant."

"I did what you asked because I loved you." My words sting. "If I had known what you were doing to me, the way you were manipulating me, I would have done what Lavens pray for every night and assassinated you."

Milo curls his fists, his face hardening as he refuses to look at me.

I stand and face him, ready to ask the question with the answer I don't want to hear. "If you didn't love me, would you do it? Would you kill me?"

He rests his forehead against the cool glass before taking one of my hands in his and for some reason, I let him.

"Yes."

Milo keeps me locked in the bedroom with the outside heavily guarded. He made up another lie that the Laven rebels—or terrorists, as he calls them—poisoned me while I was on my mission and the substance messed with my mind. So, no matter what I say to the guards, they will just consider it the delusions of some poisoned girl. It gives Milo enough time to stall while he figures out what to do with me.

The days I'm alone in the room, I try not to sulk. By now, all of the rebels' faces have been uploaded to the criminal database. Anytime one of them goes outside, the cameras will notify Ashtanaban guards and proditors to take them out, but not before they're tortured for information.

I don't like to sleep on the bed, which still smells like him. Instead, I sleep on the floor. The naps I take are restless. With my memories of the torture back, it's hard not to think about it. For some reason, it's not the pain I remember most fully, but Alarik's face.

I still have no idea why he helped me. But based on what Crux said, it almost sounds like Alarik has never wanted to be a proditor to begin with. Being a proditor is a voluntary role, so why is he here? From the stories I've heard, the five of them and Milo all grew up together on the Imnicus and even trained together, so I know he's not some spy. But once he became an adult, if he abhorred it so much, why did he stay?

I remember how he let me see the servant girl in the morgue. He knew that once I saw that burn, it was only a matter of time until I started investigating on my own. It's what he really meant when he said I could never go back once I saw her.

I feel someone shaking my shoulder. "Margot, wake up."

I open my eyes to Milo staring down at me, his arms boxing me in. Still, somewhat in my dream-state, I can't help but notice his soft lips and emerald eyes, and even as I start to feel more awake, it's hard to force myself to see his cruelty.

If it was a perfect universe, I would wish he'd lean down and kiss me. That his warm mouth would take away all my pain, and I could forget all my hatred for him. What I wouldn't give for things to be like they once were. For his lies to be the truth.

But instead, I keep my face uncaring. "What do you want?"

"I need to talk to you."

"Then get off me."

Milo pushes up and sits back on his knees. I follow suit, pushing myself up and sitting crossed-legged.

He doesn't meet my eyeline as he speaks. "I'm sending you to the Zreath region of Ashtanabo to live out the rest of your days. While you're there, you'll be guarded by proditors. It's a beautiful place. To call it a prison would almost be insulting. I will tell the arbitors that we parted ways after our whirlwind marriage."

I scoff. "And if I piss off the proditors there, I'm assuming they'll beat and torture me in all the ways you've instructed them?"

Milo's jaw clenches and his voice shakes angrily. "No proditor on any planet is ever allowed to touch you ever again. Do you understand how angry it makes me to think back to that day? Gods, even thinking of them touching you during training pisses me off. Knox is lucky I haven't killed him and Crux should be thankful I haven't ejected him from an airlock."

His words surprise me, but I don't let myself see them as caring. As far as I'm concerned, I'm still nothing but one of his prisoners. "Was your father like this to your mother? Did he lash out and beat her whenever she didn't do as she was told? Is *that* why she left?" I spit the words, no matter how low they are.

A familiar sadness falls over his face, broken up by anger at the corners of his lips. "My *mother*, like you, was a Laven. It was against Vicar law, but my father fell for her and married her anyway. My father sacrificed much for their love, and when he betrayed the Vicars, she left. Some say she's dead. But I know she isn't. She *abandoned me*, and because I have her Laven human blood, I will never fully wield the gift of the crows and can do no more than taste it."

I don't know why I didn't connect the dots earlier. Milo is half-proditor. Half-Vicar. It also explains why hyssopite doesn't seem to affect him like it would a full-blooded proditor. "Taste it?"

Milo sighs and sits back, staring out the window. "I can feel and hear things around me that others, including proditors, can't—heartbeats, breathing, even the caws and talons of other proditor's crows. It gives me cues into people's emotional states. I'm also stronger and faster than a normal human. But I cannot break into people's minds."

No wonder I could never sneak up on him, which means that time in the closet was another lie. He could probably hear my heartbeat and sense my presence from halls away.

"And what about Knox?" Gods, even thinking of Knox makes me angry. "What happened to his parents?"

"His parents died shortly before the Ashtanaban Colum was assassinated by my father. Afterwards, my father invested a lot of time into him. His crows are different. It's rare, but some prodi-tors and Vicars are born with sick crows. But sick doesn't mean weak. His crows make him as vile as he is, but they also make him strong. Even as a child, he couldn't control the darkness within, so my father used forbidden magic to help him control his crows. But once my father died, the control within Knox did too. His obsession with pain is worse than before. He's no longer satisfied with animals." Milo's jaw hardens, and I can see the pain in his face. "He's moved onto women."

Knowing Knox's condition with his crows almost makes me feel bad for him. But it doesn't change the fact that he hurt Lleu and Slone and murdered a servant. In fact, that's probably only the tip of the iceberg. I'm almost more angry at Milo for allowing Knox to have such an influential position, despite fully knowing what his cousin is capable of.

I'm reminded of the first time Milo and I slept together. Crux must have told him I was in Knox's room and then Milo searched my things after I fell asleep. Once he found the necklace, he direct-ed Knox to wipe my memory again.

The thought that he slept with me, knowing full well he was going to have Knox erase my memories afterward, makes me want to strangle him here and now.

I fiddle with the ring on my finger. Milo had the security on it disabled once my memories returned, so it's useless to me. "It seems you've made up your mind about my future, so go take care of the arrangements. I want off this ship, and I never want to see you again." I pull the ring off my finger and throw it at his chest. As it falls, it clatters and spins against the tile.

A wave of hurt passes over Milo as he picks up the ring and places it on his little finger. "If that's what will make you happy." Without another word, he leaves, letting the doors lock behind him.

Chapter 34

The next day, the door opens and I don't turn to see who it is as I stare out the window. I've already decided to accept my fate in an Ashtanaban prison.

As it is now, there is no way to escape and warn the rebellion. I would be lying if I said I've given up on them completely. But unless the gods themselves send me some idea or method, the only thing I can hope to do is die well and pray Lucinda realizes what's going on before rebels go outside and get themselves killed.

Whoever is at the door hasn't said anything yet. They simply walk up the steps of the lounge area and then come to a halt. "Margot, it's me."

I see Lleu's reflection in the window, her hair in braids and her heartbroken brown eyes. Seeing her makes me furious. She looks as innocent and elegant as always, but now I see her for what she is. All this time, she pretended to be my best friend, but in the end, she turned out to be as manipulative as Milo.

"You can cut the act." I refuse to look at her anymore, even through the reflection. "I know everything. Collect whatever payment Milo promised you and go home."

"No matter what Milo told you, I hope you know that through it all, our friendship was real, and regardless of what you may think, Milo didn't pay me anything."

I throw my hands up. "Why bother trying to rectify anything with me? I'm going to be imprisoned for the rest of my life. Just leave before I say something I regret." Even during my time in the rebellion, I never had a female friend I was close with. Knowing that the Lleu I thought I knew was all a lie is almost more than my heart can tolerate.

"Margot, they kidnapped me."

My shoulders drop and I finally turn to face her.

Lleu takes a few steps closer. "It was on the closing night of one of my shows. When I went back to my dressing room, two proditors were there, and they knocked me out. When I first awoke on the Imnicus, they wouldn't even tell me why I was here. It wasn't until I accepted that I'd die if I didn't comply that they finally told me. They needed someone good at improv who wouldn't break character, no matter what. But, of course, I couldn't help but break after what Knox did to me."

"Oh, Lleu." I walk toward her and stop shy of giving her a hug. Even though I know I shouldn't trust her, and that everything she is saying could be a lie, I believe her wholeheartedly. Mostly because there is no point in her lying at this point. I see now that she didn't have to act much at all. She probably saw me as just as much of a prisoner as she was. It's what subconsciously made our bond so tight. "But why did Knox target you?"

"Does Knox need a reason?" Lleu lowers her head. "He insisted that he needed to meet with me in one of the conference rooms. When I got there, he said he was instructed in a meeting to punish me for not notifying Milo about you leaving the medic bay. I was confused when he laced his hand in mine. I almost thought he was trying to kiss me, which I would have slapped him for, but instead I felt pain from his hand to mine. When I tried to scream, he covered my mouth and shushed me. He wouldn't stop looking at my face, and as he did, he seemed . . . aroused."

Lleu looks nauseous. "Still, he never touched me or any other girl he burned *like that.* All he wants is to cause people pain. Not just for him, but to feed his crows. Of course, after all of this, I spoke to Onyx about what happened and his face fell. He said that Milo never commanded Knox to punish me. In fact, he made it seem like Milo would be furious if he learned Knox had burned me because it could jeopardize the mission and as you know, it almost did."

I can't help myself. I wrap my arms around Lleu and squeeze her tight. "I'm so sorry. I wish you would have told me."

As she hugs me back, her arms are shaking. "Both of us would have been in even more danger."

I release her and wipe a tear off my cheek. "Is this goodbye?"

"For now. But if you think I won't conspire and seduce prodi-tors to find where they're keeping you on Ashtanabo and come visit, you're wrong."

I crack a sad smile. "Thank you, Lleu. For everything."

"One more thing." Lleu digs in one of the large pockets of her dress and pulls out a metallic envelope. She hands it to me. "Alarik wanted me to give this to you. He really liked you too, so I can only assume it's a goodbye letter."

Alarik. The mention of his name feels different with my memories back. No wonder I always felt so safe around him. There was a time when he risked his own life to save me, a girl he didn't even know. Does Lleu know how he helped me? I wish she did, but I can't risk telling her for his own safety. "Thank you."

After I give Lleu a final hug and she leaves, I sit on a chair and open the envelope. Inside is a thin piece of parchment. I unfold it, and the contents of the letter make my arms go limp.

After an hour of pacing and considering Alarik's letter, I use the intercom to page one of the guards. I tell him I need to see Milo immediately and that it cannot wait.

"Certainly, Lady Arris," the guard says back. Him using my title makes me jolt slightly and really solidifies just how far this con went. Even the soldiers and maids truly believed I was their Columess. To them, it probably wasn't even an act. A whirlwind marriage is certainly a plausible excuse. The Imnicus is large enough that him falling for a random soldier could go unnoticed.

When the doors finally do open, Milo's face is as cold as ever, but not enough to conceal what emotion he's hiding underneath. He's hurting too. Sure, he can still visit me on Ashtanabo whenever he wants, but he knows I won't want to see him. If the soldiers manage to get me off the Imnicus today and into a ship to Ashtanabo, he will have truly lost me.

"You called?" Milo asks.

I nod. "I just wanted to know when the guards will take me to the docking bay."

Milo's eyes don't meet mine. "Likely later in the evening."

Everything stays painfully quiet between us for a solid minute. I remember Alarik's letter and recite it in my head as I stand.

Dear Margot, what I am about to tell you could get us both killed, so read carefully and when you're finished, flush this letter down the toilet.

"I really meant what I said," I say.

"And what is that?"

Like any other human, Milo is a slave to his emotions. First things first, you need to get him to your room, and when you do, you need to tell him—

"That I loved you. That I *still* love you." I let myself really feel what I'm saying, which proves not to be as difficult as I thought it would be. In fact, I feel it so much that it's almost painful. No matter what happens next or what the outcome is, I won't regret it.

Milo takes a step back. "I can't hear this right now."

Before Milo can book it out of the room, I rush forward and grab his arm. "I know you love me too, and I know what you're thinking. There is nothing I can say or do to convince you to spare my fellow rebels' lives or even keep me a free woman. That's not what I'm going to ask you in the slightest. Not anymore."

He still can't seem to look at me, but he seems less eager to rush out. "Then, what do you want?"

My voice cracks as my eyes well up with tears. "I want you to hold me."

The hardness on Milo's face shatters just a bit. He doesn't even try to talk his way out of it as he pulls me into his chest, one hand wrapped around my waist and the other cradling the back of my head. His body is warm and his hold on me is tight, like he knows it just as well as I do. That this really is the last time.

The tears that were once a con really do start to fall. I don't just feel the pain of what he did to me, but the pain of losing him. That, in a perfect world where he wasn't the Colum and I wasn't a rebel, we really could be together.

Remember, Milo is half-proditor, so he can sometimes pick up on an emotional state just by tuning into your bodily reactions. If you're going to do this, you need to pretend it's real. Enough to feel it yourself.

I feel his lips on my scalp and the butterflies in my stomach. I lazily kiss his chest. When I move my head back to look up at him, his lips find mine.

His kisses are slow and angry, yet also filled with pain and long-ing, like my mouth is filled with poison that he can't help but taste. It's the same for me as I give him as much as he is giving me, as if I could enact some kind of revenge through the drag of my tongue. My breath shakes and my heart pounds.

I move to his neck, feeling every tendon and his roaring pulse as I hold on to his collar. He closes his eyes and his head rolls back. "Margot, we can't—" But his words are cut short by a low groan as I snake my hand down the front of his pants.

"I need you," I whisper.

Milo curses before losing all composure and hauls me up to straddle his waist. He kisses me furiously as he stumbles toward the wall with me in his arms, pushing every item, breakable or not, off the nearby dresser, before setting me on it. He caresses my chest and between my thighs, my body burning as much as my heart is aching. I tangle my fingers through his hair as he explores my mouth with his tongue.

I undo whatever clasps I can on his attire until I'm down to his undershirt, only breaking the kiss so I can lift it over his head. His abdominal muscles are tense as I lightly drag my fingernails down them.

Once you have him, you need to get him to the bed.

He rolls his pelvis between my legs, making me suck in a deep breath. "The bed, Milo. I want you to touch me there, just one last time."

"Yes . . . yes." Milo says it like he can't believe he himself is actually doing this. That he's choosing me over his duty.

He picks me up and carries me to the bed, laying me down on it. I sit up quickly to take my shirt off. He doesn't wait for me to get to my bra before he unclasps it himself and kisses across my breasts. I lean back and take off my shorts and panties while he does.

He tries to move me to my hands and knees, but I hold his forearm to stop him. "Milo, lie on your back."

Milo nods quickly, not second-guessing my request. After he kicks his pants and boxers off, he's on his back, and I'm kissing down his chest, along his pecs, and down his abdomen. His skin shutters beneath my lips.

Then my mouth is around his length, my head moving slowly.

"Margot—" He lets out pain-like gasps like he's already on the brink of shattering.

I stay cautious to keep him on the edge and not take him all the way as I swirl my tongue. When I release him from my mouth, he looks ready to get on his knees to beg me to keep going. Before he can, I crawl up his body and sit back, guiding him inside me.

"My gods, Margot." Milo holds my hips, rolling my hips to accentuate my movements on top of him.

I'm feeling it too, the way he feels like he was made for me. My head keeps falling into the clouds, and it takes everything in me to keep myself alert. Still, I want to lose myself in him even more than I already have.

I hate you, I hate you, I keep thinking to myself, but then a moan or gasp breaks through the mantra. I reach down and find his hands, lacing his fingers with mine and slowly moving them up above his head until my lips are just barely brushing his. I lick across his lower lip as I move his hands into position.

"Margot, I love you, I love you." Milo's lips tremble against mine.

I'm so close, but I hold back as much as I can as I remember the next part of Alarik's letter.

Beneath the pillows, you're going to hide the following—

Milo moves his hips, changing the angle of his upward thrust, hitting me just in the right place. Against any control I thought I had, I tighten up and cry out his stupid name. My mind is almost completely lost as I ride out the pleasure, no matter how much I remind myself that there is no time.

Milo's body tenses and I know this is my only shot. As he gasps and spills out, I tug on the end of the hidden belts, locking his wrists in place to the bed.

His voice is still throaty and pleasured as he jolts. "Wait . . . What are you . . ."

My body is weak and covered in chills as I make sure the belt is secured before climbing off him.

"Dammit, Margot!" Milo thrashes in bed. He tugs and tugs but cannot get out. The belts are secured with a unique four-strand knot created by the Vicars, exactly as Alarik directed. "Untie me now!"

As I stand beside the bed naked and watching him thrash, I can't help but feel a pain in my chest. There's no satisfaction in what I've done. I used his body to get what I wanted. When I look back, he never even stooped that low. In fact, I don't think he had any intention of bedding me at all as he ran his scheme. It just so happened that way.

I remind myself of who he is and what he has done. "I did what I had to do, Milo."

"I swear, if you don't let me go right now—"

"You'll what? Call for your guards? Do it."

Anytime Milo has come to see you, he always sends his guards away so they don't overhear anything. Use this to your advantage.

Milo's teeth are clenched before he pinches his lips shut.

"That's what I thought." I open the wardrobe and pull out the Ashtanaban uniform that was once a gift from him. It's not my first choice, but it's my only in-room attire with pants at the moment.

"You'll pay for this." No matter how much he struggles with the restraints, they only grow tighter.

After I dress, I step over to him and grab his hand, tugging at his black diamond ring.

"Don't you dare!" Milo tightens his fingers to try to stop me, but the leftover perspiration from his pleasure makes it slip off easily. "You won't get far, you know. Everyone is on high alert and knows you've been locked away."

"I think I'll manage." I slip his ring onto my thumb. It's loose but stays secure enough.

He stares up at me with his breaths angry and on the cusp of a growl, but his eyes tell another story. He looks wounded, like he's never known what it's like to be betrayed before. If only I could make him feel pain at the degree that I do.

I lean down and kiss him, and to my surprise, he kisses me back, his arms softening in the restraints, like he knows I won this singular battle.

He pulls away but keeps his forehead pressed against mine and his voice drops to a harsh whisper, his lips barely skimming against mine as he speaks. "You may be successful and escape, but don't think I won't come after you. I will travel regions, planets, and even galaxies to apprehend you. From now on, your entire existence belongs to me."

"And if you do catch me?" I whisper back.

"I may very well kill you," his breaths shake angrily.

"I look forward to it." One last time, I kiss him before using his ring to override the security and escape the room, leaving him bound to the bed all alone.

Chapter 35

I ignore my conflicted heart and the ache of my lips as I take the route Alarik mapped out in his letter.

Use Milo's ring to cut through the servant hallways to the west wing escape pods. He's less likely to check there.

When I finally find the hidden hallways, I keep my head low, but anytime I pass someone, nobody seems to bat an eye. It makes sense now why no one recognized me unless I was dolled up as the Columess or they saw my ring. I nearly always kept my mask while I was undercover, and most of them never met me until I first left the medic bay. Considering how many people work on the Imnicus, my employment as a full-fledged soldier and spy was an easy lie to maintain.

I return to the main hallway system of the west wing and notice a pair of patrolling guards, so I duck behind a corner before they can spot me. Once they've passed, I run into the ballroom and find the corridor to the west wing docking bay, which is mostly used for esteemed guests with smaller ships. The room has a small, unmanned curved desk with hundreds of buttons and two large screens.

I hover my finger over the buttons, trying to remember which one ignites the power to the pods from my short-lived Imnicus guard training. Not only that, but all of these pods are set to go to Ashtanabo. To escape to Lavenai, I will have to adjust the coordinates manually from inside the pod and pray I get it right.

I press one of the larger buttons, and to my relief, the pods power on. "Thank the gods."

Alarms blare, and lights in the room's corner begin to flash. There isn't much time before Milo finds me. I press a few more buttons to open the doors to one of the pods, then sprint toward it.

Soon, I'll be back with Lucinda and Dimitri, as well as the rest of the rebellion. I think of the things I'll tell them, the conversations we'll have, and the tears I'll cry on Lucinda's shoulder. Not just because of what Milo put me through, but because of the way I'll miss the lies. The friendships. His love.

"Don't think you're getting away that easily," a voice says.

His voice doesn't make me cower. Even if he has a weapon, I can still jump into the pod without even looking back. It would be so easy to lunge inside right now, secure the door, and leave the Imnicus behind me forever.

So, it's not his voice that stops me. It's hers.

As she yelps, I turn around and see Knox holding Lleu against his chest with a knife to her throat.

"Lleu!" I freeze, even as my mind tells me to ignore Knox and run as fast as I can.

The blood-red lights of the alarm reflect off of his golden hair and wicked smile. "Be a good girl and step away from the pod."

No matter how much training I have, I can't beat Knox. Even the few times I have had the upper hand, it's only because he underestimated me, and something tells me he never will again. "Keep her out of this. It's me you want."

"Margot, don't listen to him!" Lleu yells. "Go while you still can!"

"I said, step away." Knox doesn't even wait for me to obey his request before his bare hands are on Lleu's dark skin, cupping and caressing her jaw.

Lleu's eyes slam shut, seemingly by themselves as her body is overtaken by some horrible shiver. Her body bows against him, and a pained expression takes over her face.

"Knox, don't!" I curl my fists.

He smiles like he knows he has already won. "Move it."

I take ten steps forward and raise my arms above my head. Soon, Milo and droves of soldiers will be here to apprehend me. If I really wanted to, I could still turn around and dive into the pod. But I know what it's like to be tortured with proditor magic. How the body never truly forgets. It's something only those who've gone through it can fully understand, and how much we want to save each other from it.

"You're still too close." Knox laughs as Lleu tries to scream, but her throat won't let her. He presses the side of his face against hers and takes her hand. "In the meantime, I'll remind your friend of all the things I could do to her. The things I *will* do to her, if you don't comply. Remember this, Lleu?"

Black smoke surrounds his fingers just as he frees Lleu from the mental bonds of the entrancement. Lleu is screaming now as Knox burns her hand. Her legs buckle and she falls to her knees, but Knox keeps his grip tight as she tries to pull away from him.

"Fine, you win, just stop!" I take ten more steps, my window of opportunity closing. "Now, let go."

Knox unhands her, and she falls on her side. Her body trembles, falling in and out of consciousness as she whimpers on the ground.

I should have stolen Milo's gun before I left his room. My aim is decent. If I could, I would end Knox here and now. "You're a monster!"

"I've been called worse." Knox takes a few steps down the small set of stairs. "So, now you know the truth. We're not family, which means I have no obligation to keep you safe."

When he gets closer, I take a step back. "Don't touch me. I'll come with you willingly."

"I don't need to touch you to make you fear me. I've seen it in your eyes, Margot, even when you forgot everything. The way dark chills would bud on your spine in my presence, or your eyes would grow just a tad bit glassier. Deep down, you always knew what I was."

I need to stall him while I think of another plan to save both Lleu and myself. "But that wasn't enough for you, was it? When you killed the servant, you couldn't wait for privacy," I say. "You did it in the middle of the ball, while everyone was dancing just a few walls away from you."

A half smile grows on his face. "While we danced, I couldn't resist the urge to touch your scar. It reminded me of who you were because, for a while there, I even started to forget what was real and what wasn't. Touching you like that . . . did something to me. Made me want you more than ever." His voice starts to sound more breathless, like he's holding back a shivering moan. "I suppose I was relieved when Milo wanted to dance with you instead, and once I left the ballroom, I had to satisfy my urges somehow. I guess you could say that servant was in the wrong place at the wrong time."

Smoke pools around his feet. It's not possible for him to be inhabiting my mind. He hasn't even touched me yet. But I remember what Milo said about Knox. How he was Balistar's protégé for a reason.

"Just the thought of it brings me even more power," Knox gloats. "I was patient. You have no idea how long I've waited for this moment. It's why I've always been stronger than the other proditors. Stronger than my uncle. I *have* control. I always have. Even now, I can access your mind without the cool stroke of my fingers."

I know it's not completely true. If it was, he'd already have me in a mental dungeon. He may be able to cause visual or auditory hallucinations within his environment, but not tactile ones, no matter what he says to scare me.

Still, I need to keep him occupied. "I'm sorry your crows are sick—"

"Stop it." Knox's frown contorts in anger. "They aren't sick. They are powerful, just like Uncle Balistar always used to tell me. I'll never let anybody fault me for it again. Not you, not the Vicars, and certainly not the other proditors."

He pulls a gun from his belt and aims it straight at me. "You were supposed to be mine. Milo promised me that much, until he wanted you all to himself. Even now, he still won't let me hurt you. But until he finds us, I'm going to have my fun with you once and for all."

I can't dodge a gun, but I know he won't shoot. "What are you waiting for? Take your shot."

I outstretch my arms in surrender but match his slow steps as I walk backward, keeping him out of arm's reach. Now that he's out of Lleu's vicinity, I move our strides toward the pod, but I know jumping into it is still an impossibility.

"You think that's what I want? To allow you to end so mercifully? An easy shot, one and done? No, no, no," he laughs and tsks. "I want to drag my blade slowly up and down every inch of your flesh. Only when your screams are loud enough to awaken every citizen in this galaxy will I give you the satisfaction of death." Knox points his gun at my thighs.

Oh gods, he may not be trying to kill me, but he is more than likely willing to shoot to incapacitate me.

Everything feels as though it is in slow motion. One moment, Knox is aiming his gun, ready to fire. The next, my vision blurs and my body hits the ground hard.

I shake my head and my surroundings come into focus—I'm on the floor of the escape pod.

Lleu stares at me from just outside the pod, a tear falling down her dark skin.

It was her. She pushed me inside. And now . . .

"Don't you dare forget me." Lleu slams her hand onto the button of the escape pod and the door locks shut.

"No!" I pound my fists onto the window, even as the pod is counting down to launch. I try to press any button I can find to stop it from ejecting.

Knox shakes his head, smiling, like he can't believe it. But then his eyes lock on Lleu.

"Stop!" I scream the words now.

The automated voice in the pod speaks. *"Three."*

He aims his gun at Lleu.

"Two."

"Run! Lleu, run!" But I know the soundproof glass has silenced me completely.

"One."

My ears ring as blood drips down her lower belly and stains her uniform. Knox smirks at her and then at me. He mouths the words, *"You're next."*

I'm completely numb as the pod ejects from the Imnicus.

Chapter 36

I fall back into the seat and quickly buckle myself in, but it feels as though someone else—someone more rational and strong—is doing it for me.

Lleu . . . oh gods. Lleu.

The automated voice speaks again. *"Accelerating toward Ashtan-abo in five . . ."*

I don't have time to wallow or mourn, not if I want to return to Lavenai. On the touchscreen, I adjust the landing point to Merth before the countdown gets to one. I wipe away my tears as I initiate the protocol.

"Route changed. New destination: Planet: Lavenai; Region: West Betany; City: Merth."

The pod is like being in a vacuum where there is no time and no feeling. A place that forces me to think about everything I thought was real versus what actually came to be. No matter how badly I try to push out those thoughts, they still break through.

Milo was never your husband. He will never hold you again.

Knox was never your friend. You'll never laugh with him again.

And even Lleu, who turned out to be just as much a prisoner as you, is gone.

Gone. Gone. Gone.

A small, horrible part of me wishes I never regained my memory. That I could have lived out the rest of my life in ignorance. But it would have only been so long before Knox lost his mind and came after me time and time again, continuously hurting me and then erasing my memory to keep up his own charade.

An alarm blares through the pod and a screen lights up, alerting me to brace for landing. Through the window, I see the purple haze as I start to enter Lavenai's atmosphere.

I remember my Imnicus guard training and take over the manual controls as the ship slows. Thanks to Lavenai's glowing neon city, I'm able to aim the pod toward a darker area in the outskirts of the city, one near the crime district.

The only way I'm going to be able to get back into the rebel base undetected is through the sixteenth entrance, the one not documented on any tablet or computer—Sinclair's Brothel.

As I get closer to land, I must squint as a purple fog takes over the night sky.

An emergency alarm screams as the pod collides with the top of an enormous, half-dead willow tree. The pod is tossed around, spinning through the branches. I can't see anything with the flickering lights.

Dammit! I pull back on the control stick and veer off to the right, but I know I'm going too fast.

I don't bother perfecting my landing and pull back on the stick to stop the pod as quickly as I can.

I yelp as the pod thumps and slams into a mushroom field at a sharp angle. Its metal frame drags through the dirt. Shrooms splatter against the window.

I find another set of emergency breaks beside my seat and pull the lever, making the pod come to a screeching halt.

It takes me a second to gather my breath. If I hadn't had some escape pod training as a guard, and that singular flying lesson with Milo, I may not have survived the landing.

I push my sweaty curls out of my face and kick open the door. The second the air touches my lungs, a fit of coughing overtakes me. I look everywhere in the pod for a respirator, but there isn't anything in the pod except two bottles of water and some freeze-dried food.

For now, I'll have to endure the pollution. If I stay near the pod too long, the Ashtanaban guards stationed here may find me.

The mushroom field is almost pitch dark, leaving the city lights as the only guiding path back to my home.

The crime district of Lavenai is a sight of its own. Nearly every club and brothel is covered in glowing, deep-red signs that reflect off the glossy streets.

To my relief, there aren't many cameras in the crime district. Anytime one gets put up, criminals always find where they are hiding by using black market technology, and promptly shatter them. Still, I keep my head low and cross my arms over my chest to cover the Ashtanaban insignia as I push through crowds of people waiting in lines outside of clubs.

Once I'm at the entrance of Sinclair's brothel, I hesitate. He'll want something in exchange.

Joriel Sinclair always wants something.

He has run this brothel since he was twenty-one. Now, at twenty-eight, he's known for being ruthless, wicked, and he has a way of getting anything he wants no matter what people think of him.

According to Lucinda, he's everything his father Bastien was—handsome, charismatic, and also conniving. But what else does anyone expect? Behind the mask of a brothel owner, he is one of the most successful crime lords in all of Lavenai, dealing with everything from contraband to hitmen. Some say he's even been to Ashtanabo.

Inside the club, the music is loud and sensual, almost like an homage to its young owner. There is a sea of people on the dance floor and in booths. The stuffy smell of tobacco, alcohol, and various colognes waft through the air.

I stand at the far side of one of the bars to keep hidden, for now. Joriel doesn't like surprises. I want to take off the Ashtanaban jacket and strip down to the tank, but if I do, the men who already have their lustful eyes on me may think I'm one of Joriel's girls, and as I've told Joriel a million-and-one times, I'll never be his.

There's only been a handful of occasions I've been in this building, usually to hand off payments to Joriel and get the hell out as fast as I can, but every time, he always has that look on his face. The look of a man who can get any girl he wants but is dead set on getting the one he can't.

I barely have time to process before two sets of hands are on my arms, dragging me to the back of the club. Knox's shadow tries to kick in, but I push it back. I curse to myself for letting Joriel get the upper hand on me already. Two of his goons haul me through a doorway of hanging beads and force me into a chair in the center of a small room.

I hear the beads move again and the sound of his cane, one I know he isn't even close to needing. "Lucinda told me you were dead."

Joriel Sinclair circles around until he's standing in front of me, leaning on the head of his golden cane and dressed to the nines in a sculpted black suit accented with even darker imprinted roses, the top few buttons of his dress shirt undone. A chain necklace rests against his collarbone and his dark-brown hair is styled away from his youthful face. Two long earrings dangle from his lobes and rings cover his fingers, reminding me of Milo.

"Sorry to disappoint," I say.

He steps forward until he's looking down at me with that half-turned up smile he likes to do when he feels like he has leverage over me. "Tell me—" He places two fingers under my chin, tipping my head up. "Is Lucinda a liar?"

I can't tell him a single thing. Joriel is the nosiest person I know and for good reason. All information is product, one that can be exploited and sold to his network of contacts. Just because Lucinda knew him as a boy doesn't mean he's trustworthy.

"She's not," I keep my gaze hardened. If I break first, it will only give him pure satisfaction. "There's nothing I can tell you. As always, my missions are classified."

"Anything can be bought, Margot. Just name your price." Joriel lets go of me and circles me again, inspecting every crevice and every detail of my body. "Unless you're here to accept my standing offer. Is that why you faked your death? I'm flattered."

"No, I will not work for you."

Joriel stands behind me, leaning down so his mouth is level with my ear. "But you'd be only for me. There would be no sharing you with anyone else." His breath is warm against my neck. "Think about waking up every day with a full stomach and my hands soothing you to sleep at night. I know about a million Laven girls who would kill for what I'm offering you."

I shrug him off. "Don't ask me again."

"A shame. A pretty girl like you could earn much more than whatever the rebellion is offering you." Joriel paces in front of me again and moves the tip of his cane along the hems of clothes. "Now, are you going to tell me why you're dressed in an Ashtan-aban uniform? Or do I need to find a more *creative, enjoyable* way to make you talk?"

There's nothing he can do to me that would even compare to what I've already been through. But it's not his threats that annoy me. It's that I'm running out of time.

I huff out a breath. "How about this; I will give you this uniform in exchange for passage through the sixteenth entrance."

"Trouble in underground paradise? You know, I did hear from Lucinda that a few of her members have mysteriously gone missing. Do you have anything to do with that?"

Missing? It takes everything in me to keep my face neutral. "Are you going to accept it or not?"

"Any excuse to get you undressed, I'm all for." Joriel snaps to one of his goons. "Get her a change of clothes."

When the goon returns, he throws a short, golden garment onto my lap. It's made of a metal-like material that's more lingerie than dress.

I narrow my eyes at Joriel. "I'm not wearing this."

Joriel shrugs, holding back an even more dastardly smile. "It's all we have on hand."

A few goons chuckle behind me.

I know he's lying, but at this point, I only need to suffer just a little while longer. "Leave. I'm not changing in front of all of you."

"What a shame." Joriel tilts his head. "And here I was thinking you liked stripping yourself of all things Ashtanaban." To my dismay, he stays put.

"Joriel, take your goons and go."

"I'm perfectly fine where I am now." Joriel places more weight onto his cane, as if he's waiting for a show.

I mutter under my breath and undo the jacket, slipping it off and throwing it into Joriel's chest, who looks like he's getting an absolute kick out of this. Keeping the pants on, I slip the dress over my tank top, making Joriel frown.

In no time, I am able to slip the tank and pants off from under the dress, all while keeping my dignity.

"I suppose I should have expected you to be crafty." Joriel taps his cane twice against the ground. "Come."

Joriel leads me through the beaded curtains while goons follow behind us. I feel many sets of eyes raking over my exposed skin and bare back, even as I try to keep my gaze focused on the back of Joriel's chestnut hair stained red from the overhead lights. Still, it's hard not to catch glimpses of the scenes around me of people experimenting with varieties of mushrooms at tables and men going down on courtesans in booths. Apparently, when his father, Bastien, was running things, anything outside of kissing had to be done in the backrooms. Joriel, on the other hand, isn't so modest.

We pass a smaller stage made of mirrors where a young woman spins on a pole and dances to the beat of the seductive music.

A hand slips around my waist, and before I can punch whoever it belongs to, Joriel acts first, spinning around and smacking the middle-aged man's hand off me with his cane.

"Ah, ah. This one's not for sale, Bran. She's mine."

The man narrows his eyes. "Come on, Joriel, you keep all the pretty ones to yourself."

"Don't make me reinstate your ban."

The man huffs and Joriel steps back, wrapping his arm around me and resting his hand on my hip. "Just until we get to the basement door."

I nod. *He'll take any excuse to touch me*, I think to myself with a grumble.

Once we find the basement, our footsteps echo off the concrete walls. Racks of costumes and lingerie sets, metallic vanities, and wig heads fill the area. Joriel kicks out any girls who are touching up their makeup and yanks a large tapestry off the back wall.

Even with the tapestry gone, it's hard to tell that there is a secret door here unless someone has a keen eye. The only evidence are cracks in the foundation.

Joriel leans against one of the vanities. "Here it is, the passage to the rebellion in exchange for that uniform of yours."

"Thank you, Joriel." I pace forward.

"Wait," he says.

I roll my eyes. "Yes?"

His eyes look devious in a way that makes me feel unsettled. "Do you think I could just have a peek inside? Just this once. It's so invasive having a door in my own establishment that I cannot access."

"Not in a million years, Sinclair. Besides, it's impossible with the facial detection. If it senses anyone unauthorized is with me, it won't open."

"Come on, there must be some kind of override."

There is, but I'd never admit it. "Thank you for all your help, but it's time for me to go."

All is quiet. The sound of my breath is amplified from the surrounding concrete. He doesn't take his stare off me, searching my eyes. He pushes himself off the vanity and takes a step toward me.

"I'm serious." I furrow my brows. "I gave you my clothes, so let it go."

"Hmm . . . today that's just not good enough. Restrain her."

The goons whip toward me and try to grab my arms, and I feel my combat abilities click into gear as I lunge out of the way. One of the goons curses and tries to swing at me, but I duck to the ground and swipe my leg, knocking two of them onto their asses.

Joriel steps forward and I catch the scent of his hyssopite-embedded necklace. One many crime lords wear in case they ever have a run in with a proditor. Immediately, my abilities dissipate, making me curse.

He takes his cane and knocks me in the ribs, making me stumble back. With a few long strides, he wraps his arm around my lower back and presses me to his chest. He pulls a dagger from his belt and holds it to my neck.

"Screw you," I spit.

Joriel grins. "Perhaps." He spins me, facing me toward the entrance as he holds me tight. With a quick motion, he lifts his cane and presses the button disguised as a brick.

The scanner ignites, scanning up my face and my body.

"Unauthorized parties noted," says the automated voice. *"Override required."*

Joriel speaks into my scalp. "I always knew you were a liar, love. Now, do what you do best and open the door."

Dammit to hell. I hate him. But there's still a way to get around this. There is a command that has an override within itself in case any members are ever coerced. As long as the authorized member enters first, the doors will immediately close before anyone else can get inside.

For now, I need to comply.

"Intrust beta protocol," I say.

"Override accepted. Please enter."

The cracks in the concrete shuffle, stacking camouflaged bricks to the side until the sewer-like hallway is visible.

He pushes me forward, the blade grazing my spine. "Walk."

Gods, Joriel is a moron. I take a few steps forward. When the threshold nears, I pretend to trip.

"Margot—" Joriel grits.

I force my trip over the threshold into the entrance. As I do, the doors immediately slam shut behind me.

"Margot!" I can barely hear his yell through the concrete. "The next time I see you, you're dead!"

I'll add you to the list, I think to myself.

Chapter 37

The tunnel from the brothel entrance is a long walk compared to the others. It didn't even exist until years after Lucinda started the rebellion. Mold and moss cover the walls and water drips through concrete cracks, soaking my shoes.

The closer I get, the more my heart palpitates. What will Lucinda think when she sees me again? Will she assume I am back to further betray them? She must realize that it's because of me that rebels have been disappearing. Even when I tell her my memories are back, will she even forgive me for what I've done?

As the main entrance of the rebellion comes into view, everything feels like it's moving in slow motion, from the lights scanning my face to the doors whooshing open.

I run my hand along the smooth walls and almost tear up.

I am home. *Really* home.

It isn't until now that I appreciate my shared dorm room and the random power outages. My safety below ground is something I'll never take for granted again.

Everything in the base is quieter than I remember, and even after turning a few hallways, I don't see a single person.

I feel a jolt of anxiety. Did the military manage to access the base? Or have they all been picked off one-by-one?

My body tenses. To my relief, I hear the faint hum of Lucinda's voice as I near one of the meeting rooms. Still, I press my back into the wall at the sound, unable to make myself known.

As much as I've missed everyone, I am scared to face them and find out what they really think of the way I failed them. *Gods, why is this so hard?*

Even though I have my memories back, they're tainted by my life on the Imnicus. Half of me is a rebel spy, trained in the art of evasion and anonymity. The other half is still the Columess, but it feels just as real as the rest of my life. Milo's kisses, Lleu's jokes, and even Knox's false comforting words.

I cannot make out Lucinda's words through the door—the same door I entered days ago to betray the rebellion. I'm thankful she realized I was under proditor power. If it weren't for that mission, I may have spent the rest of my days tangled with the enemy and bearing his heirs, all the while working to destroy the planet that raised me.

I steady my breath and stand in front of the closed meeting room door. Before I can talk myself out of it, I press the button.

As the doors slide open, I take in the sight of rebels sitting in chairs and on the floor, listening to Lucinda's speech. The presentation on the hologram in front of her. The back of Dimitri's annoying head.

"And that's why, under no circumstances, should anyone—" Lucinda stops mid sentence as she sees me, her eyes widening. "Margot."

Every head turns and locks on me. Some people look sad and others are in shock.

When Dimitri sees me, his jaw drops.

I don't know what to say. What can I say? As far as they know, I'm supposed to be dead.

But Lucinda knew I'd be back.

Dimitri sprints across the room and wraps his arms around me, squeezing me like a grape in the way only family can. "You're alive. Thank the heavens." He hugs me one more time.

"I took the escape pod you mentioned," I joke.

A tear falls down his cheek. "See, that's why you should always listen to me."

I let go of him and then step toward Lucinda, who looks more proud than sad.

Lucinda smiles. "It's about time you showed up."

After an hour of hugs and tears, Lucinda dismisses the rebels to their dorms, with the exception of Dimitri and me.

"In time, I knew you'd be back. I just didn't think it would be this soon. How long did it take the hyssopite to work?"

"Longer than usual." All I want to do is unpack every detail with them, from my marriage to my interactions with the proditors, but I don't know where to start. But first things first. "I'm sure you realize what I've done to you. To the rebellion." I lower my head. "Milo—the Colum—knows all of our identities now. The second we walk into a Laven street with cameras, they'll torture or kill us. After what happened to me, I'm not sure which of those outcomes is worse."

"It took a few losses before I realized which file you stole. I've kept everything in lockdown since then. We have enough food to last another three or four weeks before we need to figure out something," Lucinda says.

"I'm sorry. If I would have been more careful—"

"Don't." She says the words like a caring, yet stern, guardian. "We knew the risks of sending you to the Imnicus and prepared for this."

"By the way, what the hell are you wearing?" Dimitri scoffs.

I almost forgot. I cross my arms. "Sinclair gave it to me. I had to give him my Ashtanaban uniform in exchange for passage through his entrance, and well, you can guess the rest." I look at Lucinda. "You're going to have to rectify things with Sinclair, by the way."

Dimitri folds his arms. "Pissed off that charlatan again?"

"Let's just say we will need to give him a few bribes if we ever need passage again."

Lucinda crinkles her nose. "I'll worry about Sinclair. You worry about yourself for right now."

We stand in silence for a few minutes. I know what Lucinda is waiting for, but she doesn't want to push me. If I wanted to excuse myself and lie down in my dorm for a week, she would let me.

"I . . . I got too close to people while I was there." I can't look at either of them. "I made friends. There was even a point where I started to care about the servants as if they were my own subjects."

Lucinda takes one of my hands to hold it between both of hers. "That's what they wanted. As long as they could get you to trust them, you were a pawn they could move any way they wanted. You've been through a lot. More than most people your age ever have to endure."

"But . . . Milo . . . "

Dimitri raises an eyebrow. "That bastard didn't touch you, did he? I swear—"

"He didn't," I lie. Though I know Dimitri is asking if Milo took my body by force, I'm not ready to admit that I slept with him willingly, and not just while I had amnesia, but even after my memories came back. I refuse to tell either of them that I fell for Milo Arris. It will only make them second guess my mental state. My allegiance.

"So . . . you just lived platonically as husband and wife?" Lucinda asks.

I nod. "Since my memories were wiped, it was too hard to jump into being a wife to someone I didn't know. He never pushed me for it, and now I know why." Lying to Dimitri is one thing, but lying to Lucinda is another level of sting.

Dimitri looks lost in thought before he speaks again. "And the proditors?"

I swallow, not sure if I can talk about this. But I don't think there will ever be a time in my life where I'll feel ready enough to tell anyone the details. "As you can probably guess, I got caught. After that, they tortured me. The next thing I knew, I woke up in their medic bay knowing nothing but my name. I suppose they made me the Columess to keep me close and make it easier to manipulate me into giving them the code to my tablet."

Dimitri pounds a fist onto the table, rattling the crystal pitcher of water. Though he doesn't say it out loud, I know he's not just angry about the torture. He was the one who made the decision to send me with the tablet. I should have refused it. Deep down, I knew Lucinda wouldn't have approved of me having it, yet my cousin wanted a way to know if I was all right.

But it was my necklace that had me placed in interrogation. The tablet was secondary.

Lucinda places a light touch on his forearm, the way she always has to when he loses his temper. "Continue, Margot."

"There is Proditor Knox Arris." Just the mention of his name brings nausea. "He hurt me worse than the rest and did it just for the thrill. He's psychotic, and before I escaped, he shot one of the few people I could trust. She helped me escape."

"Is she dead?" Lucinda asks.

"Presumably. Or being tortured beyond recognition."

"There are a lot of Knox's in this world. I can see the power he holds over you." Lucinda looks at my shaking hands. "Don't give him the power to haunt you."

I remember the stories Lucinda once told us of her life in crime which she was forced into. The torture she endured before Balistar even took over. But I guess that's why she's always been so collected with rebellion matters. To her, chaos has been her only constant.

I explain to them how they trained me on the Imnicus by implanting Knox's shadow into my mind. "I mapped out most of the Imnicus in my head."

I realize that my trip to the Imnicus wasn't a lost cause after all. Even through the torture and horrors, I have two things that give the rebellion more of an upper hand than ever before—Knox's shadow and a map. As long as hyssopite isn't around, I can join Dimitri on more fighting-based missions and even defend rebels against proditors.

"We'll have you draw out as much of the map as you can remember, if you're up to it," Lucinda says.

I nod. "I have one more question. While I was on the Imnicus, Milo said there was a bombing in the city that killed proditors and some civilians. What really happened? The rebellion doesn't use bombs."

"Another lie the Colum told you, I see. There was a strike of factory workers in the middle of the city that got violent and the soldiers used tear-gas to control it," Lucinda says. "It wasn't even us who initiated the protest. In the end, one of the workers sabotaged a piece of machinery and exploded the factory. One that was primarily used for imports to Ashtanabo. Unfortunately, all it's done is leave Ashtanabans without a particular variation of perfume."

"I can't believe this . . . " Even that was a lie, though one concocted by Commander Aisil, which means he was in on the whole charade too.

Lucinda looks me dead in the eye. "Margot, mark my words. The Colum and proditors will pay for what they did."

Nightmares of the proditors haunt me every time I sleep, and the more time that passes, the worse my dreams get. Now that I know their faces, the shadowy figures come to life. Crux's sneer and Knox's bloodlust. Onyx and Dune are there too. Some nights, I can't escape the dreams as they torture me again and again.

During some of the dreams, I'm outside of my body, watching them hurt me and unable to do a single thing.

In others, Alarik is there, and Crux forces him to cut me over and over.

Then, there is Lleu. In one of my dreams, she took my place on that table, and the proditors did to her what they did to me, making her scream in agony and curse the day she was born.

But even through the tortuous dreams, it's the ones with Milo that gut me the most. They're the sort of dreams you don't want to wake up from. The ones that wrap you in a blanket of comfort.

Ones that have me longing for his touch and his mouth. The sort of dreams that make waking up the real nightmare, and I hate myself for it.

One day, while I get ready to meet Lucinda in her office, I stare at Milo's ring, snug against my thumb. I want to remove it and toss it into a drawer, never to be seen again, but a painful ache in my chest stops me.

When I enter Lucinda's office, Dimitri is already there, as well as another face I don't recognize. Her peppered black hair goes well past her tailbone and she smiles at me when I enter.

"Am I late?" I ask as I secure the door.

"No, you're just in time." Lucinda motions to one of the chairs and we all take seats in a circle, but I can't help but notice the paleness in her face. Something is wrong. "I'd like you to meet Imory Nolan. She's been an Ashtanaban informant for us for years."

"It's nice to meet you, Margot." Imory shakes my hand. "Lucinda likes to keep me a secret. I'm sorry we haven't met sooner."

"Is something the matter?" I ask.

Lucinda looks at Dimitri.

Dimitri pulls out his tablet and pulls up a video, then he hands it to me. "It isn't good."

I watch the videos in an almost dissociative state. It's the only way I can get through it. One after the other, I scroll through security videos of the fifteen businesses that house rebellion entrances. Every video is the same as the last, the owner or employees going about their workday until a storm of guards and Laven-stationed proditors beat and execute every last one of them.

It's the demise of the owner of *Bevs and Shrooms* that has me the most torn up. The majority of the owners weren't even aware that we had our entrances inside their businesses. They died for no reason and no cause.

I try to hold on to my composure, but I feel it slipping. The final video is one of a few technicians trying to figure out a way to override our locks.

I hate Milo Arris. I think to myself. *I hate him. I hate him.*

"What are we going to do?" I hand the tablet back to Dimitri.

"In terms of the hackers, nothing. They aren't even close to figuring out a way in. But in terms of being stuck underground, we'll need to get our faces erased from the database sooner rather than later. That's where Imory comes in."

Imory folds her hands in her lap. "I know of an Ashtanaban base here on Lavenai that can be infiltrated. Once you're there, you can wipe all records of your names and faces."

"Would it matter?" I ask. "They could just re-upload it with the flash drive."

Imory shakes her head. "Unknown to the Colum, the flash drive has been corrupted by one of my connections. Now all that remains is the base."

"But that's not all, is it?" I ask.

Imory smiles. "You may be on the defensive now, but I have an avenue for you to launch an attack of your own. There is someone on Ashtanabo with a power to change everything. A magic that can destroy the proditor temple points and restore Lavenai's life force."

I can't believe that someone could hold such power to be able to override the work of a proditor. Like a walking hyssopite plant.

This is the push we all need. If we can somehow get to Ashtan-abo, we could end the Arris Reign once and for all, and I could find my recompense with Milo.

"But wait . . . how do you know all of this?" I ask. "And more importantly, why are you helping us?"

"I'm a Laven-born Ashtanaban." Imory smiles. "And Milo's mother."

Epilogue

Milo

Margot Tavish haunts my every dream and fantasy. She's the first thing I think of when I open my eyes in the morning and the last thing I think of before I fall asleep.

My father would have killed me in the bassinet if he knew I'd fallen for a Laven like he once did. Oh how much that mistake cost him. He never admitted it to me, but I saw how much it grieved him when she left.

I stare out the same window in my bedroom that Margot was so fond of. She'd count the stars for hours, identifying constellations she recognized from her books. The reflection paints a false image of her standing by my side, head nestled against my chest, wanting nothing more than for me to keep her safe.

But safety is something I can no longer guarantee her. In fact, I'm the reason she's in danger to begin with.

I meant what I said. When I finally catch her, I will kill her, no matter how much I don't want to. Then, maybe this infatuation will be nothing but a faint nightmare.

When Aisil enters my chambers unannounced, my fists curl. Behind me, I can hear the subtle shifting in his stance while he waits for me. He'll wait forever if I let him. Competent or not, he's a fool without a shred of ambition. Sometimes, I wonder why my father appointed him the highest of the commanders in the first place.

"What do you want?" I ask, after it's clear he will not leave.

"Is now a good time, Colum?"

"There is never a good time, Aisil."

As I turn to face him, my crows reach out, little to his awareness. I can sense the sweat forming at his pores. His pounding heart. He knows how much I hate being disturbed in my chambers.

Aisil inhales deeply and continues on. "The actress is still unconscious in the medic bay. She is stabilized, according to the medics, though her recovery could take months."

If Knox ever gets a hold of her, recovering from her wounds is the least of her worries. Thankfully, Knox isn't intrigued unless his victim is conscious. Still, he's becoming a force more and more difficult to stop.

"Keep her room under strict lockdown, even from the proditors. Nobody is to visit her except me."

"Of course, Colum." Aisil bows his head to me and disappears from the room.

Once he's gone, I pinch my nose and fall back into one of the chairs, resting one of my legs over the armrest. I study Margot's old ring, snug above my second knuckle.

That day she first entered my dining room, I hardly recognized her. Not because of the gown and jewels, but because she lacked the fire I'd seen in her during the interrogation. The second I saw her at dinner, I felt the knots in her belly and the amount of energy she had to muster up to avoid stumbling over her words. I didn't even see her as the same girl who had taken every form of torture without caving.

But for a second, she had smiled, though not in a way that was sweet or even taunting. But chilling. It was just like the smile she gave me during the interrogation, yet instead of bringing me anger, it brought me fear. I almost thought Knox made an error in erasing her memory.

It was as if, from somewhere deep within, she was peering at me as if to say, *I may not remember you, but I'm not giving up yet.*

I knew, in that moment, all the depths in which my plan could fail. All but one, it seemed.

But all of that is irrelevant. At the end of the day, Margot Tavish is still a rebel. My enemy. We're back to where we started, and as far as I'm concerned, she's a fugitive who needs to be dealt with quickly and swiftly.

Even if I have to do it myself.

Acknowledgements

Thank you to my readers who supported me during my debut and continued to read my books the two years following. When I published the first edition of this book, *Lady of the Colum*, in 2022, I really had no idea how it would perform. Little did I know that I would have people who would love my book enough to keep bugging me for the sequel. So thank you for giving me the confidence to keep pushing and not give up. Without you, I wouldn't be where I am today, and I am so glad that I have to opportunity to make it even better with the two years of writing skills I have built since.

To my husband, who has now content edited two variations of this book, thank you for being filterless with your edits. It was once I finally dropped my pride and started taking your suggestions that I really started to improve in my writing. But also, thank you for giving me grace when I was still a baby writer. I would not be an author today without your help and support.

To my sister, who has also read this book almost as many times as I have. You were the first one that obsessed over my characters as much as I do, and I'll never forget when I first told you I was thinking of writing a book. Those conversations we would have in mom and dad's living room inspired me to publish. Thank you and I love you!

To my best friend, thank you for helping me stay confident in my work, especially when I get nervous about the more morally gray scenes and characters. You truly are the voice I need to hear every time I get scared of what people think of the content of my books.

To Taylor, thank you for becoming my new editor who will help me throughout the rest of this series and the future interconnected books.

And to all my beta readers who weren't scared to tell me when things felt unrealistic or cringy. It's with feedback that books become great and an author truly is only as good as the team supporting them. Thank you from the bottom of my heart.

About the Author

Abelia Sumpter holds a Bachelor of Science in Nursing and discovered her love of writing while preparing for her national licensure exam. Her passion for storytelling began much earlier. As a child, she wrote screenplays and created short films with her friends. She currently lives in Ohio with her husband and owns a vision board the size of a novel.

TikTok: @abeliasumpter
Instagram: @abeliasumpter